to Catch a suitor

SARAH ADAMS

This is a work of fiction. Names, characters, places, and incidents either are the product of the author's imagination or are used fictitiously. Any resemblance to actual persons, living or dead, events, or locales is entirely coincidental.

To Catch a Suitor Copyright © 2020 by Sarah Adams

First edition March 2020

Book design by Sarah Adams

Cover design by Sarah Adams

WWW.AuthorSarahAdams.com

Josh, this one's for you. Thanks for being such an amazing brother and letting me steal your best friend.

Chapter One

I t was Elizabeth's torn slipper during her first ball of the Season that led her to believe that, perhaps, bad omens were real and, if so, her first Season was not looking bright. Seeing Oliver lead yet another beautiful young lady onto the dance floor only increased her worry. She had suspected the Season was going to be torturous, and she was not wrong.

But Elizabeth was not one to wallow. Or brood. She swallowed against the lump in her throat and tore her eyes away from the man she had loved since she was ten years old and searched for an exit from the ballroom.

She had only arrived at the ball a little over a half hour ago and already she was aching to leave. Not that the feeling surprised her. Crowds were the very worst. Elizabeth lifted up on her tiptoes in search of a doorway that would lead out of the ballroom, but she could not see one around the colorful swirl of satin, lace and, feathers. Really, how did women look in the mirror before a ball, assess the feathers in their hair and think *my goodness, how lovely I look imper-sonating a large bird!*

The Season was in full swing now and this ball was a horrifying crush. Despite the short amount of time Elizabeth had spent under the eyes of the *ton*, beads of sweat were already forming at the back of her neck, and the heat of so many bodies squeezed into one room together was giving her a headache. On top of all this, her rebellious little slipper was all but hanging off her foot.

Her eyes raced over the bustling room, noting each of the rosy faces, smiles plastered on, eager to prove their enjoyment in the night. How could every person in the ballroom truly be enjoying themselves? As always, her eyes gravitated to the dance floor, seeking again the tall man with sandy blond hair and a physique too wonderful for his own good. Oliver appeared to be having the most magnificent time of his life, sweeping easily around the room in spite of the overwhelming movement and noise surrounding them. In the crush, Elizabeth felt short of breath, as though she wanted to disappear and melt into the wall—feelings she was certain her older siblings never felt among society.

As the middle daughter of the Duke of Dalton, sister to both the Earl of Kensworth and the Countess of Hatley, Elizabeth had already been forced into introductions to at least fifty people whose importance made her legs wobble and her voice crack when she spoke.

This was not the plan. It was decidedly opposite of the plan.

Elizabeth had hoped that London's air would somehow change her into the outgoing socialite she longed to be. Oliver Turner was nothing but outgoing. Everything about him oozed confidence and charisma. He loved society events, flirting and dancing and then spending the summer at Dalton Park, telling Elizabeth all about his life in Town. As the younger sister of Oliver's best friend, Carver, Elizabeth had not always counted herself as his friend. But as they had grown older, the five year span between them had seemed less and less like an impediment to friendship. Now, she considered him her very best friend, and they shared all kinds of confidences with one another.

But this wasn't about him.

This was *her* Season. Her chance to show Oliver—correction, *herself*—that she was no longer the young girl who had chased Oliver, Carver, and Mary around the park grounds, begging to be included in their games. Actually, she hadn't been that girl for some time. Elizabeth now had twenty years in her dish—soon to be twenty-one. Really, if anything, she was showing Oliver that she was no longer the schoolroom miss who would listen to him talk for hours on end about whatever love he'd most recently tumbled into. He was always doing that—falling in love.

But again, this wasn't about him.

As Elizabeth had grown older, she and Oliver had turned into real friends, especially during Carver's dark years after the death of his fiancée when he refused to return home. Oliver had still come to Dalton Park every summer, however, and he spent those warm, magical months with Elizabeth and her family—but mostly Elizabeth —riding, walking, reading, and doing most all activities that unfortunately didn't include falling in love with her. However, she had come to terms with it. She wasn't one to wallow.

Elizabeth hadn't always been this comfortable with the idea that the man she had spent her whole life dreaming about would never reciprocate her affection. No, this was a new resolution. A decree written into her heart and sealed with the wax of her melted hopes and dreams.

Elizabeth had decided before she came to London for her first Season that she would not waste it wearing the willow for a man who didn't want her back. She deserved someone who cared for her just as much as she cared for him, which was why she was determined to spend her Season kicking Oliver Turner out of her heart and finally letting herself shine like a Town Diamond.

Except she didn't feel very shiny at the moment, what with her displaced shoe, and her wobbly legs, and her voice cracking as if she were an adolescent boy.

The sights and sounds and smells of the ballroom were really too much for her. She didn't understand how anyone looked forward to these events. Everywhere Elizabeth turned someone fluttered a fan, wafting the smell of sweat directly into her face. She pushed around a group of flittering debutantes. Still no exit. She did, however, have a perfect view of Oliver in his beautifully tailored blue jacket, flashing that charming smile of his to a young woman whom Elizabeth didn't actually know, but still managed to hate all the same. Someone should really tell the girl that pink was not her color. It washed her out.

Elizabeth was still seeking an exit when a large feathered coiffure swayed to the music, out of the way enough to give Elizabeth a blessed view of a door.

She shuffled across the floor—careful to slide her foot with the ripped slipper instead of fully picking it up. It was just like her to somehow manage to rip a brand new slipper during a ball. It was a subtle—or not so subtle—reminder that even though she was a daughter of the Duke of Dalton, she didn't fit in there with the *ton* and she would never get Oliver to see her as the right woman for him. *Drat.* Not Oliver. *Not* caring about Oliver's opinion of her was turning out to be a more laborious task than she had anticipated.

She pressed on toward the door, not allowing herself to glance back at the man she loved, but stopped when she felt someone grasp her arm. Elizabeth took in a deep breath.

It's not going to be Oliver. It's not going to be Oliver.

It wasn't Oliver.

"Where are you going?" Mary, her older sister and chaperone for the Season, shouted above the orchestra.

Elizabeth leaned so Mary could hear her. "To the ladies' retiring room. I just need a little air." She tucked her torn slipper a little farther under her dress.

Mary's light grey eyes pierced Elizabeth with skepticism. Elizabeth knew that look well. As the oldest of the four siblings, Mary possessed the uncanny ability to sniff out a problem when one of them was in trouble. Elizabeth wished she could plug her sister's nose. She didn't want Mary to know the truth just then. Mary couldn't know about her torn slipper. Or that she had the urge to scream every time someone addressed her as *Lord Kensworth's darling little sister.* And, most of all, Mary couldn't know that Elizabeth ached to "accidentally" spill a glass of sherry on the pretty miss currently on Oliver's arm. She was wearing a silk gown and it would stain famously.

Mary must have seen the evil look in Elizabeth's eye. "Are you feeling well?" She asked, not releasing Elizabeth's arm. Mary's eyes scoured Elizabeth's face for the truth.

"Perfectly," Elizabeth lied. "I'm simply not accustomed to a crush like this, but I'll adjust."

"You're sure? Do you want to leave early?"

Yes. Yes, she did. But Mary had been smiling all night as if she had actually been enjoying the smell of so many perspiring bodies, so Elizabeth lied again. "I'm having a grand time, Mary, so you may stop giving me that Mother Hen look of yours." Elizabeth saw a smirk begin on her sister's mouth and decided to push the conversation in a different direction. "How are you feeling? Is it too hot in here for you?" She glanced briefly to the swell of Mary's abdomen.

Elizabeth had been hesitant to accept her sister's offer to act as her chaperone for the Season when Mary had first suggested it. Mary was pregnant with her second child, and Elizabeth worried that all of the late night balls, morning callers, and constant events associated with launching a debutante into society would be too much for her sister's constitution. Especially since Mary's pregnancy was considered delicate, given the loss of her last pregnancy. But then, just before it had been time to leave Dalton Park for the Season, Kate, her younger sister, had fallen ill with influenza and Mama had not felt comfortable leaving her. Elizabeth was forced to accept Mary's chaperone.

But just now, when she was hoping to go home early, Elizabeth was feeling glad that Mama had stayed home to nurse Kate back to health instead of accompanying her to London, and hoped that perhaps her sister's swollen ankles would work in her favor.

Mary smiled broadly. "Actually, I'm feeling fantastic. It's so nice to be out in Society again now that the constant feeling of sickness has left me."

Just wonderful.

"Wonderful! Enjoy yourself. I'll only be a minute." Elizabeth mustered a believable smile and hoped it would be enough for Mary to release her hold.

Her older sister looked hesitant but then finally relented. "All right, if you're sure. Shall I come with you?"

Part of Elizabeth wanted to state that she was a grown woman and perfectly capable of taking herself off to the retiring room on her own. But instead she said, "That's not necessary, thank you."

Mary walked back to join her husband, Robert, and Elizabeth darted…or, slid…toward the inviting door on the edge of the ballroom.

No one seemed to notice her open the door and slip through. One glance around the dim hallway told Elizabeth this was not a part of the home in which she was supposed to be. The ladies' retiring room must have been through a different door.

Elizabeth pressed her lips together, looking both ways down the empty hallway. Her palms were sweating and butterflies fluttered in her stomach in the way they always did when an adventure was in the making. Thoughts of spending the remainder of the night exploring the halls played in her mind. It could be like a game, trying to avoid detection, like a…no.

Focus, Elizabeth. You are an adult now. Act like one.

She refocused her attention on the matter at hand, raising her gown and removing her slipper to inspect it. Of course. Irreparable. She flicked the limp hanging sole, no longer attached to the rest of the shoe, and silently cursed its delicate fabric.

"There you are."

Elizabeth jumped and turned toward the man who had just stepped into the darkened hallway with her. He glanced quickly over his shoulder, peeking out the door before closing it.

Oliver Turner.

Chapter Two

Elizabeth hugged the banister rails as she waited to catch sight of Carver and his new friend, returning from boarding school for the summer holiday. Miss Emma had assured Elizabeth that she would fetch her from the nursery just as soon as Carver stepped through the door. But Elizabeth was ten years old now and much smarter than her stuffy governess suspected. She knew that Miss Emma would wait until Carver and his friend had settled in and had tea with Mama and Papa before she ever went to collect Elizabeth. That's why Elizabeth snuck away from the nursery the moment Miss Emma had stepped away to fetch a book, and now waited on the second floor landing, peering through the banister rails, full of anticipation.

She didn't like that Carver had to go away to school for most of the year. It seemed unfair that she should get to remain at Dalton Park for her education while Carver had to live at Eton with no mothers and no sisters and only a slew of smelly boys to keep him company. She had missed him more than anything while he was away and was already concocting a plan to convince Papa that Carver should stay home for his studies and have a tutor rather than be sent off to school again. Of *course, Papa had tried to trick Elizabeth when he said that Carver was actually enjoying his time at Eton. But Elizabeth didn't believe him.*

She knew her big brother missed her just as much as she missed him.

A knock sounded at the door and Elizabeth pressed her face in between the spindles to get a better view. Their butler, Henley, walked to the door and grasped the knob. Elizabeth heard Mama's swishing skirts before she saw her rushing toward the door. "They're here!" Mama called out over her shoulder.

Mama had missed Carver, too. She knew because Elizabeth had seen Mama crying one day in the garden and, when she had asked her what was wrong, Mama said her heart was made up of five pieces—one for Papa, and another each for Elizabeth, Mary, Kate, and Carver. She said one of her pieces was away at school and she couldn't wait for it to return.

Elizabeth's own heart raced as Henley opened the door. Mama stretched out her arms and Carver stepped through the door to wrap Mama up in one of his big hugs. Elizabeth couldn't wait for one of her brother's hugs. He would probably even pick her up and spin her around as he always had. Elizabeth stood, ready to rush down the stairs and claim her brother's attention, when suddenly another boy stepped through the door.

She froze and sat back down, shrinking behind the banister and peeking through the rails once again. She'd never seen this boy before. Carver had written home and asked if his friend, Oliver Turner, could come stay for the summer holiday with him. Papa, of course, had agreed because he always loved to stuff the house with as many people as he could. But Elizabeth was a little worried that this new boy was going to take away Carver's attention.

Mama released Carver, after saying words Elizabeth could not make out, and looked behind him to Oliver Turner. Elizabeth thought Oliver looked a little nervous. Mama smiled and gave Carver's new friend the same hug she had given Carver. The look on Oliver's face was strange. It was the same sort of look she had seen on Miss Emma's face when Elizabeth had surprised her with a bouquet of picked flowers—like she wasn't quite sure they were meant for her but was happy to receive them anyway.

Why did he look that way?

Elizabeth continued to watch, still unsure of this Oliver Turner and not ready to announce herself yet. Papa's happy voice boomed into the room as it always did before he came into view. She could hear and see them all exchanging more hugs and greetings, but Elizabeth never looked away from Oliver. He didn't look like Carver. She knew he was the same age as her brother—fifteen years old—but his hair was lighter and he wasn't quite as tall. But then again, no one was ever as tall as her big brother. The biggest difference between Carver and Oliver was that Oliver looked a little scared. He stepped back as Papa approached him. Papa looked like he was going to hug Oliver but then he paused and, instead, slowly extended his hand. Oliver stared at Papa's hand a moment before taking it. After the handshake, Oliver smiled—a little tentative, but it was still a smile.

Everyone started moving out of the foyer and toward the drawing room. Elizabeth didn't stand up, but she hoped Carver would look up and see her, race up the stairs, and capture her in a hug like he always did. But he was laughing at something Papa had said and walked right by without seeing her. Her smile fell and she let go of the rails. It wasn't Carver's fault. She was probably just too high up for him to see her.

Elizabeth was just preparing to stand up when Oliver stopped walking. She froze, trying to remain undetected by this boy who she wasn't sure about yet. His blue eyes bounced over the foyer and then up the stairs until they landed on her. Elizabeth gasped. She didn't smile or move. Oliver seemed startled to find her there at first, but then he smiled a nice, kind smile and raised his hand to her in a soft wave.

Something strange and new happened. It felt as if a thousand flutters rushed into her stomach.

She wasn't sure about those feelings, or about the boy with the blue eyes. But he seemed nice. And for some reason, she liked that he saw her.

~

Elizabeth simultaneously relaxed and tensed, just like she always did in Oliver Turner's presence.

He walked toward her, his impressive frame even more alluring in the darkness. A subtle light played across his face—the warm glow caressing the skin of his jaw in a way that Elizabeth longed to. "What are you doing in here, Lizzie?"

Lizzie.

He'd been calling her that name since she was ten years old. Every time she heard the nickname she had to try very hard not to wince. It sounded childish, a constant reminder of how he saw her: his darling little longtime friend.

"Nothing," she said, quickly placing the torn slipper behind her back.

He grinned, his usually bright blue eyes looking as dark as midnight in the dim light of the hallway. "What do you have there?"

"Nothing," she said again. It was a solid alibi. She was sticking with it.

Oliver wasn't quite as massive as her brother Carver, but when he stepped in front of her and towered over her as he was doing just then, he felt very much like a giant. Elizabeth's heart stumbled as she smelled his familiar scent—like mint and fresh rain and something else masculine and spicy that she couldn't name. She wanted to bottle it up and carry it on a chain around her neck so she could inhale it whenever he wasn't around.

"Then let me see your hands," said Oliver, nodding toward her hands still tucked behind her back.

"No. They're cold. I'm trying to warm them up."

His eyes narrowed. "Mary said you left the ballroom because you were overheated."

"Mmhmm. I am. But my hands are…cold." She winced. She was a terrible liar and always had been.

As he spoke, he gave her the half smile that always made Elizabeth's stomach turn inside out. "What scrape have you gotten into this time?" Before she could answer, he darted his hand behind her back and retrieved the broken slipper.

She sighed and looked on, a little crestfallen, as he held the pathetic accessory up to the flickering candlelight. He began to chuckle. Elizabeth tried to snatch the slipper back from his hand but he just lifted it higher. "How in the world did you manage to tear your slipper?" Well, he didn't need to make it sound as if it was *such* a fantastic situation. In fact, it had torn quite easily.

As it turns out, when a lady stands on her tiptoes to get a good look at a gentleman across the ballroom, the back of her slipper might fall off. And when the back of the slipper is lying limply on the ground, another gentleman just might step on it. And when she goes to take a step, the heel of the slipper will remain pinned under his boot and the whole thing will tear. It was accomplished quite easily. But she couldn't tell him that, because it had been Oliver who she was lifted on her tiptoes trying to see.

It was his fault for looking so ridiculously handsome in his evening attire.

"I must have snagged it on a chair or something. Who knows?" She shrugged, and Oliver simply raised an eyebrow, knowing her too well to believe such a docile story.

He turned his attention back to the slipper and flicked the fabric once again. "I'm afraid I can't fix it. I've left my sewing kit in my other reticule." This was what she loved most about Oliver: his sense of humor. That—and his eyes, as blue as the North Sea—and his laugh, the way it rumbled in his strong chest—and his nose, the way it sometimes crinkled when he was reading. And everything else about the man.

Oh, she was pathetic. This was exactly why she had decided to come to London: to find another recipient for her heart. She didn't even feel too particular about who that someone might be—she just needed him to be a gentleman other than the one in front of her, someone who would return her love rather than continually dash her hopes of reciprocal feelings.

Elizabeth cleared her throat and extended her hand. "Never mind the slipper. I'll manage with it as it is."

But the handsome fool just smirked and held it up over his shoulder as if he expected her to make a lunge for it again. "How?"

"The same way I've been managing it for the past half hour. I slide my foot instead of picking it up."

His face was too serious to be trusted. "I don't know, I can't picture it. Let me see the walk."

She gave him a flat look. "Not going to happen. Give me my slipper, Oliver."

"I must insist you show me your sliding walk, so I may judge whether it's a sufficient cover or not. I cannot let my dearest friend parade about a ballroom looking as if she were mentally deranged."

"I'm not performing the walk for you."

He gave her a look that said, *I think you are.* She refuted his look with a challenging one of her own before rushing up to him, rising up on her tiptoes, and grabbing for her slipper. He, of course, being the ever-playful Oliver, raised it high above his head. But then he did something surprising. Oliver reached out and snaked an arm around her waist, pulling Elizabeth up close to him. She froze, feeling shot through the chest as her heart tried to recover, beating an unnatural rhythm.

Elizabeth expected him to let her go.

He didn't.

Oliver was only teasing. He was always teasing or playing some amusing game with her, although never a game quite like this one. But, still, he must have simply been teasing her. However, when she willed herself to meet his gaze, she saw something entirely new reflected in his eyes. She was dry brush and his eyes were a loose flame. There was no teasing glint. No smirk. His face was solemn and his eyes bored into hers. Knowing exactly what to do—because she had dreamt of this moment a million times before—her greedy hand raised to rest on his chest. She sucked in a breath when his hold around her waist tightened. She could feel the warmth of his hand searing through the fabric of her gown.

Her lips parted and her breath shook when his eyes fell to her lips. She pressed her hand a little heavier against his strong chest and felt his heart beating a rapid rhythm not so different from her own. If Oliver hadn't been holding her so firmly to him, she would have undoubtedly melted into a puddle on the floor by now. Someone would have needed to mop her up. Fortunately, he was holding her as if the last breath of humanity lived within her body.

Was he going to kiss her?

"What?" Oliver's slightly husky voice broke through the moment, to her horror, alerting Elizabeth to the fact that she had spoken the question aloud.

Oliver abruptly released her and stepped away, the fire in his eyes dying, replaced by a new, closed-off expression.

No, no, no, no.

She saw a muscle in his jaw jump as he cleared his throat. "I'm sorry, Lizzie. That was…"

She shook her head, feeling the flush of embarrassment creep up her neck. "No! Of course it was nothing." A forced chuckle left her mouth and she smiled awkwardly. "Nothing at all. We both understand that neither of us feels that way about the other." Elizabeth resisted the urge to grimace from the pain of those words that were only half-true.

He stared at her for a moment. Usually she could read every expression that flashed across Oliver Turner's face—a talent she had developed from spending countless hours with the man over the course of ten years. But just then, she hadn't the slightest idea what he was thinking. "Right." He handed her the slipper. "I'm glad we are both in agreement. Because, honestly Lizzie, you mean so much to me, and…" she wanted to shut her eyes against the words she knew were coming, "…I would never want to lose your friendship."

She wasn't exactly sure why falling hopelessly in love with each other would mean they had to sacrifice their friendship…but it didn't truly matter because she had already prepared herself to hear those words.

Because Elizabeth refused to be a lovesick, pining woman, and also because this little situation only added to her resolve to find someone new to whom she might give her affections, she said, "I agree whole-heartedly." For good measure she added, "Besides, I'm completely convinced kissing you would have been exactly the same as kissing my brother."

His head kicked back a little and his brows stitched together. "Well…perhaps not *exactly* the same."

She moved past him toward the ballroom door, relishing his offended scowl a bit more than she should have. "Oh, yes—*exactly the same*. It would have been stale and boring and just plain unremark-able." She heard him let out a scoff.

It felt a little too good to make him pay for that almost-kiss.

She paused, her hand on the knob of the door, and looked back. "I think you ought to find another entrance back into the ballroom. I'd hate for someone to see us entering together and assume the worst." She paused for dramatic effect. "Then you would be forced to marry me. A dreadful fate for us both."

Elizabeth slipped quickly back into the ballroom and shut Oliver behind.

Chapter Three

Oliver's boots clacked against London's sidewalk, a haunting echo in the deserted street. It was quiet—almost too quiet compared to the usual bustle of Town. But it was six o'clock in the evening on a Wednesday, which meant most everyone on this elite side of town was inside, dressing and preparing for dinner and a night full of dancing and socializing at Almack's Assembly Rooms.

He was of course going as well, because he always went. London counted on him to go and flirt with their daughters and dance with their wallflowers. It was his unofficial job to make aging mothers blush and smile and become more pliable toward whatever demand the young ladies were hoping to make on their pitiable guardians. Oliver wasn't exactly sure when that had become his post in life but, nevertheless, it was.

To say he disliked his situation in life would be a lie. Was it taxing at times? Yes. Did it sometimes demand more of him than he felt he could give? Yes. Did it sometimes land him in courtships, the thought of which made him shudder? Absolutely. But somehow, Oliver still didn't mind. In fact, he felt a small satisfaction anytime he contributed something to lift another's day, something to lessen their burden, make them smile. To make them pleased with him.

And thankfully, none of those courtships ever lasted.

Every flirtation or courtship Oliver entered followed the same pattern. They started with a hope so bright he felt the need to squint in its direction and ended with a false conversation about how their relationship had grown into a friendship much too dear and they were better suited for a platonic life. *As your friend, I could never ask you to sacrifice a future full of love and devotion for a life of mere friendship.*

Which was a little ironic considering he was hopelessly in love with his best friend. But he had to push those thoughts away. He couldn't marry Elizabeth because—well, he simply couldn't. Recently, Oliver had even decided to put the whole idea of marriage behind him.

Thankfully, romance and love-filled marriages had become quite in mode over the past few Seasons. Every lady who received his heart-melting speech looked at him as if he were the very manifestation of Eros, sent to earth with the sole purpose of helping her find true love. And perhaps he was. Not a god—but sent to earth to set up love matches among his friends and acquaintances. Because, honestly, he was deucedly good at it.

Nearly every lady Oliver had ever courted had ended up married within two months of their separation. Even Lord Kensworth—or Kenny, as Oliver had nicknamed him ten years ago when they had first become friends—had profited from this odd talent of his. A woman who Oliver had briefly harbored a tendré for—which, admittedly, happened more often than not—had ended up falling in love with Kensworth. They had been married one month ago to the day and Oliver liked to think his presence in the situation was the catalyst for making it happen.

There was a reason people of the *ton* had nicknamed him "Charming." Some thought it was because of his smile or the way he flirted, but that wasn't it. The lesser-known reason was because he seemed to be young ladies' lucky charm. Oliver was sought after because to court *Charming* was to find oneself married and well situated swiftly after. But he didn't mind...for the most part. It was nice to be wanted. And nice to know that in the end, he wouldn't be responsible for that woman's happiness. Oliver would never have to worry over becoming his father.

Oliver quickened his steps as the sight of Hatley House—where Elizabeth would be staying for the Season—came into view. But, then he realized that his steps had quickened and forced himself to slow down. Rushing to see Elizabeth was ridiculous. On the other hand, she was new to London and likely feeling a little alone. As her best friend, surely rushing to make certain she was settled and happy was the honorable thing to do? He let himself hurry his steps again until he was standing in front of Hatley House. The home belonged to Mary and Robert, the Countess and Earl of Hatley.

He drew in a deep breath, willing his thoughts and emotions to all line up where they ought to be. Elizabeth was his friend—Kensworth's younger sister—and that was all. Nothing more. There could never be anything more between them.

Before Oliver took another step toward the front stoop something caught the corner of his eye. He turned to face the small alley that separated Hatley House from the neighboring home and looked up. His body tensed when he realized that a woman was hovering half out of a window on the second floor—a line of knotted bed linens dangled from the window, forming a sort of rope. He didn't even need to see the woman's face to know who it was.

Elizabeth.

Oliver jogged into the alley and craned his neck to look up at his friend, who had apparently gone mad enough to risk her life climbing out of a second story window.

"Lizzie!" Oliver called out as quietly as he could and still have his voice reach her. He glanced sideways toward the street, hoping his voice hadn't alerted any bystanders to Elizabeth's madness.

"Oliver?" said Elizabeth, pausing her descent and peering down over her shoulder with such a pleased smile that it made a warm sensation spread through his chest.

No. No warm feelings, Oliver.

But then her smile fell away and she just looked annoyed that he had caught her. "What are you doing here?" she asked.

"I could ask you the same thing," he said, resisting a grin at the sight of her—skirts bunched up in her hand, excitedly scaling down a wall using bed linen as a rope, with more length of her legs showing than he was comfortable admitting he had noticed. Granted, it wasn't actually much. No more than he had already seen when she would lift her skirts to walk with him through the streams of Dalton Park during the blissful summers of their youth. But the difference was, Oliver no longer felt the same way toward Elizabeth as he had during most of those summers. She had been a child back then, but certainly was not now.

Which is why he cleared his throat against its sudden dryness and focused his eyes on her face.

"I think the answer to that question is self-evident. I'm escaping through my window." She was moving down the wall much faster than he thought prudent. Oliver would have asked her to be careful, but he knew that would be to no avail. The woman was fearless.

So instead, he stood directly below her and prepared himself to catch her if she fell—his customary position for most of their friendship. He held his breath when her boot slipped off the wall, but she clung tighter to the makeshift rope until she was able to regain her footing.

"Aren't you going to tell me to take care?" she asked, a smile in her voice, as she continued moving.

"No, I'm much too fond of my breath to waste it on those words." He held up his hands as she neared the top of the first floor window. Having to fix his eyes on her like that really wasn't helping his determination to deny his feelings for the woman. She possessed a natural grace and elegance that the average woman had to refine for years to achieve. Elizabeth, however, accomplished the look with no effort at all—while scaling down the side of a house.

It made his stomach clench to think of how she would draw the eye of every eligible male in London. Elizabeth was going to be an instant success this Season, of that he was certain.

Elizabeth neared the ground but then paused, realizing what Oliver had noted from the moment he walked up. Her makeshift rope did not reach the ground. Instead, the end dangled to just above Oliver's head. Elizabeth would not be able to reach the ground on her own without letting go and jumping from a height that would most likely leave her more than a little bruised.

Her eyes reluctantly slid to his. Oliver had to bite the inside of his cheek to keep from smiling. He folded his arms across his chest and leaned casually against the wall, gazing up at her, letting his eyes convey his triumph.

Elizabeth took in a long slow breath and narrowed her eyes. "Oh, just say it."

"Say what?" he asked in an innocent tone.

She rolled her eyes and adjusted her hold on the linens. "That I do not think before I act."

He gasped playfully. "I'm offended, Lizzie. I would never say something so stuffy."

"You would and you have. At least a dozen times over."

Oliver grinned. "Hmm. I think you're mistaking me with some other prosy fellow." He had in fact said that very phrase too many times to count, but it had never done a bit of good, so Oliver had decided to stop saying it. Besides, if he were being honest, he liked rescuing Elizabeth from the scrapes she continuously found herself in.

"Well, if you're finished acting as if you're posing for a Grecian marble, could you possibly help me down from here?"

Oliver unfolded his arms and pushed off the wall, moving just below Elizabeth again. "Is that your way of saying I'm looking rather handsome today?"

"I would, but I'm afraid that if I tend to your ego any further you will combust." At that moment, Elizabeth reached the end of her rope and peeked over her shoulder down at Oliver.

He—being of a tall build—was able to reach her lower legs, though he really *shouldn't* reach her legs. He stared at the brick wall in front of him, trying to work through the problem. In his mind, he thought he would just take hold of Elizabeth's legs and let her slide down in his arms to the ground. But now, when faced with a very real Elizabeth, it felt too improper. And his racing heart wasn't doing anything to help convince him otherwise.

"Lizzie, I think you should—" However, he didn't have time to finish that sentence or formulate a new plan.

"I'm letting go," she said, leaving him barely enough time to reach up and take hold of her legs. In a blink, she was sliding down through his arms until her feet gently and safely reached the ground. Oliver's heart pounded against his chest as Elizabeth spun around, still encircled by his arms, and faced him. He was struck by how incredibly right it felt to hold her.

If he held her in his arms a moment longer, he would be forced to kiss the woman and show her just how wrong she had been. Like kissing her brother, indeed! In fact, Oliver was certain that a kiss shared with Elizabeth would be nothing short of devastating.

Using impressive amounts of will power, Oliver dropped his arms and took a small step back on the pretense of inspecting his jacket. "Well, I hope your shenanigan was worth it because I don't think this jacket will ever recover. You ripped off a button."

He heard her chuckle, but it sounded a little forced. Or was he just reading too much into her actions? Blast. He needed to get a hold of himself.

"It was more than worth it, believe me," she said playfully. "Your button sacrificed itself for a noble cause."

Oliver stopped pretending to care about his jacket and turned his attention back to Elizabeth. She wrapped her arms around herself, trying to keep warm. He almost pulled her into an embrace to warm her, but he refrained. Instead, he squinted up at the top window. "Are you going to tell me what you have escaped from? Is using the door too much of a bore for you now?"

Her light pink lips pulled into a grin. "Doors *are* rather average. But, no. Mary has been put to bed."

Oliver's face sobered at the thought of Elizabeth's older sister— who also felt very much like his older sister—taken ill. "Is everything all right with her and the baby?" Oliver knew that Mary was increasing and that she had lost a baby during her last pregnancy. Neither of those things were public knowledge, but Oliver had spent enough of his life at Dalton Park with Kensworth and his family that they considered Oliver one of their own and shared most everything with him. They loved him in a way that his own father never had.

"Thankfully, she and the baby are both well. However, she began to have a few startling pains after the ball a few nights ago, and the doctor thought it best for her to remain abed until her time comes. And you know how inept Mary is at sitting still." Oliver couldn't help but laugh at the way Elizabeth said those words—completely serious, and as if she was not exactly the same way.

"I'm failing to see where the window comes into play."

Elizabeth's eyes widened in horror. "The woman is a nightmare, Oliver. She is bored to death, laid up in that bed of hers, and has taken to putting all of her energy into managing my every move—even more than usual. Not to mention the many, *many* times a day she pulls me into her room to discuss my hopes and dreams for the Season." She shuddered. "She's suffocating me. I just needed a little walk, but I have to pass by her room to get to the stairs. I simply couldn't risk alerting her to my exit, or else she'd call me into her chamber again." Elizabeth *would* rather risk her life climbing out of a window than discuss her feelings. Or at least, discuss her feelings with her older siblings.

He knew that Elizabeth had always felt overshadowed by them— even though she had never said as much to him outright. But there was a lot Oliver knew about Elizabeth that she had never spoken. He just wished her feelings toward him were one of those things.

Actually, no. Oliver didn't wish that. Because even if she did share his feelings, it wouldn't change his mind about the future. Oliver would never marry. He wasn't going to marry Elizabeth or any other woman, for that matter.

"I can see how the window was an appealing choice…but not perhaps the safest. If I hadn't been here to catch you, what would you have done?"

She shrugged a shoulder, a half smile on her mouth. "Why should I waste my time with what if's? You *were* here and that's all that matters." Her eyes held to his, a secret message that either read as thankful or annoyed flashing through her sky blue irises. "You're always there to catch me," she said in a frosty tone. *Annoyed, then.*

Suddenly a voice called from the window above them, drawing their eyes up to Lord Robert Hatley, who was leaning out. "Elizabeth, did you climb out of this window?"

A pause. "Yes."

Hatley let out a short laugh and shook his head lightly. "Of course you did. Well, get back in here because I will not let you leave me to fend for myself with your sister." In any other noble family, Elizabeth would have been scolded, punished, and caged until she could learn to act as a proper society lady for ever doing something so reckless as climbing from a window. But Oliver had learned from a young age that Elizabeth's family was quite unlike any other.

"Is Lady Hatley truly that miserable to be around in her state?" Oliver asked, looking back and forth between Elizabeth and Hatley.

Even from the ground Oliver was able to see the flat look Hatley was giving him. "She's insisting that I try on every single outfit I own, inspect each one from head to toe, and purge the things that are out of fashion."

Oliver let out a laugh, imagining his stoic friend parading around his room for Lady Hatley to judge. "Is it too late to cast my vote? I've been itching to burn that grey waistcoat of yours for at least five years now."

"I was going to invite you to stay for dinner, but now I think I'll let you starve," said Hatley. He pointed at Elizabeth. "Back inside in five minutes, Miss Escape Artist. But leave the imp outside." Hatley disappeared back into the house and pulled the makeshift ladder back in with him before shutting the window. Apparently, he didn't trust Elizabeth to not re-enter the house the same way she left it. Smart man.

Oliver rested his eyes again on Elizabeth. She had a way of smiling that made it impossible for him to not return it. "Are you coming in?" she asked, gesturing with her thumb toward the front of the house.

"Didn't you hear Hatley? I'm banned from admittance."

"You know, I do have a bit of pull with him. Or perhaps we could simply lie and say that I was attacked by footpads and you fought them off. He will be honor-bound to give you dinner then."

Oliver chuckled. "No sense risking the goodness of your soul for my benefit. I was planning on dining at White's before I made my way to Almack's anyway. I only stopped by to see how you are settling in."

"I'm pleased you did." She held a soft smile for a moment before it changed into mischievous. "But only because I would have fallen to my death had you not. It has nothing to do with being pleased to see you."

He laughed. "Of course not." But inwardly, he wondered if there was some truth to her words. Did she only view him as she would an older brother, always around to protect her and help her down from walls, apple trees, old ruins, and other obstacles of great height?

Oliver peeked around the corner to make sure no one would spot them before exiting the alley together. His steps slowed as they approached the door. He didn't want to leave Elizabeth—a recurring theme of the past few years. And that was precisely why he had to go.

They said their goodbyes but, before they parted, Elizabeth turned back. "Oh! I almost forgot to tell you. Since Mary is sentenced to her bed, she can no longer act as my chaperone for the Season."

Oliver raised an eyebrow. "And you're happy about this because you've finally found a way out of having to endure a Season?" Most of her life, Elizabeth had grumbled and complained at the thought of having to come to London for the Season. Adventure and freedom meant more to Elizabeth than fine gowns and stuffy ballrooms.

Her face didn't brighten like he had anticipated. Instead she looked toward her slippers and fidgeted a bit with her skirts. "I do not feel that way anymore, Oliver." Her eyes darted back up to his—something like uncertainty in their depths. "I fully intend to enjoy my come out, and… hopefully even make a match."

"Good," he said in a tone that sounded odd even to him. He wasn't sure what she wanted him to say, or why her eyes seemed to challenge him. "So is the duchess coming to Town after all?"

"No." Elizabeth shook her head lightly, loose blonde curls that had slipped from her pins bouncing around her face. "Kate is still ill. And you know how dreadful Kate is when she is ailing. Mama cannot leave her."

"And yet you still look happy after all of this rather depressing news."

"That's because the solution is going to be much more entertaining."

"Oh?"

Her eyebrows lifted and lowered. "Rose and Carver are returning to Town early to act as my chaperones."

For a moment, Oliver couldn't say anything. His mind was too busy racing with images of Rose—Kensworth's new bride, who was also a newly rehabilitated con woman—returning to London in the new role of countess. Elizabeth was correct—it was most definitely going to be entertaining. And then he thought of Elizabeth and Rose living under the same roof together and he couldn't help but laugh.

"What?" asked Elizabeth.

"Nothing," he said, backing down the stairs with a grin on his face.

Her brows pulled together with suspicious amusement. "I know that grin, Oliver Turner. What are you off to do?"

"Oh—nothing important. I simply want to get my name in the betting books at White's. There's no chance Kensworth House is still going to be standing at the end of the Season with both you and Rose living under its roof."

Her eyes narrowed, but she smirked. "If I had a something in my hand I'd throw it at you."

"My point exactly."

Chapter Four

Elizabeth entered the house and closed the front door as lightly as possible before hugging the wall as she ascended the stairs. The middle of the stairs were the creakiest, therefore she needed to avoid them at all costs. Once finally at the top level, Elizabeth tiptoed across the floor, holding her breath and praying that Mary wouldn't see her pass by. She loved her sister dearly, but Mary seemed intent on discussing every aspect of Elizabeth's life, and she could not stand it any longer that day. Her well of patience had run dry.

Elizabeth had almost made it to the opposite side of Mary's door, holding her breath and pursing her lips together in quiet concentration until she was stopped by Mary's voice. "Elizabeth, love? Is that you?"

Elizabeth shut her eyes tightly and she let out a defeated breath. Caught by the mother hen again. "Yes. It's me," she said, turning to walk into Mary's room, resigning herself to an afternoon of smothering and unwanted conversation.

"Oh, good!" said Mary, with a bright smile, sitting propped up on her bed by a mountain of pillows and surrounded by dozens of fashion plates.

Elizabeth chuckled at the sight and moved toward her sister's bed.

"Are we trading in our coverlets for fashion magazines now? I'm not sure that will keep us as warm in the winter."

Mary's light grey eyes squinted in a mock smile. "Very funny. But no—I've just been rethinking your wardrobe for the Season."

Elizabeth groaned and pushed a pile of papers aside so she could dive onto the bed beside her sister. "No more talk of gowns, please. I've had quite enough of that with Mama over the past three months of preparation." Elizabeth snuggled up to Mary and looped her arm around her sister's. If she was going to listen to Mary's constant interference, she was going to listen while resting comfortably.

Mary was ten years older than Elizabeth, and often acted more like a hovering mother to her than even Mama did. In fact, Mama was more like Elizabeth in temperament, always quick to dive into an adventure and slow to enter a ballroom. That was how Elizabeth knew Mama was likely not sorry in the least to have to stay home and nurse Kate back to health. Elizabeth almost envied Mama. Almost. But knowing she was most likely having to hear at least fifteen times a day how Kate was near her death, and that the family should be brave after she passed, made her feel grateful she was in Town and not back home at Dalton Park. She could practically hear her younger sister declaring that if the family harbored even an ounce of affection for her, they would not touch that dreadful black—because to Kate, wearing black was the equivalent of torture.

Mary picked up a picture of a lady in a bright pink dress and eyed it closely. "I'm just not certain you have enough color in your wardrobe."

Elizabeth snatched the picture out of Mary's hand and tossed it off the bed. "Leave my wardrobe alone, Mary," she said with a playful scowl before she wrapped her arm back around her sister's. "Believe me, I have more than enough color variations." Thoughts of that turquoise dress came racing back to mind and Elizabeth cringed. Despite her sisters' attempts to sway her dislike of it, Elizabeth still thought it made her look like a trifling piece of shrubbery.

"Why don't you let me fetch your sewing and you can focus all of this obnoxious—er, I mean, *endearing* attention on making new gowns for the baby?"

Elizabeth grinned at her sister, but Mary's body stiffened. She looked up from the fashion plate she had been studying, and for a brief moment, stared out into the room before turning her attention back to the image again. "Are you sure you don't like this one? I think the pink would really set off your blue eyes." Was that it, then?

Flags raised in Elizabeth's mind at her sister's blatant attempt to change the subject. Something was wrong with Mary—the rock of the family, the sibling who always had everything well in hand. Elizabeth had no intention of telling Mary how much she admired her, looked up to her. Mary was accomplished, loved, prepared and confident in the face of all trials. At least, that was always how she had appeared when she would swoop back in from London with all of her fantastic tales of Society and culture.

In those moments, Elizabeth had always stood by, silently admiring her older sister and wishing she could be her. She also wished she could be one of Mary's friends and confidants— and Carver's as well. Instead, it often felt as if her older siblings only interacted with her when it was required. The older Elizabeth became, the more strained her relationships with her siblings felt. Although they were close, there was still a wall between her and Mary that she wasn't sure how to scale. And if she were being honest, she was a little afraid to even try.

When Elizabeth did not acknowledge the picture of the horrid pink gown Mary was holding, Mary held it closer to Elizabeth's face. "What do you think? Shall we have it made for you?"

"Absolutely not."

"Why? I'm certain it will make your eyes look dazzling." Here was Mary pushing again. Was there ever a time when Elizabeth had asserted her opinion and Mary had accepted it without argument?

"I do not doubt its ability to bring out my eyes. My fear is that those who have to look at me in it will not be too pleased when they are left blinded."

Mary smirked down at her. "Now you sound like Kate, with your dramatics." She paused and squinted. "Or Carver, with your sarcasm."

"Or Robert, by combining them?"

Mary chuckled and finally pushed aside the fashion magazines to nestle down into her pillows next to Elizabeth. It was in those small moments when Mary would relax her shoulders that Elizabeth saw hope for the two of them as friends. "I think it would be more like Oliver. I don't think Robert is capable of dramatics."

At the mention of Oliver's name, Elizabeth's mind flew back to how it felt having him hold her in his arms standing in the alley. And the way he had looked at her—it almost gave her hope for a future with him.

But did she really want hope? No. She was quite finished hoping. What she wanted was to move on and stop torturing her heart like she had every summer Oliver spent with her family. He had started out as a brother figure—a protector. But as the years had progressed, he had gone from someone who simply watched over Elizabeth to a genuine friend. A close friend. Someone who shared everything with her. Someone who laughed with her. Someone who valued her opinion. Maybe someone who—no. She couldn't let herself finish that thought. All of those things were true, but they all simply pointed to their close friendship. Elizabeth wanted nothing more than for Oliver to return her romantic sentiments, but she knew that was a wasted dream.

Mary's voice broke into Elizabeth's thoughts. "I'm so sorry I won't be able to be with you this Season after all. I feel as if I have let you down." Mary sounded defeated. It made Elizabeth feel a tiny bit guilty that she was glad to have Rose as her chaperone instead of her over protective sister. Rose never smothered or inserted herself into Elizabeth's problems as Mary did. In fact, Rose only ever listened and gave opinions when asked. It was a novel idea, really.

Elizabeth forced herself to wear a somber expression. "I'll miss you dearly, Mary. But I wouldn't risk anything happening to you or the baby for the world. We need to keep you resting so you are ready for all the sleepless nights our newest little lord or lady will bestow on you." Elizabeth looked down and rested her hand on Mary's wonderfully round stomach. Usually, Mary would smile and place her hand over Elizabeth's and say something like, *"I cannot wait to hold this little darling."* But she didn't do that this time.

Mary cleared her throat and changed the subject again. "I think I will have Rose over for tea when she and Carver arrive."

"Oh?" Elizabeth asked, inwardly trying to make sense of Mary's avoidance of any topics pertaining to the baby. Perhaps it was simply coincidence? Perhaps Mary hadn't heard her?

Mary shifted on the bed, forcing Elizabeth's hand to fall away from her middle. "To fill her in on all of her duties as your chaperone. She is new to this life, you know. I'm sure the idea of launching you into society, all while trying to establish herself as the new wife to the Earl of Kensworth feels daunting." Elizabeth wondered if she and Mary were thinking of the same woman. She never knew Rose to be daunted by anything.

"I'm sure Rose will manage well enough. This life is not exactly foreign to her, given all of the identities she's assumed. I dare say she will manage better than I."

"True." Mary agreed a little too quickly for Elizabeth's comfort. Did she not think Elizabeth was up to the task of becoming a Society lady? "Still, I will rest easier knowing that she is thoroughly apprised of her responsibilities. Oh, and Oliver. I must remember to have Robert speak to him."

Elizabeth sat up a little. "Why must Robert speak to Oliver?"

Mary sat up as well. "About the Season. To make sure he keeps you in his sights."

"In his sights?" Why did Elizabeth not like the sound of that?

"Yes—I know Carver will be a diligent guardian, but I would feel more comfortable knowing Oliver acts in a similar manner."

Elizabeth let out an incredulous laugh. "As my…*guardian*." Was Mary blind? Could she not see how much Elizabeth adored Oliver, and how offensive that idea would be to her? Elizabeth was torn. In many ways, she had no desire for her sister to learn of her sentiments toward Oliver. Mary would surely meddle and tell Oliver regardless of Elizabeth's own say in the matter. But another part of her wished that Mary would see her as a grown woman, capable of loving—as well as attracting—a man such as Oliver Turner. Obviously not Oliver Turner himself, since he was not in fact attracted to her, but one like him, perhaps. Surely Mary didn't think it completely beyond the realm of possibility?

"Of course. He's always kept a hawk-like eye on you. And since you two are close friends, I think he will be a wonderful blockade for unwanted suitors."

Elizabeth couldn't stop an incredulous laugh from bursting forth. Not only was Mary going to ask Oliver to act as a guardian to her during the Season, but she was going to ask him to *shoo* away other suitors?

"Mary, I beg you not to ask that of Oliver. I'm sure his time this Season will be monopolized enough without the added burden of holding on to my leading strings."

Mary waved her off as always, landing on a decision without truly hearing Elizabeth's objections. "Oliver is always happy to help where you are concerned."

Elizabeth cleared her throat and tucked a wayward curl behind her ear. She could assert herself further, but what was the point? At the end of the day, Mary would still do as she thought best. They needed to change the subject, and she decided now was the opportune moment to see if Mary's avoidance of a certain topic was coincidence or not. "I never did hear if you and Robert have settled on a name for the child."

Mary tensed and looked around the bed. "Have you seen the plate of the cream dress with burgundy embroidery? I wanted to have a second look at it but I seem to have misplaced it." *Not a coincidence, then.*

Elizabeth knew she shouldn't press it, but her desire to be more than simply Mary's little sister held sway. She wanted Mary to see that she was capable of helping to bear some of her burdens. "Are you thinking of passing Robert's name down if it's a boy and yours if it's a girl?"

Mary was almost wildly shifting through the papers scattered around her. "Perhaps. Oh—it must be around here somewhere. Have you seen it?"

"Do you have a hunch as to what the sex will be?"

"Just wait until you see the embroidery. I've never seen more elaborate floral stitches." This was getting ridiculous.

"Mary, stop searching for a moment." Mary paused but would not meet Elizabeth's eyes. "Is something the matter? You seem a bit out of sorts today. Is it…because of the baby? Are you worried—?"

Mary's eyes shot anger at Elizabeth. "Leave it alone," she said, speaking with such force that Elizabeth took a retreating step back.

An unwanted stinging touched the back of Elizabeth's eyes and she blinked against the sensation. "I was only trying to—"

"I know what you were trying to do. And I wish for you to stop. My affairs do not concern you."

Elizabeth gripped her skirts and willed herself not to cry. Tears would only make her appear even more childish in Mary's eyes.

After a moment, Mary's posture relaxed and she let out a breath. "What I mean to say is, you have enough to think about with your come out and all that is expected of you as a debutante. No need to overload your mind with things that do not pertain to you." Yes, Mary had made that sentiment perfectly clear. Elizabeth was in no way needed by her sister and should focus all of her efforts on not making a muddle of her Season.

Wonderful. Perfect. Then that was precisely what she would do.

The air felt heavy. Elizabeth wanted to breathe but she was afraid that if she did, it would come out shaky and tearful, and tears would do no one any good. "Very well." She looked down and smoothed her skirts, hoping her sister couldn't see just how much her rejection had stung. "I shall leave you then. I have a letter to Mama to finish writing."

Mary nodded but would not meet Elizabeth's eye again. "Send her my love." She gestured toward the copy of *La Belle Assemblée*. "Will you hand me that one before you leave? I don't believe I've looked through it yet," said Mary, using one hand to point toward a fashion plate at the bottom of the bed and the other to retrieve a pillow and cover her middle.

Something was most definitely upsetting Mary, and Elizabeth's heart ached at the sight. She hurt for her sister and also at the distance she felt between them. She had hoped this Season would change things between them, but clearly she had been wrong.

Chapter Five

I t had been five days since Oliver had found Elizabeth climbing out of her window, and four days since he had promised himself he wouldn't spend every single day of the Season with her. Too bad he apparently had the will of a child in a room full of biscuits, because he had spent every single one of those four days with Elizabeth. It wasn't good. And it wasn't doing anything to help him lessen his growing feelings toward her.

He knew from Elizabeth that Kensworth would be back in Town today. In fact, he and Rose had been expected at Kensworth House the previous evening. Oliver had intended to pay them a visit when they first arrived, but had gotten stuck at that blasted ball, guilted into filling every young debutante's dance card. Most nights, he didn't mind. However, ever since Elizabeth had arrived in Town and been without a proper chaperone, thus unable to attend any social events, he had felt as if London had suddenly lost some of its magic.

Ballrooms didn't feel quite as dazzling knowing that Elizabeth was only a ten minute carriage ride away. He had pictured her curled up next to a fire reading a gothic novel that Kate had lent her and dying to talk to someone about it. Elizabeth never could just read a book. No, that would be far too docile for her. If Elizabeth was going to open a book, she was going to pause every minute to recount whatever nonsense she found, or animatedly read the funny bits or…*Wonderful.* He was still thinking about her. Of course he was, because that seemed to be all Oliver had been able to do for the past several months. Which was why he needed to go visit Kensworth. Seeing the physical evidence that Elizabeth was only his friend's younger sister would help shift his thoughts back to where they ought to be.

Oliver dressed quickly, left his rented apartment and walked toward Kensworth House as if the ground beneath him was on fire.

It was probably a little ridiculous how much Oliver was looking forward to reuniting with his friend. The two men had been thick as thieves until Kensworth married Rose a little over a month ago. Which was ironic since Rose really had been a thief before their union. And now, this had been one of the longest stretches Oliver and Carver Ashburn, Earl of Kensworth, had gone without seeing each other in a decade. That pitiful fact alone proved that it was good that Kensworth had married Rose.

Oliver looked down at his pocket watch and smiled as he approached the massive familiar townhouse. Kensworth hated mornings. And he especially hated seeing Oliver in the mornings. That's precisely why he made it a priority to show up in Kensworth's bedchamber at the earliest hour he could manage. Just then, it was only a quarter past eight o'clock in the morning, so he knew his friend had likely not yet even opened his eyes. *Perfect.*

Oliver ducked into an alley that led behind the house and headed to the servants' basement entrance. The trick to achieving the prank was getting in the door without alerting Kenny's butler. He'd been caught a few times and then made to sit in the parlor like a misbehaving child until *his lordship was ready for visitors.*

Oliver slowed his steps and quieted the click of his boots against the pavement as he rounded the house. He slipped down the small set of cement stairs that led to the servants' entrance. When he opened the door, he could hear the staff bustling around in the kitchen, so he turned the handle while closing the door to prevent it from making a loud click. He then hunched down as best a man of his exceptional height could and inched quietly toward the stairs.

With Kensworth House's immense size and lavish furnishings it was exactly the opposite of Oliver's small bachelor's quarters. Oliver's father owned a fine townhouse right on the edge of London's elite West End but Oliver refused to stay there. It wasn't that he was afraid of Frank Turner ever coming to stay in the townhouse, because Oliver knew better than that. His father preferred to stay holed up with all of his anger and hatred at Pembroke—the country estate. Oliver refused to live in the townhouse because he simply would not take one penny from that man until the day his father died, and he would inherit the lot of it. Luckily, he had an aunt who had liked Oliver enough to leave him her fortune (small though it was) after she died. It kept him fashionably dressed, properly housed, and adequately fed until he could inherit the fortune his father was loath to give him.

Oliver made it up the narrow set of stairs that led to the ground floor without detection. Peeking his head into the vast main foyer, he found the familiar sight of the large crystal chandelier, a green ornate rug spread over the marble floor, and the longcase clock ticking in the corner. And, thankfully, no disapproving butler.

A grin pulled at his mouth as he eased open the door and stepped fully inside.

"Mr. Turner," came a voice that made Oliver jump and spin around. He found the disapproving butler emerging from the coat closet. Had he been lying in wait for Oliver?

"Blast, Jeffers," said Oliver, tugging on the lapels of his jacket and straightening to his full height. "I wasn't expecting to find you emerging from the closet."

The man's face was impressively smug. "I, however, am not surprised at all to find you emerging from the servants' stairs." Yes. He had definitely been lying in wait.

"Well," said Oliver with a grin, "it's lovely to see you as always, Jeffers, but I can see myself up to Lord Kensworth's rooms."

"Mr. Turner," said Jeffers in a lazy tone, most likely weary from having to utter the same phrase he had said dozens of times before. "His Lordship—"

"—Does not receive visitors before the hour of ten o'clock. I know, I know," said Oliver, waving a dismissive hand in the air. "But surely, by now, you know me well enough to make an exception?" Oliver flashed his most charming smile.

"No."

His smile fell. "Fine. I will go wait in the parlor until his lor—" but then he spun around the scowling butler and ran up the stairs, taking them two at a time. Oliver didn't look back. He knew he would find Jeffers wearing a black look and possibly muttering profanities under his breath. It never failed to make Oliver grin. Elizabeth would have been proud of that spin maneuver.

Oliver paused and took a moment outside of Kensworth's room to collect himself. He tugged at the bottom of his light blue waistcoat, ran a hand against his hair attempting to put it back in place, and rolled his shoulders in preparation for waking the esteemed Earl of Kensworth.

Once, Oliver had thrown a basin of water on Kensworth and then taken off, running out of the house before his friend had time to catch and murder him. Another time, he had woken him by placing a live chicken in his bed. The lengths he had gone to catch and find that chicken were perhaps a little mad—but it had been worth it to see Kensworth's face when he opened his eyes. Today, however, he was going to settle for the simple run and jump. Startling, yet effective.

The moment after Oliver turned the handle and opened the door, something soft and fluffy smacked into his face. Apparently the butler wasn't the only one who had been expecting him. Oliver blinked down at the pillow lying innocently at his feet.

He chuckled and stepped into Kensworth's darkened room. "Well, good morning to you too, darling."

"Go away, Oliver," said Kensworth, his voice muffled by the pillow covering his face.

"Did you just throw a pillow at me?" Oliver asked, moving more fully into the room to stand next to the bed.

"No. That was Rose."

Oliver froze. Rose? His eyes shifted for the first time to the opposite side of bed. Sure enough, he saw the form of Rose under the coverlet pulled all over her head, leaving only the ends of her brown hair visible. Heat rushed to Oliver's face as he realized he had just barged in not only on Kensworth but also on his new wife in bed.

"Oh, blast," he said, quickly turning away so that his back was to the bed. "I'm sorry, Rose. Er—Lady Kensworth. If I had known that you…well, I wouldn't have come in here."

He heard her laugh a short laugh as well as the sound of covers shuffling. "Don't you dare start calling me Lady Kensworth. And, yes —how could you possibly have known that Carver's *wife* would be in his bed with him in the early morning?"

He grimaced at her words. It was so obvious that she should be there with him now. Why had that thought never occurred to him before? "Right. I'll just be on my way then," he said, charging toward the door.

"No, no. I'm already up and going into my own room so you two ladies can have your morning chat," said Rose, followed by the sound of feet shuffling against the floor and then a door shutting on the far end of the room. Assuming that meant it was safe, Oliver turned back around slowly until his eyes landed on his friend.

Kensworth was now sitting on the edge of the bed looking as annoyed as ever. "Oliver. Do me a favor and go get your own wife so you can have someone to talk to in the mornings who isn't me."

Oliver smirked. "But you know me so well. Imagine how long it would take for a wife to learn all of my complexities?"

"Believe me, you're not as complex as you think."

"Is that your way of saying I'm daft?"

Kensworth ran his hands through his hair with a small grin. "I think you must be if you thought you would find me alone in my bed after marrying Rose only a month ago."

Oliver couldn't help but chuckle. It really was stupid of him. "Don't worry. It won't happen again."

"I don't doubt that. Rose will shoot you if you do it again."

"Relying on your wife to be your body guard?" Oliver tsked. "Shabby, my man."

"I'm debating calling my guard back in here to take care of you right now."

Oliver smiled and moved across the room toward the parlor that connected to Kensworth's room. Before he opened it, he paused. The room no longer connected only to Kensworth's room. It also connected to the bedchamber of the lady of the house.

As Oliver stood there, his hand poised on the knob, he was hit with the realization that he could no longer move with freedom through his best friend's house as he had done nearly every day since they had both moved to London. An uncomfortable feeling settled over him. It was heavy and cold and told him that he had been replaced.

There weren't many places in Oliver's life that felt like home. His own home—Pembroke—felt like anything but a home. It's why he had been avoiding the place—and the man who occupied it—since he had met Kensworth all those years ago at Eton. He had learned from the Ashburn family what a peaceful home looked like—what caring parents looked like.

Dalton Park and Kensworth House felt like two pillars in his life holding him up—giving him a place to belong and feel wanted. And, suddenly, he felt as if one of those pillars had just been ripped out from under him.

"What is it?" asked Kensworth, coming to stand behind him.

Oliver forced a smile. "You probably should go in first. Since… that's your wife's parlor as well now."

Kensworth didn't seem to be feeling the same significance of that statement, because he just smiled and nodded. "You're right. I'll go in first."

Oliver stepped back, falling into his new place as he watched Kensworth enter the parlor, and then waited for the cue that it was clear for him to enter. A fire lit in the grate made the room feel warm and soothing to the gnawing sense of change Oliver felt prickling at him. He breathed a quiet sigh of relief as he and his friend both sunk into the old, worn leather chairs, and everything felt a little more normal again.

He looked down and ran his finger over the familiar large crack in the leather. For the first time in the history of their friendship, Oliver was at a loss for what to say. There was so much buzzing around his mind, but he couldn't give voice to any of it.

"No smiles for me today, sunshine?" said Kensworth.

"Am I frowning?"

"Yes, and it's a rather disturbing sight. I haven't seen that face since childhood. What's made you pull it today?"

Oliver took in a deep breath, keeping it captive in his chest as his mind raced with reasons. Elizabeth. Kensworth's marriage. His boredom with Society. Feeling lost and uncertain of who he was or where he belonged anymore.

Instead, he voiced what was most bothering him at that moment. "Your hair."

Kensworth's head kicked back slightly. "What the devil is wrong with my hair?" he asked, grinning and reaching up to run a hand through his long locks.

Oliver scrunched up his nose theatrically. "It's too long. Looks as if you're letting yourself go, living at the orphanage." It had been no shock to Oliver when Kensworth had announced they would be living full time at the orphanage Rose and her uncle Felix had founded. Kensworth hated Society and had been looking for a way out of it since the day he had stepped into it. Boxing had been his escape before he met Rose—something Oliver wondered if his friend would pick back up now that he was home for the Season.

Kensworth just grinned deeper. "Rose likes it."

"Hmm. I don't."

"Well, it's a rather good thing you're not the one I'm trying to get to kiss me, then."

Oliver shrugged. "Your loss. I'm a fantastic kisser."

Kensworth shook his head, but Oliver didn't miss the hint of smile that slipped over his mouth. "Speaking of, who is the newest lady to catch your fancy?"

Oliver tensed, his finger pausing midway over the crack in the leather. "What do you mean?"

"Oh—don't act the innocent. The Season has been in full swing for almost two weeks. Usually by now there is someone you are professing your undying love for." It was annoying how well Kensworth thought he knew Oliver sometimes. Even more annoying that he wasn't wrong. Oliver was in love again, but this time it was different. His feelings for Elizabeth were frightening and longstanding. It was because of these feelings for Elizabeth that he was constantly trying to lose himself in London flirtations. He couldn't marry Elizabeth—he simply didn't trust himself with her. So trying to forget her every time he returned to London felt like his only choice.

But now, she was here in London and he couldn't escape her— or his feelings for her.

"I'm sorry to disappoint you, but no lady has caught my fancy this time." He tried not to let his eyes dart away from Kensworth's steely grey gaze, but he was unsuccessful. He looked to the fire and stretched his boots out to it, pretending he was only shifting in his seat to warm himself, and not because he was as uncomfortable lying to his friend as he would be on a bed of needles.

"No one?" asked Kensworth, eyes narrowed suspiciously.

"What can I say? Maybe I'm outgrowing my love sick ways."

"Doubtful." Kensworth continued to eye him for several uncomfortable minutes as if waiting for Oliver to crack under the pressure. Beads of sweat began to form at the base of Oliver's neck but he refused to look away. Finally, Kensworth broke his gaze and readjusted in his seat, suddenly intrigued by his fingernails. "Elizabeth is coming to stay with us. Moving in today, in fact," he said, as if it was the most natural and spontaneous topic in the world and had nothing to do with what they had been previously discussing.

Which meant he knew. But how? Oliver had said nothing to his friend about his feelings for Elizabeth. And he absolutely wouldn't now, either. There was too much risk that Elizabeth would find out. Kensworth and his entire family were wretched secret keepers. "Yes— she told me." He opened his hands, indicating his presence. "How else would I have known you had returned to Town?"

"I thought perhaps you had caught my scent on the wind or something." He smirked. "So you've seen her, then?"

Oliver chuckled. Did it normally sound so high and bubbly? He didn't think so. "Of course I've seen her. Is that surprising?"

Act natural. Don't let him see you sweat.

"Not in the least, actually." Kensworth rested his chin on his fist and Oliver almost rolled his eyes at the look directed at him. It seemed his friend was in a mood to prove something. Well, not today. Oliver was a closed book, but Kensworth continued to try to crack him.

"I think we both know I am getting to the point in the conversation where the gloves come off."

"I assumed it." The air felt too hot.

"Olly, do you love Elizabeth?"

He curled his toes inside his boots. It wasn't fair of Kensworth to ask him outright like that. He didn't want to lie to him, but he must. If Oliver admitted his feelings, he knew his friend would be elated and encourage the match. But there would be no match because Oliver loved Elizabeth too much to marry her. If there was even a chance his father's words were right—the words that had haunted him everyday since he had finally confronted to the man three years ago—he would never let himself come anywhere close to forming an attachment with Elizabeth. She deserved the best. Oliver would never be that for her.

Pushing his feelings for Elizabeth away was his only focus now. He took in a discreet breath through his nose and looked his friend in the eyes before he lied to him. "No. I do not love Elizabeth."

Something flickered across Kensworth's eyes. Skepticism? Or maybe disappointment? It definitely wasn't relief—which at least made Oliver feel a little pleased. It would have been difficult to see his friend sigh with relief.

"That's too bad," said Kensworth. "You could have saved me from the many insufferable balls I'm going to have to attend." Oliver learned long ago that Kensworth covered his feelings with a jest. He always had to squint to see the truth, but when he did, he could find it buried beneath the sarcasm.

Oliver smiled and clasped his hands behind his head. "You could have just said that you are disappointed I won't be your brother-in-law."

"I could, but lying is such a terrible habit and I'm trying to break it." Kenny smirked, and Oliver felt himself relax into his favorite leather chair for the first time.

His comfort was short lived. A moment later, there was a short knock at the parlor door followed by the entrance of a footman holding a silver tray. "I apologize for the interruption, my lord, but there is an urgent missive for Mr. Turner."

Oliver sat up straighter in the chair, wondering what sort of message could have been urgent enough for its sender to track him down at Kensworth House? Not that it would have been that difficult to do. Most people knew it was where he spent most of his time outside of Society functions.

The footman approached Oliver, extending the silver tray that held the suddenly ominous-looking letter. Oliver picked it up and nodded his thanks to the footman. His eyes caught sight of the handwriting on the outside of the letter and his stomach twisted.

Waiting until the footman left and closed the door behind him, Oliver broke the seal.

Oliver, I am writing to you because this is the end for me.
I do not expect you to come but, nevertheless, I thought
you should know.
Frank Turner

Two sentences. His father had caused him nothing but pain for his entire five and twenty years of life and, now that he was almost dead, all the man had to say to his only son was contained in two sentences. It wasn't that he had ever truly expected his father to be remorseful for the way he had treated him, but he at least expected…well, he wasn't sure. But it definitely wasn't that.

Oliver folded the small letter back up and shoved it into his jacket pocket. Really, he ought to have just thrown it into the fire.

"Who's it from?" asked Kensworth, leaning forward in his seat.

Oliver pursed his lips together and looked to the fire. "My father."

Kensworth knew Oliver was estranged from Frank Turner, but he didn't know why. It was an implied rule that Oliver's home life was an untouchable topic. Well, untouchable with everyone besides Elizabeth. Kensworth knew enough, however, to understand that receiving a letter from the man was shocking.

"You don't really expect me to be content with that short answer, do you?" Oliver just looked at him, wishing very much his friend would be content to not prod. "Well? What did it say?" Kensworth asked again.

"He's dying, but he doesn't expect me to go see him."

A heavy, uncomfortable pause filled the room. "And will you?"

Oliver looked to the fireplace and watched the flames dance, running his thumb against the crack in the leather. "No."

Chapter Six

Elizabeth finished tying her bonnet under her chin and assessed her outfit in the looking glass. Kensworth House had become her new home earlier that morning and she was a little ashamed to admit how much she was already enjoying the freedom that came along with being away from Mary. Things felt strange between them. Mary was unreasonably closed off, unwilling to share anything of herself with Elizabeth, but all too eager to manage every breathing moment of Elizabeth's life. The space would be good for them. Maybe it would even give Elizabeth the chance to show Mary that she was a grown woman, capable of managing her own life and even—*gasp*—contributing to others' lives as well. But no, Mary would probably think it was far too ridiculous a notion that Elizabeth was capable of offering wisdom to another human being.

Wonderful. Now she was stewing. Elizabeth hated to stew. It made her feel a little too unhinged and very much like her younger sister Kate. What she needed was a walk. That had to be the reason for all of her agitated feelings. She had simply been cooped up too long.

Grabbing her shawl, Elizabeth headed toward the door. Suddenly, a loud bang exploded through the air, making the walls rattle and a picture frame fall off of the nightstand. Elizabeth gasped and clutched her chest, feeling her heart pound against her palm as the reality of what she had just heard sunk in. It was a gun shot, she was certain. But, from where?

She rushed to the door and flung it open. At that exact moment, Carver was running out of his room. His eyes were wide and filled with fear, his enormous body poised for battle. He swept his gaze quickly over Elizabeth, checking for any signs of harm before he glanced down the hallway.

Their eyes met again, worry and questions reflected in both. "Rose is downstairs," Elizabeth said, remembering she had left her sister-in-law in the drawing room earlier that morning.

Carver's whole body went rigid. "Stay here." His large shoulder brushed past her as he advanced toward the stairs.

He must have been mad if he thought Elizabeth was going to just stay put while he ran head first into what could be a very dangerous situation. No. She picked up her skirts and followed quickly behind Carver down the stairs. "Do you think it was an intruder?" she asked in a loud whisper, trying to let her voice carry over the loud thumping of their feet against the stairs. Should they be tiptoeing? Was announcing their presence a mistake?

Carver darted a glance back at her over his shoulder. "I told you to stay put."

"But you knew I wouldn't." Perhaps he saw her as a reckless little girl, but Elizabeth was too full of concern to care.

He paused briefly, as if thinking everything through and coming to the conclusion that there was not one scenario in which Elizabeth would remain upstairs. "Fine. At least stay behind me."

She nodded and obeyed as they approached the closed drawing room door. She could feel the pulse in her neck and hear a whooshing sound in her ears. Was an intruder on the other side of that door? Was Rose harmed?

Several petrified maids and a few nervous footmen had formed a group in the foyer. They advanced toward the drawing room door but Carver waved them away. They agreed, each looking ready to be of service to their master, but utterly dreading the idea of confronting a gunman. It was good of him not to send them in first.

Sometimes Elizabeth wished she possessed a bit more healthy fear. But the only fear that touched Elizabeth was for the safety of her sister-in-law. Because, if she was being honest, Elizabeth felt alive at the possibility of what waited beyond that door. Possibly too alive. Danger and excitement always felt like a siren calling to her. She was all too aware that was *not* a quality the daughter of nobility ought to possess.

Carver put his hand on the door and looked back at Elizabeth: *Are you ready?* She nodded firmly and he pushed the door open. Immediately, laughter rose in Elizabeth's throat. Carver's eyes widened momentarily before he pulled Elizabeth into the room and then kicked the door shut with his heel before the staff had a chance to spot their new countess.

"Rose," said Carver, on a sigh that could be interpreted as relieved, amused, and exasperated all at once. "I should have known."

Elizabeth had never assumed that her new sister-in-law's transition from criminal life to the peerage would be easy, but she had never imagined she would find Rose standing in the drawing room, clothed in a lovely lilac morning dress, wicked smile, and holding a smoking pistol in her hand. Clearly, there was no intruder. Elizabeth looked to the other end of the room where Rose had been aiming her pistol. There stood a footman with his eyes shut tight, holding a playing card as far away from his body as his fingers could manage. Elizabeth had to press her hand to her mouth to hold back a laugh as he cracked open his eyes. A heavy dose of relief washed over his expression as he looked at the playing card and confirmed that all of his fingers were still attached. The playing card, however, had a hole blown straight through the center.

Unfortunately—or fortunately, depending on how one felt about crabby old ladies—there was also a big black hole in the portrait of Great Aunt Willowfred hanging on the wall behind him. Oh yes, Elizabeth was feeling much better in her brother's house than she had under Mary's roof.

Rose lowered her gun but held up a finger at Carver with her opposite hand. "Now, wait just a minute before you throttle me," she said, taking a step away from his advance toward her.

"You have approximately ten steps before your chance to explain ends," said Carver, sounding none too happy with his new bride.

"You remember Ben, don't you?" Rose had told Elizabeth about Ben earlier that morning. He was somewhere around eighteen years old and she had known him from her days on the wrong side of the law. He had wanted a better life, but was too old to enter Rose and Carver's orphanage. Instead, they had hired him on as a footman.

Elizabeth had a feeling that before too long the entire staff of Kensworth House would be composed entirely of rehabilitated thieves.

"I remember him," said Carver, taking another step, not looking away from Rose.

Rose's eyes were wide and alert. "Well, he had the audacity to suggest that the stories about my shooting abilities were all a hoax! That they were all just made up tales, because according to Ben—" she flashed the footman a menacing look, "—a *woman* could never actually live up to the reputation of my marksmanship."

"So you decided to punish him with the fear of being shot dead by a woman in our drawing room?"

"No." The innocent look Rose flashed Carver was laughable. He was stalking toward her—a wolf, fangs bared—and she was nothing but a baby lamb. "I simply wanted to give him the opportunity to witness firsthand just how fine a shot a woman can be. And, also, that I can indeed shoot a playing card out of a man's hand from twenty paces away."

"You're abusing your power," he said, but Elizabeth could hear the amusement in his voice now.

Rose gave a mock gasp. "Never! Ben volunteered to hold the playing card."

Carver looked back at Ben, who looked very much like a man who had *not* volunteered to hold a playing card. Carver looked back at Rose with a lifted brow and she gave a deep, resigned sigh.

"Very well," she said with a sulky pout that would make Elizabeth's three-year-old niece proud. "Please forgive me, Ben. I'll never shoot a playing card out of your hand again."

"Thank you, my lady."

Her eyes narrowed at him. "And this is the part where you apologize for your folly."

"No," said Carver, drawing the word out for emphasis. "This is the part where we remember that we are trying to keep the whole world from learning of your past and beg Ben to not tell any of the other staff what happened in here. If anyone asks, Rose was going to surprise me with the gift of a new pistol, but it misfired when she was looking it over."

Rose scoffed. "I would never mishandle a pistol."

Carver grinned before looking back at her. "I think you've proven that point already today, darling. Your ego can stand to be knocked down a bit. Do I have your word, Ben?"

"Yes, my lord," said Ben before he bowed and rushed out of the room, looking like a dog with his tail between his legs. Poor pup.

Carver finally walked fully up to Rose and stopped just in front of her, holding out his hand. "A deal is a deal. You promised you'd hand it over if there were any more shooting shenanigans." Any more? And Elizabeth thought she was the one with an over inflated love of excitement.

Rose rolled her eyes and placed her pistol in his palm. Then Carver smiled with such tenderness and intimacy that Elizabeth felt a little uncomfortable at being its witness, wrapping his arms around Rose and pulling her firmly up to his chest, pistol still in the hand draped behind Rose's back. Elizabeth looked away, feeling that the moment had become a little too private for her to witness. She started to quietly back out of the room. With every retreating step, her mind pulled to Oliver. She wondered what it would feel like to be held by him the same way Carver held Rose.

That brief moment, when Elizabeth had been encircled in Oliver's arms, had felt like coming home. It felt like hope and belonging and safety all wrapped up together. How much more wonderful would it feel to be really held by him, with real intention? Held because of a mutual love, too strong to keep them apart. No, Elizabeth needed to stop thinking about Oliver. It wasn't going to happen. One day, she would be held as she dreamed, only it would be with someone else. Hopefully, a gentleman as equally wonderful as Oliver who would be worthy to receive her heart.

She *did* worry, though, that someone equally as wonderful did not exist.

"Elizabeth, wait!" Rose's voice caught Elizabeth just before she escaped the room. Elizabeth paused and Rose tried to wriggle free of Carver. "I need to talk with your sister," she said, looking up at him.

Carver just adjusted his arms more securely around Rose. "Go ahead, love. Don't let me stop you."

She narrowed her eyes at him. "Alone. In fact, I think now would be the perfect time for you to revisit that boxing saloon you've been missing so much."

He pretended a face of heartbreak before turning his eyes to Elizabeth. "Do you see how she treats me, Elizabeth? Kicking me out of my own home." He shook his head, looking again to Rose. "Such a cold hearted woman."

Rose chuckled, pretending to squirm out of his arms again. "And you're entirely too lovesick. I think a good round of boxing is exactly what you need."

He smiled mischievously. "I don't think that's what I need."

Elizabeth pretended to cough to cover the embarrassed laugh that came, unbidden, from her mouth. She wasn't alone in those feelings. Rose's face turned a bright shade of pink that Elizabeth had never seen on her confident sister-in-law before. Perhaps coming to stay with a newlywed couple wasn't the most intelligent plan after all.

"Out," said Rose, looking as if she was torn between embarrassed, angry, and amused.

"All right, all right. I'll go." Carver leaned down and briefly kissed Rose's cheek. But then he quickly pulled away, touching his fingers to his mouth and pulling a deep, put on frown. "Just as I suspected. Ice cold."

Rose gave him a flat look before trying to kick him. Carver laughed fully—a sound that Elizabeth had never thought she would hear from her brother again, before he had met Rose—and jogged away from his wife and out the door.

Elizabeth let out a sigh. "You two are going to be difficult to live with."

"Hopefully you won't have to live here and endure it for too long," said Rose, taking a seat on the settee.

Elizabeth pretended to be offended. "Already wishing me gone?" She sat on the opposite end of the settee with Rose, tucking her feet up under her skirts.

"You know what I meant. Hopefully, you won't have to wait too long before your hand is claimed by a certain someone who shall remain unnamed."

Elizabeth was glad that she had confided her feelings for Oliver to her sister-in-law when they were last at Dalton Park. Usually, Elizabeth kept her feelings to herself, more comfortable with them remaining hidden than exposed, especially in a family of Elizabeth's size where keeping a secret seemed to be optional. She had no doubts that the moment Mary or Kate or Carver learned how she felt toward Oliver, the rest of the family would be in the know before the end of the day. It's simply how things went in their family. And it's why Elizabeth tended to keep things bottled up.

But Rose...she was different. From the first day Elizabeth had met Rose, she had proven herself to be a solid confidante. Not only was she a trustworthy secret keeper, but she was a good listener. And in a family where everyone was talking, it was nice to be heard.

Elizabeth let out a tense breath, recalling the last time she and Rose had discussed this topic. Rose's suggestion had been for Elizabeth to encourage the attention of other gentlemen, to hopefully open Oliver's eyes and help him see her as more than the child who used to tag along on his adventures with Carver. But the more Elizabeth considered the idea of trying to make Oliver jealous, the more uneasy she felt. Only a sad, pathetic sort of woman could be satisfied with love gained through manipulation.

"That certain someone shall remain unmentioned because there will never be a reason to mention him again," said Elizabeth, deciding it was more comfortable to look at the floral print on her dress than to meet Rose's eyes.

"What do you mean by that?"

"It's nothing. I've simply decided it's time to move on from my feelings for…the aforementioned man."

Rose's expression pinched. "Has something happened between you two?"

"No." Well…an almost-kiss that was hardly worth mentioning. Which was the problem. There was never anything worth mentioning. "Frankly, I'm tired of harboring a love which will only ever be one-sided. He sees me as his dearest friend, and that's all. I'm ready to broaden my horizons and look for someone who will return my affections." She should be awarded a medal of some kind for managing that speech in an unaffected voice.

Rose remained quiet.

Elizabeth fidgeted with the fabric of her dress. "Which is why I am hoping that you might help me."

"Help how?"

"Well, I was hoping that you would help me become more confident as a Societal woman. Stand out a little more." Oh, she felt ridiculous asking this. "I want to catch the eyes of eligible gentlemen, but I don't think I can do it as I am now."

Rose laughed. "Why ever not? Elizabeth, you're stunning. I will be very shocked indeed if you do not catch *every* gentleman's eye—not only the eligible ones."

"That's only because you haven't seen me in social situations. I'm a bumbling nightmare of awkward interactions."

"I've seen you at Dalton Park. You seem just fine to me."

"That's different. I'm comfortable there. And I'm only ever surrounded by family at home."

"And Oliver. You've never seemed awkward or uncomfortable around him." That's because Elizabeth never felt more comfortable in her life than when Oliver was near. But that was beside the point.

"Oliver doesn't count. I'm trying to forget him, remember?"

Rose sighed. "Yes. I just…" she broke off and shook her head. "Never mind."

"No, tell me what you were going to say." Perhaps it was because Rose listened more than she offered advice, but when Rose did offer her thoughts, Elizabeth always wanted to hear them.

"Before you completely push Oliver out of your heart, are you sure you do not wish to simply tell him the truth about how you feel? See if perhaps he—"

"No," Elizabeth cut her off. "I cannot."

"But why?" Rose's voice sounded a little pleading. "What if he does return your affection? You could both avoid the whole Season and get on with your life together that much sooner."

"Or he might tell me he does not return my affections and will never be able to look me in the eyes again. Then, I would lose my best friend as well as having to live with the humiliation of it all for the rest of my life."

"Kate would be proud of that tragic speech."

Elizabeth smiled. "She would, wouldn't she? The point is, it's too great a risk. One that I'm not willing to take."

"Fine," said Rose, but she didn't sound happy about it. "I suppose I see your reasoning."

"I knew you would. So will you help me become more of a Town Diamond? Look more confident and sophisticated?" Rose had been assuming various identities for years. She was a master at morphing into whomever the occasion called for. Elizabeth knew there would be no better tutor for feigning confidence.

"I suppose I can teach you a few tricks. But Elizabeth, I also feel that if you have to change yourself for love, it's probably not a love worth having." She became a touch smug. "Besides, I think it's a silly reason to not tell Oliver of your feelings, and a tad bit cowardly." This was yet another reason why Rose was so dear to Elizabeth. When asked for her opinion, Rose never tried to sweeten her words. She spoke them, honest and true, without any coddling or manipulation.

"Once again, you're making me feel so welcome here," said Elizabeth with mocking smile.

Rose chuckled and leaned over to squeeze Elizabeth's hand. "I *am* happy you're here, Elizabeth. There is no one else for whom I would even consider coming back into London so soon."

"And you won't say anything to Carver about my feelings for Oliver?"

"Your secret is safe with me."

Those words brought an immense amount of relief. The last thing she wanted was for her brother to confess her feelings to Oliver on her behalf. "Thank you."

"Just promise me one thing," said Rose, softening her voice. "Don't lose out on a wonderful life with Oliver because you are too afraid of rejection."

"Would you have been able to make that same promise to me a month ago, when you left Dalton Park because you suspected Carver didn't love you?"

Rose's lips pressed into a line, but Elizabeth could tell that her sister-in-law was trying to hide a smile. "You're not supposed to question my profound statements. You're simply supposed to marvel at my wisdom."

Elizabeth couldn't help but laugh. She stood from the settee, already weary from the emotional weight of their conversation and eager to move on. "I'll just go to my room now and think about the importance of your wise words until the soirée tonight." Elizabeth had almost forgotten about the soirée at Miss Loxley's home. She cringed at the thought of attending what would surely be the event of the Season. She thought immediately of at least ten different ways she could bungle the evening.

Rose picked up a small embroidery hoop from the basket beside the settee and nestled back into the cushions. "No, you won't. But you could at least pretend to find me wise beyond my years."

Elizabeth paused in the doorway, eyeing her usually spirited sister-in-law sitting in the drawing room, docile as a fawn, needle in hand. Somehow the picture before her was at odds with the Rose she had known when she had first come to Dalton House. Elizabeth chuckled.

"What happened to, '*If you have to change yourself for love it isn't worth having?*'"

Rose just grinned and continued with her embroidery. "If there is anything I've learned in the short time I've been married to your brother, it's that there is a difference between changing yourself for someone to love you, and growing into a better person." She paused and looked up at Elizabeth, eyes twinkling. "Now go away and don't say anything else before you ruin my wonderfully profound statement."

Elizabeth decided to take her walk after all. After a quiet—and rather dull—walk in the park with her maid, who seemed too nervous to engage in even the most trifling of conversations, Elizabeth returned to Kensworth House. Really, she didn't understand what was so exciting about London or why everyone raved about it so. The air felt uncomfortably thick and hazy, and it smelled of the manure that filled the streets. Everywhere she looked—everywhere besides Grosvenor Square, where she stayed with her titled brother—she saw poverty and deprivation, and no one paying a whit of attention to the needs of those who suffered.

So far she was thoroughly unimpressed.

As she returned to her bedchamber, untying the bonnet strings from her chin, Elizabeth heard her name spoken from within Rose's bedchamber. She paused by the door for a moment, wondering if maybe Rose had called out to her, but when she recognized the hushed voice of her brother, she knew she was the subject of a conversation she was not meant to hear.

To keep moving would have been the proper decision. Eavesdropping was not exactly the habit of an upstanding member of society. And yet—they were talking about her. Her feet remained glued to the rug outside Rose's door.

"…you've spoken with him about her?" asked Rose. Spoken with whom about what? Propriety be hanged. Elizabeth pressed her ear to the wooden door.

"I did," said Carver.

"And what did he say?"

Who was this he? If Elizabeth pressed her ear any harder into that door she was going to fall right through it.

"Oh, you know Oliver…" Oliver! Elizabeth pressed her hand to her mouth to keep from audibly gasping. She, without a doubt, had heard her name mentioned a moment ago. Did that mean that Carver had asked Oliver about her? "He's not one to be tied down. I think even just the question made him feel faint." What question?

"Really?" Rose sounded a little sad. There was a pause before she spoke again, sounding more energetic than before. "Well…perhaps you misunderstood him. Tell me your conversation, word for word." Bless her. Elizabeth wanted to fling open the door and hug her sister-in-law for requiring such clarity.

"I asked, '*Do you love Elizabeth?*' To which he responded, '*No.*' I hardly think there is room to misconstrue his words." Elizabeth's heart dropped. There was her answer. Oliver didn't love her. Hearing the words out loud hurt more than she had thought possible.

"Did he say why he didn't love her? Did he give a reason?" asked Rose.

Carver gave a short soft laugh. "May I know why you are so inquisitive about this topic, Mrs. Bow Street Runner? Is there something I should know?"

Elizabeth held her breath, wondering if this was the moment Rose would disregard her promise and break confidence.

Rose chuckled, sounding completely at ease, the exact opposite of how Elizabeth felt. "Nothing to tell. I suppose I'm just a little disappointed by this news. I'll admit I've been hoping that Oliver and Elizabeth would make a match of it."

Elizabeth heard Carver let out a strong breath. She could picture him running his hands through his hair, as he did when he felt overwhelmed. "I've been hoping for that same thing." This was news to

Elizabeth. "Oliver has always taken excellent care of Elizabeth. I know she would be safe with him." *Oh.*

Of course that would be the reason he wanted Elizabeth and Oliver to marry. Not because she had anything to offer, but so that Oliver could be a *guardian* for her for the rest of her life. He and Mary must be in cahoots.

The weight of her feelings pressed hard on her heart, forcing her to acknowledge them—something she wasn't even sure how to do. She pushed away from the door and quickly walked back to her room. Only after she was safely inside with the door shut did she allow a tear to fall down her cheek. She pressed her back to the door and shut her eyes against the emotions swirling within.

Oliver doesn't love me.

Well. At least now she knew for sure. There would be no more wondering. Easier to move on this way. She swatted away a tear and looked around her room without really seeing it. Her mind constantly switched tracks, between unwanted emotion and options for her future. Firm in her belief that feelings were nothing but thorns in the flesh sent to remind a fallen humanity of their sin, Elizabeth pulled herself together and pushed away from the wall. She decided to put everything she had into carving out her future—without Oliver.

Elizabeth felt a new resolve. She *would* put Oliver out of her heart. She *would* find someone else to love her. And she absolutely would *not* end the Season a pitiful woman, pining over a man who didn't love her.

Elizabeth moved across her room and threw open the doors of her wardrobe so aggressively that her hair blew away from her face. If only Kate were there to see her—she would have been so proud. Elizabeth reached inside and removed the turquoise gown. She took in a deep breath and held it as she firmed her resolve that, tonight, she would finally wear the gown that made her feel like a trifling bit of shrubbery.

Chapter Seven

Oliver stood outside Kensworth house for the second time that day. This time, however, was different because he knew Elizabeth was somewhere on the other side of the door. And he knew her beauty would take his breath and he would have to, once again, smother his inconvenient feelings for her.

He cleared his throat, feeling both his nerves and his cravat strain at the effort. He was being ridiculous. What did he have to be nervous about? This was Elizabeth—*his* Elizabeth. His dearest friend, his most beloved confidant.

But—no, not his Elizabeth. Yes, she was still the same Elizabeth with whom he had spent countless hours, the same Elizabeth in whose boots he had once put worms, the same Elizabeth with whom he had cheated at hide-and-seek. But there, once again, was the problem. Elizabeth may have been the same girl, but she certainly did not look like her anymore. He needed to find a way to the more simple feelings he had had for her when they were children. Perhaps if he forced himself to picture her with bows tied at the ends of her braids, like she had as a girl, it would help him to put these feelings behind him and he could finally move on.

Something inside him whispered that he hadn't felt normal around Elizabeth for three years now, but he firmly—and finally—ignored it.

Oliver felt the tension in his shoulders ease the moment he stepped through the door of Dalton Park. It was Oliver's seventh summer at the park, but his first one without Kensworth at his side. Oliver understood why Kensworth didn't want to go home. The unexpected death of his fiancée was still fresh and, since it had taken place on the grounds of Dalton Park, his friend couldn't bring himself to go anywhere near it. Kensworth had moved to London and Oliver had followed him there.

But it was summer time and Kensworth had given Oliver his blessing to return to Dalton Park without him, for which Oliver was grateful since it had become home to him in a way he'd never experienced before. He had missed the room that had been his ever since his first holiday there. He had missed the duke and duchess. He had missed Kate. And he had missed Elizabeth.

She, especially, was like the little sister he had never had. She was full of fun and pluck and just the right amount of obnoxiousness to keep things interesting. Sometimes Kensworth found Elizabeth to be a pest, always following them around the grounds and inserting herself into their activities. Oliver, however, never felt that way. He didn't mind spending his days with little Lizzie. She had been darling, with her bouncing curls and endless zeal for life.

After greeting the duke and duchess, Oliver made his way up the wide staircase of Dalton Park, feeling his burdens melt away with every step. It had been that way since he was a young buck. The duke and duchess fostered an environment of love and peacefulness in their home—so different from anything he had ever felt in his own home. Pembroke had felt like a prison from the day Mama died. Of course, Frank Turner had still been every bit as hateful and violent before Mama died as well—but Mama had shielded Oliver from most of the man's anger.

Now, there was no love contained within the walls of Pembroke, which was why Oliver had decided, after his last trip to visit his father, that he would never return. Unfortunately, what he hoped would be a cathartic trip to confront Frank Turner ended up being a hopeless journey that ended with him feeling more fearful than when he started. As much as he wanted to have outgrown being so affected by his father's bullying—he hadn't. Frank Turner had still gotten into his head, and now he feared he would never be rid of that hateful voice.

But he didn't want to think about Pembroke or Frank Turner now. And he certainly didn't want to think about the last words his father spat at him on his way out. No, Oliver would not pollute Dalton Park with even a hint of his father's influence.

He reached out and traced a path with his fingers over the wood molding lining the walls of the hallway that led to his room. So much time had been spent here that he could find his way around with his eyes closed. It felt quieter, though, without Kensworth. Normally, they would have so much pent up energy from a long journey that they would spend most of their walk to their rooms wrestling down the halls.

And usually Elizabeth would have been waiting for them by the front door. Where was she?

Oliver stopped in front of his door and smiled. It was good to be home.

He opened the door and walked into his room. The light was low and it cast a golden glow across the—

"Boo!"

Oliver started and whipped around, heart racing, breath short. Elizabeth emerged from behind his door and, judging by her doubled over laughter, she was enjoying his reaction.

"You wretched girl!" he said, chuckling and putting his hand on his chest to still his heart. He should have known better than to trust her absence at his arrival. "How long have you been—" but his words fell flat when his eyes finally focused on Elizabeth's face for the first time.

She was still laughing but had emerged from the shadows and stepped fully into the golden light he had been admiring only a moment ago. His breath left him. Along with all of his words. He blinked, unsure that he was even looking at the same girl.

He wasn't. Blast. Elizabeth was not a girl anymore.

"What is it?" Elizabeth asked, her amusement starting to die away as she registered the shock on his face. "What's wrong? Is there something on my face?" She started brushing at her cheek.

What happened to the girl he had left behind last summer? Elizabeth was much taller and slimmer—and yet somehow had more of a figure. She had filled out in places that had most definitely not been filled out when he last left her. The way she looked now made him breathless and evoked feelings in him that the girl from last summer had never stirred.

It was not good.

"Oliver, you're scaring me! Do I have a spider crawling on me somewhere?" But he couldn't tell her what was running through his mind. Thankfully, she had already provided him an excuse.

He smiled and stepped toward her. Blast, blast, blast. She even smelled incredible. "You...have a bit of an ink smudge. Here, I'll get it." Oliver wasn't sure if telling that lie made his predicament better or worse. Because now, he was running his thumb along her soft cheek and noticing how her lashes were so dark against her light blue eyes. And her lips were full and entirely too kissable. Which was ridiculous because they were not actually kissable. Meaning, absolutely under no circumstances, could he kiss Elizabeth's lips. Running his thumb across them was also unacceptable.

Oliver suddenly realized his hand was still resting against her face and she was looking up at him as if he had lost his mind. Maybe he had...

Air and space. Those were two very important things he needed at that moment. Oliver took one large step away from Elizabeth and cleared his throat. How old was she? He'd never really cared to know before because she had always just been little Lizzie to him. Now it felt like a very important question. He quickly added up the years in his mind and realized she was now seventeen years old. It made being alone with her in his bedchamber highly inappropriate.

"Are you feeling all right?" asked Elizabeth, taking a step toward him. That single step did things to his heart.

"Never better." He looked in her twinkling blue eyes and wished he hadn't. She was stunning and she smelled fantastic. Had she usually smelled like oranges? He was mesmerized by her. Bewitched. "Actually, no," he rushed to say when his thoughts turned again to kissing her. "I think I may be coming down with something. Feels like influenza. You should leave straight away so you don't catch anything." He began to push her from the room. Another monumental mistake. He didn't have his gloves on and she felt so warm beneath his touch. No, no, no. What was happening to him?

Elizabeth spun around to face him once across the threshold of his door. "Shall I have Mama call for the doctor?" Her big blue eyes blinked up at him. His legs felt unaccountably weak.

"No. Definitely not." The doctor wouldn't find a fever—but he may diagnose an infatuated fool. "A good night's sleep will set me to rights."

She stepped a little closer, setting her sweet orange scent on the air again. Everything about Elizabeth intoxicated him. And when she smiled, he was a goner. "I'm glad you're back, Oliver. I've missed you."

He would never forget the way Elizabeth looked while saying those words to him. He could feel all of it—every little detail—etch itself into his soul.

"I missed you too, Lizzie."

∽

Feeling rather good about his plan to picture Elizabeth in bows and braids, Oliver ran his hand over his own hair, making sure everything was in place, and straightened the lapels of his most well-fitting coat. He wore it because everyone else seemed to enjoy the sight of him in it, certainly not at all because he hoped Elizabeth would find him irresistible in the deep green tailored jacket.

Oliver knocked on the door and smiled cheekily when the disapproving butler answered.

"Jeffers," said Oliver, stepping inside Kensworth House. "Always a pleasure." It was never a pleasure.

Oliver could have sworn he heard Jeffers grunt, but he wasn't entirely sure. "Just so, sir. I have been instructed to ask you to remain waiting for the family in the foyer. They will be down momentarily." Jeffers eyed Oliver closely, as if expecting him to dart from the room and run up the stairs again. Jeffers's reprimanding look rather tempted Oliver to do just that. Were all butlers so supercilious?

"No need to fix me with that glare, Jeffers. I am here as Lady Elizabeth's escort tonight, so I shall be on my best behavior." Another grunt. Oliver supposed he deserved it. It had been his unofficial mission in life to get under the butler's skin. It was just a little too much fun to watch him scowl.

"Lady Elizabeth will be down momentarily." Somehow those words, coupled with the menacing look the butler was giving him, only intensified Oliver's buzzing nerves.

He fumbled with the folds of his cravat as an excuse for something to do while he waited. *Bows and braids.* He just needed to fix that mental image in his mind and this whole Season would go by in a flash, friendship not just intact but unscathed.

Movement caught his eye at the top of the staircase and, when he looked up, his heart stopped. All thoughts of bows and braids fled his mind at the image of ethereal beauty gliding down the stairs. Elizabeth wore a silk gown in an indescribable color, some mix of green and blue. All he knew was that whatever color it was, it made her eyes stand out like a beacon in the night. They called to him as if he had been lost at sea and was finally seeing the promise of land.

Oliver's heart beat an unnaturally fast rhythm as Elizabeth drew closer. This felt far too much like that day several years ago when Elizabeth had changed in his mind forever. Just like that day, he had a feeling this would be a memory he would never forget. He formed a smile he hoped didn't look as if he were harboring an undying love for this woman.

Oliver spent every London Season for the past three years trying to overcome his desire for Elizabeth. She had awoken his heart that summer at Dalton Park. Any other woman had paled in comparison to Elizabeth after that. He ached to think she would never be his.

"Well?" she asked with a searching smile as her silver slippered foot reached the ground floor. "Will I do?" There was some new tentativeness—an insecurity he'd never seen before lingering in Elizabeth's eyes. Which was absurd because the woman looked like some sort of otherworldly faerie from lore—to look at her would grant eternal youth or riches or—

"Oliver?" she asked again. Her brows pinched together nervously when he didn't respond the first time.

"Hmm? Oh—" He let out a short laugh and readjusted his stance. "Lizzie you look…" but what could he say? His instinct was to tell this woman how absurdly beautiful she looked and spill all of his feelings at her feet. But that would be dramatic, not to mention impulsive, which was what he had promised himself he would not be with her. With Elizabeth, he was Oliver—not the flirtatious *Charming*. "You look well."

Her brows pulled deeper together, and she seemed even more unsure of herself. "I look well?"

He nodded, feeling like the ground between them was shifting back into something uncertain. He could feel another pillar falling. What he needed to do was find some way to put them back on firm, friendly footing.

Bows and braids. Bows and braids.

Blast. That still wasn't working. Her soft, golden curls were intricately braided and pinned beautifully around her head in a way he hadn't seen on her before. A single curl hung loose, dropping down to graze her lovely, slender neck.

Which he could not stop staring at. *Wonderful.* He needed to get ahold of himself. He'd been resisting this woman for three years. He could certainly resist telling her how he felt for one more night.

Oliver cleared his throat and forced his eyes up the stairs to where he hoped Lord and Lady Kensworth would emerge momentarily. "Do you suppose the love birds will be much longer?"

He saw Elizabeth shrug out of the corner of his eye—only the corner because he didn't quite trust himself yet to look at her again. "I'm not sure. To be honest, I'll be surprised if they even emerge from their blissful bubble to join us tonight."

Oliver whipped his head to look at Elizabeth. "You think they might not come with us? Why not?" He could hear the sharpness in his voice, and saw the evidence of it registered on Elizabeth's face. He cleared his throat and forced himself to speak in a more normal tone. "I just think Miss Loxley will be terribly disappointed to do without Lord and Lady Hatley *as well* as Lord and Lady Kensworth."

Elizabeth took a step toward him, but he instinctively took a step back. *Wonderful, Oliver.* He hadn't done that since he was twenty-two and she seventeen. Could he be more obvious? Oliver felt like he needed to go run around the block just to relieve some of the tension he felt building. Would he never grow used to Elizabeth's beauty? But it wasn't just her beauty. This woman was incredible to him in every way.

"Are you all right, Oliver? Is something wrong?" It was as if it was three years ago and they were back in his room all over again.

"Oh, no, I'm just fine," he said, reaching out to rest his hand on the wall behind him. Unfortunately, he completely missed the wall and nearly fell to the ground. He was able to right himself quickly with a springy little jump that made him look even more insane than he already had. He forced a smile. "I think I'll just go tell the coachman that we'll be another minute."

Elizabeth's eyes were wide and her mouth was slightly open as he turned away from her and darted out the door. Oliver flew down the steps and paced at least ten circles before he felt he had gained enough composure to go back in the house.

Never once had he denied himself the ability to flirt with a woman whom he found attractive. Or to court her as soon as she had caught his eye. But he had never allowed himself the privilege of either of those things with Elizabeth, because he knew that if he courted her, he would never be able to let her go.

Anytime he even remotely contemplated the idea, Frank Turner's words pierced through his mind, angry and unwavering. The memory returned unbidden of Oliver's last meeting with his father: he had finally summoned the courage to tell his father just how much he had been hurt by his violence and hatred. And what had Frank Turner done? He had laughed. His father had laughed in his face and said, "I wouldn't be so judgmental if I were you, boy. My blood runs through your veins. One day you'll be just like me, and my father before me, and his father before him. We Turners are all the same and there's no use pretending you're any different."

Oliver clenched his fists at his sides and looked back up at the now ominous-looking front door. He would never hurt Elizabeth the way his father had hurt his mother. The way his father had hurt him. Oliver would make sure Elizabeth got the very best in life, which meant letting her go.

Chapter Eight

Everything was under control. Kensworth and Rose finally made their way downstairs, and the four of them settled in the carriage. Seeing Kensworth and Rose had helped Oliver regain some of his composure and steeled his determination. The only problem was, now they were in a dark carriage and he couldn't really see Kensworth anymore, but he could certainly feel Elizabeth sitting beside him, her arm brushing against him every time the carriage bumped and swayed.

Oliver was torn between wishing the carriage ride was a little less jostling, and hoping they never met a smooth patch ever again. Because, blast it all, he liked the way Elizabeth smelled tonight and the way his arm felt as if it had caught fire every time hers brushed against him.

But he had the situation completely under control.

"Any more news of Mr. Turner?" Kensworth's voice mixed with the sound of his father's name felt like a bucket of cold water dumped over him.

"What's happened to your father?" asked Elizabeth, concern coloring her tone.

Every so often, they passed a street lamp and its light would cast a brief warm glow across Elizabeth's face. In those moments, he could see the questions in her eyes. Elizabeth was the only one in the Ashburn family who knew the true extent of Frank Turner's abuse toward Oliver. Many times over the past few years, when he had continued to summer at Dalton Park without Kensworth, he and Elizabeth had spent their days walking for hours over the grounds, talking about anything and everything. During those summers, he had let Elizabeth inside the walls of his heart that no one else even knew existed.

Kensworth knew that Oliver's father was difficult to be around. He knew that his father was harsh—and that they had an unfixable relationship. But Elizabeth knew more. She knew that Frank Turner was never awake without brandy coursing through his veins. She knew that Frank Turner had a heavy fist and a short temper. She knew that Oliver was hated by his father. And that the only words ever spoken to Oliver by his father were of his worthlessness.

Oliver looked toward Elizabeth. "I received a letter from him not long ago. He's…not well."

He heard her take in a deep breath. And then in the dark carriage, Elizabeth reached over and took his hand. She squeezed it once and then pulled hers away. Oliver almost reached back for it again, but thankfully Rose's voice stopped him. "We're here," she stated as the carriage pulled to a stop outside of Miss Vienna Loxley's home, in line behind at least ten other carriages.

Oliver relaxed a little. He had been to several of Miss Loxley's eccentric dinner parties over the past few years and he knew that inside that four-story townhome would be plenty of entertainment to distract him.

"I'm not quite sure you're prepared for this evening," he said, pulling himself away from the heaviness he had been feeling before, and grinning at Elizabeth.

Elizabeth's head turned quickly to look out the window at the home of her sister's oldest and closest friend. Vienna Loxley was a woman quite unlike any other in London—possibly the world.

"I think I am actually feeling a little excited about this event," said Elizabeth.

"Hold on to that feeling. It's likely the only event you will truly enjoy the whole Season," said Kensworth. His bland tone made it clear to everyone listening just how he felt about having to attend any of the *ton* events.

Rose nudged him in the ribs. "Be nice."

He sighed. "Must I?"

"Yes."

Kensworth leaned across the carriage toward Elizabeth. "Darling, are you sure you wouldn't rather skip this whole entire come-out and return to the orphanage with Rose and me? We could always use another teacher. I'm sure we can find you a very nice farmer to settle down with." He wagged his eyebrows playfully.

Rose pulled her husband back into the seat. "Any more unhelpful comments like that and you'll be finding yourself sharing Oliver's bed tonight rather than mine."

Kensworth's eyes widened and he pretended to button his lips.

"Why must he intrude on my goodnight's sleep?" asked Oliver. "Doesn't he have his own bed you may sentence him to?"

"Yes—but I don't think that would be punishment enough."

Oliver squinted a smile at Rose. "Very flattering. Thank you for that."

"You're quite welcome." She smiled sweetly back at him. Rose was certainly throwing a new dynamic into his and Kensworth's friendship.

Elizabeth and her brother laughed at the bickering. The carriage inched forward again as the other equipages were emptied and began to drive away. Finally, it was their turn to exit the carriage. A footman opened the door and Oliver quickly stepped down to help Elizabeth out of the carriage before wrapping her hand around his arm and escorting her inside. Rose and Kensworth followed closely behind. Oliver wished he and Elizabeth could be the ones to walk behind. It would give him a much better view as his reclusive friend and new bride re-entered Society. Oliver had rarely ever been able to drag Kensworth to an "insufferable puffed up society event full of preening debutantes and obnoxious mothers"—Kensworth's exact words—and he wished he could see his friend's face as he was forced to smile and do the pretty. Oliver, however, had mastered that particular talent.

They all made their way up the front stairs of the home behind the line of invited guests, and just before the door opened, Oliver leaned toward Elizabeth's ear. "Prepare yourself," he said, quiet enough for only her to hear.

He felt her shiver beside him. Because of his breath against her ear or because of nerves? She turned wide eyes up to him and he felt as if they were voicing a question to him, one he couldn't interpret. His gaze dropped briefly to her lips, which were, at the moment, tantalizingly close to his.

But no—thoughts of her lovely mouth were not allowed. He looked toward the open door of Miss Loxley's home. It was time to focus on the evening ahead of them, helping to launch Elizabeth into Society.

Chapter Nine

Elizabeth stood in the entry hall of Miss Vienna Loxley's London townhouse and gaped. She had heard her sister speak of Vienna, but never had she actually met the woman. And never had she imagined a home that could only be described as *eccentric*.

The warm light of many candles illuminated the space, allowing Elizabeth to see with perfect clarity the many jaw-dropping features of the room. Her eyes first settled upon a gigantic round table in the middle of the foyer. The table itself was nothing impressive, but the base had Elizabeth blinking: a massive and quite startling carved lion head held up the large mahogany table, realistic enough that she wouldn't have been surprised to hear it roar. She turned to take in bright green drapes—the exact shade of a lime—hanging over the two main windows to either side of the front door. An ornate longcase clock stood in the corner of the room, fashioned to look as if the base were a woman wearing a dress, complete with slippers peeking from underneath.

"It is something, isn't it?" asked Oliver, pulling Elizabeth back into the moment.

"I cannot find the words to describe this home," said Elizabeth, turning her wide eyes to Oliver.

He grinned mischievously. "Look up."

Elizabeth obeyed and then gasped at a scandalously painted ceiling. Those musicians were so very naked behind their lyres and harps that Elizabeth wanted to blush or laugh or wrap a shawl around herself. They did look very merry, though.

"Ah—you've arrived!" A cheerful, fluttering voice called from across the foyer.

She tore her gaze from the provocative ceiling and resisted the urge to gape when she finally laid eyes on Miss Vienna Loxley. Elizabeth had of course heard many tales of her sister's friend. She was prepared for Vienna to be a little out of the ordinary. *This* woman could never be described as anything so pedestrian. Vienna was an angel in the flesh.

White-blonde curls peeked out from beneath Vienna's elaborately decorated gold silk turban, adorned with glittering jewels and one single large ostrich feather rising from the back. Elizabeth had never appreciated fabric head wraps before. Vienna, however, elevated the style and made it look entirely different and highly appealing. Her skin was nearly as milky white as her hair, giving her an appearance more porcelain than flesh. Her bright green eyes glittered as much as the emeralds dotting her turban. Most striking of all was the thin flowing cream gown draped over her willowy figure. Vienna was nothing less than striking.

The woman swept over to Elizabeth and took her hand and kissed it. "Lady Elizabeth, I presume. I cannot believe this is our first introduction. But I feel as if I already know you from all the stories Mary has told me over the years. You look exactly as she described: a beauty, with mischievous eyes." She winked and turned her attention to Oliver. He bowed and she curtsied. Even her curtsy was impressive. It was both lazy and regal at the same time. Elizabeth slowly awakened to an uncomfortable sensation growing in her stomach. It was ugly and pinching.

"Mr. Turner, you are going to be the most envied man in the room, walking in with Lady Elizabeth on your arm." Elizabeth's eyes followed Miss Loxley's hand as it reached out and landed on Oliver's forearm. "I predict she is going to be the Diamond of the Season. And my predictions are never wrong."

"When is Turner not the most envied man in the room?" said Carver from behind them.

Vienna laughed, a lovely, soft, fluttering sound. "Quite right. Such a flirt!" She tossed a saucy look at Oliver that peeved Elizabeth. Her feelings toward Vienna were shifting rapidly, and they were beginning to smell terribly of jealousy. "Lord Kensworth, I almost feel as though I'm seeing a ghost. How many years has it been since you've been out in Society?"

Elizabeth felt Oliver's arm stiffen at the exact moment that she did. Elizabeth and her family knew to the day how long it had been since Carver had become something of a recluse. His fiancée had died a little over three years ago, and for those three years, her brother had felt lost to all of them. It wasn't until Rose had come along and helped Carver heal that he had been able to surface from his grief.

"It's been too long," Carver said. It was enough. He looked down to Rose with a look of deep adoration--a look Elizabeth very much wished that Oliver would give her. "Miss Loxley, allow me to introduce you to my wife, Lady Rose Kensworth. Love, this is the famous Miss Vienna Loxley, Mary's closest friend."

Vienna laughed again. "I doubt Lord Hatley would appreciate me still holding that title, but I do love Mary dearly, so I shall claim it proudly. Lady Kensworth, welcome to my absurd home! I hope you find it...amusing." Shocked by those words, Elizabeth looked at Miss Loxley to judge her meaning. But she looked neither sarcastic or self-deprecating. Instead, she looked rather pleased and joyful.

"I can honestly say I'm pleased to be here," said Rose with a curtsy, looking at ease and confident, as always. "I have heard endless tales from your parties. I am extremely intrigued about what entertainment we may encounter this evening."

Vienna smiled a little wickedly. "All I will say is, you will not be disappointed."

Just then, the butler opened the front door again and a new line of guests gathered behind them. Vienna excused herself to welcome the newcomers. The four of them moved into the expansive drawing room, and Elizabeth watched with dismay as Carver and Rose were almost immediately pounced on by those already assembled. Would she be next? She didn't feel ready. Her legs felt weak and she feared she looked ridiculous in her brightly colored gown.

Oliver must have sensed her nerves because he guided them toward the edge of the room, farthest away from the other guests. Part of her hated that he knew how she felt before she expressed it. Actually, all of her hated it. It was annoying for him to be so in tune with her and yet to not have more tender feelings toward her. It made not loving him anymore all but impossible.

"What do you think so far?" he asked in a hushed voice.

"A little stunned. Does Miss Loxley know her decor is ridiculous?"

Oliver chuckled a little and retrieved two glasses of champagne from a tray as a footman passed. He handed one to Elizabeth and she eyed it, realizing she had never tried champagne before. Wine, yes. Although, if she was being honest, she didn't much care for its bitter flavor. This drink, however, looked light, airy, and promising.

"Would it surprise you to know Miss Loxley had this whole house designed with only the intention of making her guests laugh?" Elizabeth watched Oliver put the champagne flute to his lips and take a sip. Never had she envied glassware before.

She forced her mind back to Vienna Loxley. "Actually, it does not surprise me in the least. She seems like a fun sort of person, and so confident." She eyed Oliver, searching his face for any signs that he harbored feelings for their beautiful and eccentric hostess. Not that she had any right to care about such things. Oliver was her friend. Nothing more. Heavens, she was growing weary of having to constantly remind herself of that fact. The sooner she could find someone else to distract her mind, the better.

Elizabeth took a tentative sip of the bubbling drink and was surprised to find that she liked it. She liked it quite a lot, in fact.

"She does give that impression. But when you look closer, you'll see something different," said Oliver.

"What do you mean? You do not find Miss Loxley to be confident?"

He shrugged and took another sip of champagne. "She will try her best to convince you that she is. But in my experience, sometimes confidence can simply be a mask—something to hide behind so others can't hurt you." His eyes locked with hers and Elizabeth suddenly felt like maybe they weren't talking about Vienna anymore. Oliver was the epitome of confidence. His manners were engaging, his whole person was beyond attractive, and Elizabeth was certain Oliver could flirt with a fern and make it blush. But she also knew the parts of him he kept hidden—his deepest injuries. She had always assumed his personality was a product of overcoming his childhood hurts. Never, until that moment, had she considered it could be his mask.

This, however, was not the place to engage Oliver in a deep discussion.

She raised her glass to her lips again, casting her eyes out on the quickly filling room. "This is an annual party that Vienna hosts, is it not?" She took another sip, realizing for the first time that the walls were pink. Actually—everything in the room was pink. The curtains, the settee, the rugs. Had there ever been a more absurd room?

"Yes. She's been hosting it since she inherited her fortune from her uncle several years ago. You must count yourself lucky. It is ridiculously difficult to secure an invitation to one of her parties."

"More difficult than procuring a voucher to Almacks?"

Oliver chuckled. "Exceedingly. In fact, Lady Jersey and her whole set have never once been able to garner invitations to Miss Loxley's. It's rumored that she's been so ill about it that she's tried to have the Watch shut it down for several years now."

Elizabeth laughed, feeling a little lighter with every sip of her new favorite drink. "And what is it that makes this party so fantastic?"

Oliver's eyes filled with amusement. "The entertainment. She converts her ballroom into a staged theater for the occasion." Elizabeth's excitement grew at the eagerness in Oliver's voice. "Every year, Vienna hires some sort of entertainment, but manages to keep it completely under wraps until it is revealed the night of the party. One year, Lord Byron performed a reading of one of his poems that scandalized the entire room. The next year, Vienna somehow arranged for an exclusive bout between two prizefighters. No less than five ladies fainted dead away at the sight of so much blood." Elizabeth could easily imagine it. Mary was always saying the ladies of the *ton* adored fainting. It made them interesting, apparently.

"Last year's party," continued Oliver, "was much less bloody, but certainly no less shocking. Beau Brummel himself walked onto the stage in his underclothes and proceeded through his dressing routine, step-by-step with his valet, for the next three hours. Gentlemen all through the crowd requested pencils and notepads to record the way he tied his cravat." He chuckled. "At least three ladies fainted that night as well."

Elizabeth laughed, feeling a bit lighter and more at ease. As much as she adored the country, it was wonderful to finally be in Town sharing this moment with Oliver. Her nerves calmed a trifle, and her trepidation receded a touch. For once, Elizabeth hadn't been left behind. She wouldn't have to hear the tales second-hand from Oliver when he came to stay for the summer. She was here, experiencing the eccentrics of London with him—her best friend, the man she loved.

Elizabeth stared at Oliver with her lips poised against her champagne glass. If only she possessed a bit of Rose's confidence, perhaps she would be able to tell Oliver how she felt about him. Risk everything and declare her love. She wasn't sure how she could feel so bold when it came to climbing out of windows, but act like complete mush when it came to sharing her heart. Because at that moment, wearing the brightest color gown she had ever worn, and standing amidst an event that she felt like she was sneaking out of the nursery to attend, she didn't feel at all confident.

And she still wasn't sure what to make of the way Oliver had reacted to the sight of her. It certainly hadn't done anything to lessen her anxieties. He had reacted so strangely when she first walked down the stairs, as though he wanted to be anywhere but there with her. Perhaps it *was* pathetic, however, despite her confirmed suspicions regarding Oliver's lack of romantic feelings toward her, that part of her was still hoping he would see her in that gown and find her breathtaking.

It wasn't fair that instead, she felt exactly that way about him. Really, must he wear such formfitting jackets? Did he perform some sort of exercise to build the muscles tugging against his jacket? What would it feel like to run her hand up his arm and over those broad shoulders?

"What are you thinking of that's making you blush so suddenly?" asked Oliver, his deep blue eyes sparking with amusement, a devilish smile on his lips. *Drat.* He'd caught her ogling him.

Elizabeth shook her head lightly, "Oh nothing. I'm simply…" She was going to say that she was simply warm, but the sound of another woman's voice interrupted her.

It seemed they had finally been discovered in their blissful little corner.

Chapter Ten

"Mr. Turner!" A petite, dark-haired young woman moved to stand far too close to Oliver. Did every woman have to look at him in that kiss-me-here-and-now way? She certainly understood the desire, but must they wear it so plainly across their faces? "I hoped you would be in attendance tonight. How dashing you look in your dark green jacket. It is quite my favorite of your wardrobe." She reached out and ran her hand slowly down the length of his arm. Elizabeth narrowed her eyes. Did every woman pet him in such a way?

"Ah—Miss Barley. You are also looking radiant in your lovely gown." Huh. Miss Barley looked radiant while Elizabeth simply looked well? Elizabeth bit the inside of her cheek. This was precisely why she must move on from Oliver. She needed comments such as those to lose their sting.

Miss Barley feigned embarrassment as she coyly sidled closer to Oliver. "I knew I could count on you to notice my new frock. It was made especially for the occasion. And, if I am remembering correctly" —the blasted woman bit her lower lip—"this particular shade of blue is your favorite, is it not?"

Elizabeth could only blink at her forwardness. And also at how

startlingly long her lashes were. Good heavens, but they looked terrifying—like spiders perched above her eyes, waiting to crawl off and
bite someone at any moment.

Even more startling was the charming smile Oliver returned to her.
"Your memory serves you well, Miss Barley. It is indeed my favorite
color." This party was becoming less and less enjoyable by the minute.
As though he could hear her thoughts, Oliver looked her way. How
good of him to remember she existed. "Forgive me, Lady Elizabeth,
have you and Miss Barley been yet acquainted?" With that look, Elizabeth's heart sank even further. His face looked different—his smile
bright and welcoming, of course, but also devoid of the intimacy and
warmth she usually felt from him. It was as if he had put on a new
man, one too pleasant for his own good, suddenly treating Elizabeth as
if she were nothing more than a mere acquaintance.

"I have not had the pleasure," said Elizabeth, burying her feelings
down deep, to be examined later.

Miss Barley's eyes slid to Elizabeth, deliberately assessing her
slowly from head to toe in a way that made Elizabeth wish to hide
behind the drapes. She felt ridiculous enough as it was in this dress.
She didn't need Miss Barley's help to feel any more a spectacle.

"A pleasure, my lady." Somehow Miss Barley managed to make
even that small statement sound condescending. Her dark—nearly
black—eyes turned back up to Oliver and she fluttered her spider-
lashes at him. "Now that you are back in Town, I do hope you will join
Mama and me for tea one day soon." She turned her eyes to Elizabeth,
a sneer marking her pouty lips. "Of course, you are also welcome,
Lady Elizabeth. It's only that Mr. Turner has always been a frequent
visitor to our home, and Mama does so dote on him." The woman's
face molded back into a flirtatious smile as she looked up at Oliver.
"She will be most disappointed if made to endure another week
without your company."

Could the woman be any more obvious? Her meaning came
through loud and clear—she was staking her claim on Oliver Turner.
Well, Elizabeth had news for Miss Barley. She would not be entering
the competition. A friend was all she would ever be to Oliver. Unless,

of course, he were to…no. It was past time for her to stop wishing for the impossible.

Oliver's eyes darted to Elizabeth—holding her gaze for the briefest of moments—and then back to Miss Barley. "I should not wish to disappoint you or your lovely mother for the world, Miss Barley. I will call within the week," he said. His words felt like daggers to Elizabeth. But why?

Elizabeth had known Oliver was a flirt. That was nothing new. But some small part of her had hoped that maybe, just maybe, when she came to London, he wouldn't flirt with anyone but her. Now, she felt stupid and small for ever entertaining such a hope.

The last few bubbles slid across Elizabeth's tongue as she finished off her drink. She cast her eyes out over the now crowded drawing room and thought of the plan she had been concocting in her mind all day. It was time to act on it.

Her eyes raced over each of the different well-dressed ladies and gentlemen in their finery. She was vaguely aware of Oliver and Miss Barley continuing their flirtations, but the sounds around her all faded to a muffled hum as she searched for the right person—the right man.

Her eyes bounced, sorted, and measured each person in attendance until her gaze landed on a tall gentleman in the back corner of the room. And there she lingered. He was much taller than the other men gathered around him, and he was dressed in the height of fashion. He had brown hair—closer to the color of honey than true brown—and a nice lazy sort of smile. He was handsome, exuding a quiet confidence. Elizabeth was determined to detach her heart from Oliver, and this man just might be the one to help her do it.

Miss Barley's voice suddenly cut through Elizabeth's thoughts. "I see you've noticed Lord Hastings." Elizabeth chose to ignore her smug tone and use the opportunity to her advantage instead.

"Yes—I admit I have." Elizabeth resisted the urge to look at Oliver. She turned her eyes to Miss Barley instead. "What can you tell me about him?"

Miss Barley let out a short laugh and managed to move even closer to Oliver, casting her eyes toward Lord Hastings. Elizabeth's feet itched to step on the woman's toes, but she refrained. She had no claim on Oliver.

"Only that he is a viscount and referred to as the Unobtainable. Many a woman has set her cap for him, but none have ever caught his eye." *Interesting.* For some reason, Elizabeth liked that thought. It was exciting, and goodness knows she liked excitement. "Not only has he never courted a woman, but he never dances at balls and very rarely pays attention to any females." Her eyes slid like serpents back to Elizabeth. "But by all means, try your hand at the man, my lady."

Elizabeth could feel Oliver's gaze burning into the side of her face. Did he disapprove of her forward questions? It didn't matter. She couldn't allow his opinion to hold weight anymore. As much as it pained her, it was time for their relationship to undergo a change.

"Are you acquainted with the viscount?" Elizabeth asked Oliver this time.

He held her eyes—face nearly expressionless. "A bit." His voice was quiet.

"If you will both excuse me, I see a friend who has just arrived. But do find me later Mr. Turner. We have much catching up to do." Miss Barley fluttered her lashes at Oliver and dropped a curtsy before walking off. But Elizabeth did not miss the way Miss Barley's fingers lightly trailed over Oliver's elbow as she passed him. A possessive fire swept through Elizabeth's body, and she had to force her gaze to her feet in an attempt to smother it.

Jealousy. Anger. Hurt. Longing. It all washed over Elizabeth like a wave. She didn't want to feel these things, but her mind insisted on replaying every single moment that had transpired between Oliver and Miss Loxley, Oliver and Miss Barley, and Oliver and every other woman with whom she had seen him interact. It wasn't fair. She had shared so much of her life with him, and he had this whole other life in London that he lived without her. Now that she was here and seeing it first hand, it made her ache. She was present with Oliver, but she *still* was not truly able to share it with him. They were friends. Nothing more. She could not trail her fingers across his elbow. She could not dance fluttering eyelashes in his direction.

He will never love me in that way.

"You're frowning," said Oliver.

She lifted her chin and forced herself to meet his eyes. *Friends.* She knew her place. "No. Only lost in thought."

"And what thoughts would those be?"

"I was only thinking of Miss Barley, and wondering what your opinion is of her?" For so many years she had been forced to hear about the latest young woman to steal Oliver's attention. By reopening that line of communication, she was inserting herself back into the role of devoted friend.

His boyish grin made her insides ache. "I think her eyelashes are quite fantastic. Do you agree?" She couldn't answer the question, and she was angry at him for finding the woman—and her obvious attention—attractive.

Elizabeth dug her nails into her palm. "Mr. Turner," she forced her voice to stay calm and unwavering as she faced him. His smile dropped entirely at the formal use of his name. She hoped he wouldn't notice that her hands were actually trembling. "I would like to make Lord Hastings's acquaintance. Would you be able to make the introduction for me?"

His eyes remained fixed on her for two breaths—his face unreadable. Was he contemplating? Was he irritated at the idea? Jealous? No. Elizabeth wouldn't let herself hope for such a thing.

The same cold and disconnected smile from a moment ago spread again over his mouth, and he nodded. "Of course. I'd be more than happy to make the introduction. Hastings has a good reputation. I think you two would…deal well together." She noticed Oliver tug at the top of his cravat, but other than that, he seemed completely at ease with the idea.

"Wonderful." She smiled, and then took another glass of champagne from a tray when a footman came around again. She was going to need all of the liquid courage she could get if she was going to attempt to become exactly what Miss Loxley had predicted.

Elizabeth was done being the adventurous young girl from Dalton Park. She was quite through being infatuated with Oliver. It was time to shake off her nerves, step into the role Miss Emma had worked for years to mold Elizabeth into, and claim her heart back from a man who would never love her in return.

She was going to become the first and last woman to catch the eye of the Unobtainable Lord Hastings.

Chapter Eleven

How had Elizabeth gone her whole life without ever having tasted champagne? It was magnificent. And the more she consumed, the more she enjoyed it. In fact, the more she consumed, the more she enjoyed everything. Even Miss Barley's eyelashes were beginning to look more appealing. Elizabeth especially liked the way the feather, in the hair of the matron with whom she was conversing, seemed to be dancing. How amusing, to have a dancing feather! Where had the woman even found such an accessory? Was there a bird still attached to it somehow?

She had just opened her mouth to ask the woman when Oliver's voice boomed, seemingly out of nowhere. When had he even walked away? They had just finished dinner and were waiting again in the drawing room for the butler to announce them into the ballroom for the entertainment portion of the evening, and then Oliver had excused himself and left her in the care of...oh, right. He had left her with Rose. Rose! She had lost Rose! ...No, there she was, right beside Elizabeth, where she had left her. Ever-faithful Rose.

"Lady Elizabeth, Lady Kensworth, may I present to you, Lord Hastings."

Elizabeth's eyes widened when she realized the man she had

decided to make fall in love with her was standing just in front of her. And he was staring at her. Why was he staring at her? Had he already fallen in love with her?

Oh. No. It was because she wasn't talking. Were all of these words simply in her head, then?

"Pleased to make your acquaintan—" Rose started to say but Elizabeth's voice suddenly realized how to work again and it shot out of her mouth like a cannon.

"So wonderful to meet you, my lord," said Elizabeth, with a confident smile and a curtsy. There. She'd spoken and she had done such a fantastic job of it that she rewarded herself with another big sip of the lovely, bubbly drink.

Lord Hastings cleared his throat and bowed. "A pleasure, Lady Elizabeth. And Lady Kensworth, I offer my sincere congratulations on your recent marriage."

"Thank you," said Rose, and again Elizabeth was amazed at Rose's poise, despite the fact that she had been a wanted thief only a month ago.

Oh, dear. Elizabeth was suddenly worried she was going to blurt out that Rose used to be a wanted thief. She covered her mouth to protect the words from escaping on their own. "I feel very lucky to be joined to such a wonderful family," continued Rose. She glanced at Elizabeth, frowning ever so slightly at the hand pressed over her mouth. "And to have gained such lovely sisters." Rose removed Elizabeth's hand from her mouth and wrapped it around her own arm. How nice that she wanted to snuggle.

Only Elizabeth couldn't really focus on snuggling Rose just then because Oliver's face looked pinched, and she wondered why he should be scowling in such a way. "Is your cravat too tight?" she blurted out.

Oliver's eyebrows flew up and he looked between Rose and Lord Hastings before settling his gaze back on Elizabeth—a small tentative chuckle escaping from his mouth. "No. Why do you ask?"

"You look grumpy." She noticed everyone's faces suddenly looked as if they had just peeked again at the painting on Vienna's ceiling, and she wondered if she had said something wrong. But…what was it she had said again? Elizabeth's memory suddenly escaped her. And had her tongue always felt so heavy?

"Perhaps it is a bit too tight. I believe I'll go and attempt to retie it before we move into the ballroom." Tie what? And why was Oliver always trying to get away from her lately? Because, he clearly was. It was probably her offensive shrubbery dress.

"Lady Elizabeth," said Lord Hastings, in his lovely baritone, after Oliver walked away. "I understand this is your first Season?"

"Forgive me," Rose interrupted, placing a hand on Elizabeth's arm. "I must leave you for a moment. I can see that Lord Kensworth finds himself backed into a corner with Lady Humphrey, and he keeps flashing me the look of the desperate, in need of rescue."

Lord Hastings chuckled. "By all means, go save your husband. I, myself, have succumbed to the same fate once or twice and would not wish it upon anyone."

Rose smiled and, with a curtsy, hurried over to Carver. They were wonderful together. Elizabeth wanted to be wonderful with someone. She looked back to Lord Hastings. Now was her chance to win him over. She took the last gulp of her friendly drink and noticed he was watching her with the hint of a smile. He extended his hand toward her now empty glass. "Allow me." He retrieved it from her and handed it off to a servant.

Handsome and chivalrous!

But then when he chuckled and thanked her, Elizabeth realized she had said that thought out loud. Why was she always doing that? Her cheeks filled with heat—or rather, continued to heat, because she felt as if her face had been on fire ever since she had finished her first glass of champagne. She placed her gloved hands on her cheeks to try to cool them, but there was nothing for it. Still hot.

Lord Hastings cleared his throat. "As I was saying, this is your first Season, is it not?"

"Yes."

"And…are you enjoying it?"

"Quite." She wanted to say more, but suddenly the room was

starting to feel a little wobbly and she was having to use a great deal of energy to remain upright. And her tongue…so heavy. This wasn't normal, was it?

She noted Lord Hastings pressing his lips together as if to keep from smiling at something again. But she had no idea what it could be since neither of them had said anything funny. Lord Hastings was nice but not at all as funny as Oliver. "And…may I ask what aspects of London you are most excited about experiencing?"

"None of it." Oh, blast! She shouldn't have said that. "I mean, all of it."

He gave a half-smile. "No, I don't think you meant that."

"No," she sighed. "I didn't." She wished the bloody floor would stop shifting.

"You are a daughter of the Duke of Dalton, are you not?"

Elizabeth narrowed her eyes, focusing on Lord Hastings's dark green ones and trying to block out the way the room was starting to turn on its end. "Yes, one of three. My younger sister is Lady Kate, and my eldest sister is Lady Elizabeth." She paused. "Wait, no. That's not right. Lady Hatley is my eldest sister! That's it."

Again, he pressed his lips together, as if holding back a fierce laugh. "I am well acquainted with Lady Hatley. I believe my eldest brother vied for her hand during one of her seasons."

Elizabeth gave a short snort. "He and every other man in Society. They all wanted her dowry." Again, the words flowed freely from her mouth, completely unbidden. And why had Miss Loxley made her rooms so wobbly? Horribly rude.

"I don't believe my brother was after her dowry, if that helps remove his name from your black books," said Lord Hastings.

Elizabeth waved him off. "Doesn't matter a drop to me. Mary will be the first to tell you she can take care of herself. Trust me. She doesn't need my help in the least. And you can tell your brother she settled for nothing but a love match, so there's no need for him to feel slighted by her."

Lord Hastings's brow pulled down. "My…brother is no longer with us. He died two years ago, I'm afraid."

A large puff of air released from Elizabeth's cheeks. "Well, then it's rather a good thing Mary didn't choose him, isn't it?" Wait a moment. Was that a rude comment? Yes. Her hand flew to cover her mouth as she realized her words had once again exited instead of staying in her head where they belonged. And why was she talking so loudly? How did one lower one's voice? Just another thing she failed at. "I'm terribly sorry," she said, trying to lower her voice unsuccessfully and deciding to convey her apology by grabbing his arm instead. But it felt wrong—so she placed her other hand on his other arm to balance out the gesture. There. Steady as she goes.

What was that snooty matron scowling at? Elizabeth nearly told the woman to pull the tack out of her slipper before she was distracted by Lord Hastings. He must have heard something funny again from someone else, because Elizabeth could see him chuckling behind his closed lips, shoulders slightly shaking. She wished he would share the joke with her. She loved to laugh!

"Lady Elizabeth," he said, barely hiding his amusement, "are you feeling quite well?"

She pulled away with wide eyes and placed her hand on her chest. "Moi? Oh, I'm feeling phemmminonial." She frowned at her words. "Phem-en-om-in-al. Oh, you know what I mean!" She leaned in to whisper to him. "But I do wish Vienna had not made these rooms so wobbly. They are *quite* frustrating."

Chapter Twelve

Was Elizabeth swaying? Yes. She definitely was. Something was off. Oliver had tried to keep his distance that evening—distance for himself, and distance for Elizabeth. Flirting with Miss Barley seemed like the most natural way to remind himself that his destiny had already been carved out before him as *Charming*, not as Elizabeth's husband. In fact, she had expressed interest in Lord Hastings, and as much as the idea hurt, Oliver knew it was for the best. If Lord Hastings began courting Elizabeth, and then married her, Oliver would never have to acknowledge his feelings for her.

Of course, he would then have to spend the rest of his life looking on as Elizabeth shared her life with another man, which did not sound too appealing either. What choice did he have? He wasn't willing to tell Elizabeth of his own feelings. She deserved nothing but the best, and the truth was, Lord Hastings fit the criteria much better than he did.

But then why was his heart protesting so much at the thought of Elizabeth in the arms of another man?

Oliver re-entered the drawing room and pushed through the crowd. A buzz of excited energy filled the space, in anticipation of the moment when the doors to the theater room would open to reveal whatever eccentric entertainment Miss Loxley had planned for the evening.

As he drew closer to where Elizabeth stood in the corner of the room, he could verify that she was indeed swaying like a tree in the wind. And also that Lord Hastings was still with her. The man had claimed her attention ever since Oliver had introduced them after dinner. His teeth clenched together even though he knew he was being ridiculous. Good for Elizabeth, catching the eye of the Unobtainable. If anyone could, he knew it would be her. Which is why he had wanted to shake the annoying Miss Barley for even suggesting it. He felt like an invalid, faced with a horrible yet necessary remedy. Elizabeth being taken off the market was the cure, but he just couldn't bring himself to swallow the medicine. It tasted too much like poison.

Oliver had almost made it to Elizabeth's side when he heard her laugh such a boisterous, shrill laugh that it caused him to cringe. This was not at all like her. Something was definitely amiss.

He stopped beside Elizabeth and Hastings. "Enjoying yourself tonight, Liz—Lady Elizabeth?" he corrected, feeling unnecessarily angry that he must address her formally.

Elizabeth's eyes went as wide as saucers and she leaned toward him. "Oh, yes!" Oliver blinked at the smell of champagne heavy on her breath. "The mooost fun! Lord Haplings is verrry gentlemanly." She winked at Hastings, unaware that she had mispronounced his name.

Oh no. Was she…? Blast. The woman was completely foxed!

Oliver looked hesitantly to Hastings, wondering what he thought of Elizabeth's lack of decorum, and was a bit—though he would deny it until the day he died—pleased to think that maybe this would scare the man off. But why did he feel that way? Oliver couldn't—wouldn't— act on his feelings, and he couldn't reasonably expect Elizabeth to remain single her whole life.

No. He cared deeply for Elizabeth. He wanted her happiness. Which is why he needed to save her just then.

However, Hastings spoke first. "Turner. I believe Lady Elizabeth has suddenly"—he gave Oliver a meaningful look that said he would be the one doing the rescuing—"taken ill. You are a close friend of her family, are you not? Would you be able to escort her to Lord and Lady Kensworth and inform them of her illness without the room raising questions?" Hang Hastings. This was what Oliver had already planned to do. Now it sounded as though Hastings was the one to ensure Elizabeth's wellbeing.

The man continued, leaning closer to Oliver so Elizabeth would not overhear. "I would escort her myself, but I do not wish for Lady Elizabeth to feel any more embarrassment than she likely already will tomorrow."

Oliver smiled tensely. "Of course. I'm *exceptionally* close with their family, so it would only make sense if I were the one to inform them." Oh. Wonderful. He was going to act like a jealous fool now.

Hastings lifted a brow in the haughty way of the aristocracy and smiled tentatively before turning his attention back to Elizabeth, who appeared to be deeply enthralled by something on the ceiling. "My lady?" Her head flew down, and the sudden movement seemed to knock her off balance. Hastings and Oliver both lunged to grab an elbow, and she giggled—the sound jolting him back to a time when a ten-year-old Elizabeth had begged Oliver to help her play a lark on her brother by gluing his boots to the floor. Oliver wished he could glue Hastings's boots to the floor right then and run away with Elizabeth.

"Lady Elizabeth," said Hastings, "I will leave you with Mr. Turner now."

Elizabeth pulled her dark blonde brows deeply together. "*Mr. Turner...*" she said slowly and with a heavy slur, "...is not here." She leaned in to Hastings and whispered conspiringly—and loudly. "Apparently, he is not well, but Oliver didn't think me important enough to inform me sooner." Oh, good heavens.

Oliver pulled her to his side and flashed a tight smile to Hastings. "I'll take the lady from here. Good evening, Lord Hastings."

The viscount bowed and watched as Oliver wrapped Elizabeth's arm securely through his arm and then managed to somehow get her safely out of the drawing room. He caught Rose's eye, however, just before they exited the room, and she immediately noted the urgency of his look. He watched as she quickly excused herself from the group of tabbies surrounding her and rushed from the room with an elegance that would make the duchess proud.

Once into the hallway and safely away from the judgmental eyes of Society, Oliver wrapped his arm around Elizabeth's shoulder and guided her toward an empty parlor at the front of the house.

"What's happened?" asked Rose in an anxious tone, after stepping into the parlor and closing the door behind her.

Oliver sat Elizabeth down on a settee and she immediately started to fall over. He sat down beside her and wrapped his arm around her shoulder again to keep her upright. And then Oliver met Rose's wide eyes.

"She's foxed," he said bluntly.

"Oh, blast." Rose crossed her arms in front of her. "We need to get her out of here or this will follow her through the whole Season."

"I agree."

Elizabeth seemed to become alert to the world around her for the first time. She sat up straighter and looked at Oliver, "I'm not ddrunk!" she nearly shouted. She gave a crooked grin and then put her finger on the tip of his nose. "You're drunkk, Olly!" She chuckled. "Drunky, Olly."

"All right, Lizzie, I'll make you a deal," he said, removing her finger from his nose and trying not to laugh. "I'll let you call me Drunky Olly, but only if you promise to walk with me out of this house to the carriage and be very, *very* quiet."

She saluted him. "Yes, sir, durnky Olly."

Rose's face reflected both the amusement and the horror of what they were about to attempt. It would be a miracle if they got her out of there without anyone realizing Elizabeth was drunk as a wheelbarrow. "I'll go fetch Carver. It's not even necessary for me to ask you to remain here with her, is it?" She gave him a smile that said she meant more by that statement. Did she know? How? He'd been so careful the past couple of days to not show his affection. He'd even been forcing himself to flirt with other ladies all evening.

He shook his head and tightened his arm around Elizabeth's shoulders. Rose left and Elizabeth laid her head on Oliver's shoulder, the sweet smell of her hair flooding his senses. Must she make this so difficult for him? Only Elizabeth could make intoxication look lovely.

He felt Elizabeth take in a deep breath, her shoulders rising and falling in a way that reflected contentment. He relished too much her closeness. And the realization that she fit perfectly beside him made him ache. Oliver peeked down just as Elizabeth shut her eyes and nestled into his side, the heat of her body radiating into his. She was smiling softly. Did she feel as comfortable tucked up next to him as he felt holding her there?

This was a frozen moment, a stolen bit of time that he knew would take yet another piece of his heart and surrender it to the woman who he would never let himself have.

His eyes traced a line from her earlobe, down her neck to the top of her shoulder where it lingered on the cap sleeve of her gorgeous gown. She had been too much for him that night. Forcing himself to stay away and allowing her to befriend Hastings felt like the worst sort of torture. But it was what was best for her—his sweet, wild-hearted, Lizzie.

Oliver lifted his hand and without thinking, wrapped one of her soft, dangling curls around his finger. The tips of his fingers brushed against her neck. He noticed that her smile broadened and the hairs stood up on her arms. "Olly," she said with a sleepy slur.

He allowed himself the moment to rest the side of his face against the top of her head. "Yes, darling?"

"Do you find my dress repppulsive?" That last word was a mouth full for her but she eventually got it out.

He shut his eyes and smiled. "No, Lizzie." For a moment, he considered leaving it at that. But the night and the smell of her hair and the realization that she would not remember anything he said was bewitching him. He could not hold his words inside him any longer. "You must know, the way you look tonight, and every second of every day for that matter, is driving me mad." He held his breath, waiting for her response, but she only sighed. He looked down and ran his knuckles against her jaw, eliciting a dimpled smile. He whispered, "You are beautiful, my darling." He was counting on the promise of her inebriation that she would not remember his words tomorrow. But if he were being honest with himself, part of him hoped his words would sink into her heart and she would never forget them.

A second later, the door opened and the moment was pierced. Oliver dropped his hand to wrap around her shoulder once again while Rose and Kensworth snuck into the parlor. Kensworth paused and gave Elizabeth a pitying look before squatting in front of her and taking her hand, coaxing her to open her heavy eyes.

She blinked at her brother with a frown.

"My poor little love," said Kensworth, smiling kindly at his nearly incoherent sister. It wouldn't be long until the room was spinning wretchedly. He doubted the carriage would come away unscathed from their trip home. "You mustn't feel too badly. We've all been a little jug-bitten at some point in our lives." Kensworth placed a hand under Elizabeth's elbow and gently pulled her to her feet. "Let's get you home." It was selfish, but Oliver wished Kensworth and Rose had not been so hasty in coming to Elizabeth's rescue. He would have liked a few more minutes to sit with her in his arms.

"Here," said Rose, taking Elizabeth's arm in hers. "Let me be the one to escort her out. It will look more natural and I can hold her up without anyone thinking it too odd."

"No," Oliver's voice shot out too quickly. "I shall escort her out." He felt reluctant to leave Elizabeth in her state.

Rose shook her head. "We need you to stay behind and spread the rumor of Elizabeth's sudden illness. Hint at a fever and let everyone begin to draw their own conclusion. But whatever you do—do not outright say that she has influenza, or else no one will believe you. People like to feel as if they are intelligent enough to crack a code on their own." Leave it up to Rose to concoct a scheme. And as much as he didn't want to leave Elizabeth, he knew Rose was right. He needed to give a reason for Elizabeth's sudden disappearance that would draw sympathy for her rather than raise eyebrows.

Elizabeth stumbled a little bit to the side, her eyes looking glazed and heavy as she swung them to Oliver. "I don't know what you all are talking about. I'm perrrfectly sober. In fact, I have something I wish to say to Oliver." She stood straighter and squared her shoulders at him, but still looked like she could fall over at any moment. "Oliver, I'm tired of hiding it. I—" but he didn't know what Elizabeth was going to say because Rose clapped her hand over Elizabeth's mouth.

"Shhhh. Yes, darling, I'm sure you are quite sober, but let us wait until we've had a good night's rest to talk with Oliver."

It was on the tip of Oliver's tongue to protest, but Elizabeth spoke again. "I'm not tired," she said with a yawn, stumbling over her own steps as Rose dragged her toward the door.

Kensworth moved ahead of them and peeked his head out the door, and then waved them forward when the hallway was clear.

"Thank you for your help, Oliver," said Rose before the three Ashburns slipped out the door.

Then they were gone, and Oliver was alone in the parlor. He was thankful for Rose, he really was. But he would be a liar if he said he didn't miss the way life was before Kensworth had married. He missed the time he had spent with his friend. He missed how uncomplicated his relationship had been before he was aware that Elizabeth was maddeningly beautiful and he would have to let someone else marry her. What was his place in that family now? The Ashburns had been Oliver's grounding force for the past ten years.

But now, he felt a little washed out to sea—unsure of who he was or where he belonged.

Chapter Thirteen

I t was official. Elizabeth despised champagne. It was a vile devil drink that swept her up in the moment with the promise of confidence and happiness. That was not what she had received—not at all.

She pulled her legs up under her and nestled further into the settee in her favorite room of Kensworth House: the gold parlor. Situated in the back of the house, it was the room least frequented by any other members of the household. Which she thought was ridiculous because it had the most wonderful little settee in front of a large bay window overlooking the back gardens. She liked this room—and she could be alone here. Today, it's most important feature. And, despite being surrounded by walls, she still felt free.

Elizabeth—head full of galloping stallions notwithstanding—had been unable to sleep a moment past seven o'clock this morning. But oh, how she wished she could have slept away the entire day. Her stomach still reeled from the previous evening's overindulgence and every bone in her body ached, not to mention the creeping sense of mortification that grew in inverse proportion to her sobriety.

Elizabeth had opened her eyes that morning, recalled the previous evening as a hazy nightmare, and promptly decided to slip back into an ignorant slumber and avoid facing reality ever again. But she couldn't. Her head throbbed and sitting upright seemed to be the only thing for it.

Knowing that Rose and Carver would not likely leave their rooms for another few hours, Elizabeth dressed in a simple cream walking dress and retrieved the ridiculous novel Kate had lent her. Kate, of course, had sworn it was the most romantic story ever told. Elizabeth could not stop laughing at the silliness of it, but it would provide just the kind of mindless diversion she needed today. She needed an escape —to somewhere far from the reality of her bungled attempt to catch the eye of any gentleman, much less garner the attentions of Lord Hastings.

She winced as she remembered how many times she had grabbed his arm. And...oh, goodness. Had she told him how fortunate it was that Mary had not married his recently deceased brother? She had surely ruined her chances with him. Utterly ruined.

Elizabeth groaned, running her hands over her face, wishing that was all it took to scrub away her dreadful memories. Well, never mind. She would find a way through it. She would find some way to recover —as long as Lord Hastings was good enough to not besmirch her reputation.

She picked up her book, determined to put all bad thoughts out of her mind and lose herself in a silly novel. She read an entire page before she realized she was comprehending exactly none of it. No, her mind was instead playing—or replaying?—a scene she wasn't sure was a dream or a memory. It was of Oliver, his strong arm wrapped protectively around her. She closed her eyes and could smell him. She could almost feel his fingers brushing against her neck. But when Elizabeth remembered his whispers of how beautiful he thought her, she realized it must have been a dream. A wonderfully blissful dream—the only good thing that had come of her run-in with the devil's drink. She tilted her head to the side and touched her fingers to the nape of her neck, remembering a touch that had felt all too real.

Elizabeth sighed. Reclaiming her heart was going to be more difficult than she had imagined.

~

Oliver stepped into Kensworth House as Jeffers closed the front door behind him. The dour butler turned back to level his ever-present glare at Oliver.

"Simmer down, man," said Oliver. "I'm aware of the time, and I have no intention of being seen yet. You will be pleased to hear that I learned my lesson the last time I attempted to intrude on Lord Kensworth's morning."

Jeffers grinned—the sight making him somehow even less attractive. Really, he must talk to Kensworth about finding a new butler. "Pleased, sir? I should never be pleased to hear that you have had an unsatisfactory visit."

"Shouldn't be…but you are nonetheless," Oliver said, turning away from the butler and walking toward the drawing room. "I'll await his lordship in the drawing room."

"Very good, sir," said Jeffers in a way that made Oliver feel as though he was being patted on the head and given a biscuit.

Oliver had almost made it to the drawing room when a familiar sound caught his ear. He paused. A light chuckle drifted down the long hallway and settled over Oliver like a fresh breeze in summer. He smiled and looked over his shoulder, making sure Jeffers wasn't skulking around the corner, tracking his every move. He then hurried down the hallway toward the parlor at the back of the house.

The door was slightly ajar and Oliver peeked in, the sight stealing his breath. Elizabeth was curled in the corner of a settee, bathed in a warm glow of sunlight. Her loose curls glinted like gold in the sun. Her fingers were pressed to her mouth, a book in her other hand, and she was smiling—trying to stifle another laugh.

Oliver knew he should walk away. But his heart was practically grabbing him by the lapels of his jacket, demanding he go in. His heart and mind warred.

This is London. Rules are different here than at Dalton Park, and she is alone. Do not go in.

But he could leave the door open…

It would still be inappropriate.

He could leave the door wide open *and* sit far across the room.

Turn around and leave.

But goodness, she was beautiful. And captivating. And humorous. And he didn't entirely trust himself to not walk right in that room and blurt out, "I adore you, Lizzie. I cannot be simply your friend any longer."

He expelled an annoyed breath. What was he, a foolish young buck with no self-control? No. He was a grown man. He could go into that room and be Elizabeth's friend just like he'd been doing for the past ten years. Besides, it wasn't as if he could avoid her forever. Now was the time for him to school his feelings—until those feelings fled altogether. Because they would. He would make sure of it.

But he seriously doubted they would dissipate at all today with her looking like the goddess of beauty. For this reason, he officially decided that he would turn away and wait in the drawing room, as far away as possible from Elizabeth Ashburn.

"Good morning, Lizzie," he said, pushing the door open. Blast. No control. And now her bright blue eyes were flying to him and her smile was blooming and he was walking to her. Walking right to her. Not to the chair where he had promised himself he would sit, but to the very settee where she was already perched.

"Oliver!" How did she always manage to make his name sound so remarkable? She made to stand but he waved her back down. "You weren't planning to jump out and scare me, were you? Because I don't think it would be in your best interest to begin a battle of that sort again," said Elizabeth.

She wasn't wrong. Elizabeth took scaring a man to a whole new level. He had always hoped to one-up her but somehow she always managed to outdo him instead, hiding away in the most unexpected places and then scaring the living daylights out of him when she would pop out with a loud noise.

He chuckled. "No, no. I forfeited those wars a long time ago and I'm still waving the white flag." His eyes fell to her book. "Am I intruding? Shall I leave you to your reading?"

"No," she said, snapping it shut and moving her bare feet to the floor. She started messing with her hair, tucking strands behind her ears and looking self-conscious—much like she had last night before the soirée.

His brows furrowed and he grinned. "What are you doing?"

She paused her fidgeting and her eyes met his. "I just realized how I must look. I haven't even run a brush through my hair yet this morning." Something about those words—knowing that he was seeing her just as she had awoken—sent a thrill through him.

No. No thrills.

He attempted a light chuckle and gestured toward the seat beside her on the little settee. She nodded and he sat down, refusing to acknowledge the empty chair mocking his weak will from across the room. "You do realize that I've seen you with your hair down more than pinned up throughout the course of our friendship?"

"Yes…but it's different here."

"Still looks blonde to me."

She gave him a flat look. "You know what I mean. It's different in London." He did know. He had just been thinking that before he walked in. "Here, in Town, I must be *Lady Elizabeth*, and you are Mr…" She paused a moment, her thoughts seemingly moving to his father just as his did, every time he heard his own surname. "Turner."

His chest tightened. Why did he have to share that man's name? Why could hearing it always jolt him back to his father, shoving him up against a wall, face purple with anger. Telling him he was a burden, a weight, an albatross, how much better life would have been had he not been born.

"Anyway" she continued, "I don't think we are allowed to be quite as familiar with each other as we are at Dalton Park." He was thankful she had changed conversational tacks, ignoring the tension surrounding his parentage.

He finally relaxed against the settee and draped his arm over the back. "Are you suggesting we implement some new rules for our friendship?"

Her blue eyes sparkled. "Exactly."

Rules were exactly what they needed. A few mutually understood guidelines would help him put Elizabeth back inside the friendship box where she needed to stay. And as much as he didn't want to admit it, lessening his presence around her would ensure that she was given more of a chance to make a match with someone else. It would be best for both of them.

"What did you have in mind?" he asked.

"Well, for one, I suppose we should not be in here alone at this hour of the morning without my chaperone's knowledge."

"Oh, definitely not," he said with a grin, making no attempts to move.

In fact, he was trying to stay very still. Elizabeth's curls were only a whisper away from brushing up against his hand where it was draped over the back of the couch, and it was taking all of his will power to not run his fingers through it again. It was soft. He knew not only because of last night when he had wrapped a strand around his finger, but because of a time last summer when he'd had to gather it up for her after she had come down with a stomach illness during one of their morning horseback rides. He had held her hair back while she had retched into a bush. The fact that he had never forgotten how it felt, and that he hadn't minded holding her hair for her while she was violently sick, spoke of just how much he adored her.

"What other rules shall we put in place?" he asked.

"Addressing me formally while we are in public is a must. No more calling me Lizzie in ballrooms or at dinner parties."

He gave an offended huff. "I've never addressed you as Lizzie in front of anyone else but your family."

"I know," she said, lifting her shoulder and peeking at him playfully over it. The flirtatious look made him want to groan. "But you must admit that you do call me Lizzie when we are talking alone at dinner parties or balls." She paused, her brow crinkling together. "Which puts me in mind of another rule." She rotated a little on the settee, placing herself even closer to him. His eyes drifted to his hand where his knuckles now rested lightly against her arm.

He should not be feeling sparks at the slightest touch of her. And why did he not move it? Did she mind? She didn't seem to. In fact, she was still going on about the newest rule they should implement. Honestly, he was only half listening because his mind was wandering to her lips and imagining what it would be like to throw all of his resolve out the window and kiss her. Give himself a chance to prove that he wasn't like his father. He was roused again to reality when he heard Elizabeth say, "...I cannot have you scaring away my other suitors by calling me Little Lizzie in front of them." The words *other suitors* felt like a punch to his stomach.

He pulled his hand away. "I haven't called you Little Lizzie in years. But what's this about other suitors? Do you already have one in mind?" Somehow, he already knew the answer.

Her eyes flicked to his before her gaze turned away and she fidgeted with the pages of the book in her lap. "Well...not exactly another suitor. Not yet, at least. But I will admit that someone has caught my eye." She paused and bit her bottom lip before releasing it, turning determined eyes to him. "Actually, it's Lord Hastings. He was very kind to me last night." Her shoulders slumped. "Though I'm afraid I completely bungled that." One could only hope. *No.* He wasn't supposed to be thinking things like that. He was supposed to be glad for her to be courted by other men.

She looked down at her lap and a lock of hair fell from behind her ear. Oliver reached out and tucked it back without really thinking. Surely that wasn't strange for him to do? Surely he'd done that before? But the fact that her eyes turned wide, questioning him, told him that it was the first time he had ever touched her like that before. He wanted to box his own ears.

Rules. Implement the rules.

Oliver cleared his throat and stood up, forcing a smile. "I sincerely doubt you have deterred Hastings by indulging in a little too much champagne."

She pulled a pained look and put her face in her hands. "Oh, Oliver. I was so stupid. How could I have had so much to drink? I said the most mortifying things to him. I will be surprised if he ever looks in my direction again." Was he a terrible man to be fighting a joyful smile? Yes. Terrible.

"You're being too hard on yourself, Lizzie. I doubt he thought a thing of it. But I must ask...Hastings? Are you sure he is the one you wish to court you?" What was he doing? Why was he asking that?

"Why shouldn't I wish for Lord Hastings to court me?" Her tone was curt.

He tipped a shoulder and stood to mindlessly assess a few books on a nearby shelf. "Just seems a rather dull fellow to me. I doubt he could keep up with you or your sense of adventure."

"What's that supposed to mean? I am not such an untamed creature as you may think me, Oliver."

He turned around at the sudden edge to her voice. "No, Lizzie, that's not what I meant."

Her eyes were fixed on his, the blaze sparking in them all too familiar. Everyone had always found Elizabeth agreeable and docile, but he knew a side of her that no one else did, all fire and ferocity. It had put them in any number of rows over the past few years of their new, closer friendship.

"I think it's exactly what you meant." She stood up abruptly and winced a little, touching her hand to head. He knew it must ache like the devil. "I'm a grown, refined—"

"—Now wait a moment," he said, cutting her off and taking a step closer. "I never implied that you were not grown or refined."

She crossed her arms. "Didn't you?"

"I said Lord Hastings was dull."

"And that he couldn't keep up with me."

He shrugged. "You run fast."

"And my *sense of adventure.* What was that supposed to mean?"

"It means that you climb out windows."

She let out a heavy breath and released her arms. "Must you keep bringing that up?"

He grinned, trying not to find her agitation attractive. "Yes—if you continue climbing out of them."

She held up a finger. "That was *one* other time, Oliver. One!"

He stepped closer to her and folded her finger down. She watched the action closely. "Elizabeth, there's nothing wrong with your sense of adventure. It's who you are—that's all I meant. I don't want to see you settle for someone who will not bring you happiness."

Her gaze held his and then dropped to his mouth before returning to his eyes. That was all it took to send his heart racing. "I just"—her voice was quiet—"would hate for *anyone* to think I am not capable of making a good wife because I am too reckless."

He swallowed, becoming aware of a sudden conviction to say all the things that he had resolved should remain unsaid. "I don't believe *anyone* would think such a thing about you."

Their stares fixed and neither broke away for several breaths. "I... had the strangest dream last night," Elizabeth said, reaching up to lightly rub the side of her neck. He watched her movement, knowing she was remembering what he had hoped she wouldn't from the night before. He and Elizabeth had always had a way of speaking with their eyes. He could see her questions. He could see her wondering if all he had said the previous night was true and real. Did she hope for that?

"Was it a good dream?" he asked, even though he shouldn't have.

She smiled softly. "Wonderful, in fact."

The air closed in. The world outside of them disappeared, and it was just he and Elizabeth standing in the sun-drenched room. He wondered, now more than ever, if she loved him in return. What would he do if she did? What if he told her how he felt, and they kissed, and he courted her, and married her, only to find out Frank Turner had been right about who he would become? Oliver had never struggled with temper or alcohol thus far. But what would happen when children came along and life grew more stressful? What about when he was living in close quarters with a wife? What if he felt angered by her?

His father's words haunted him. *My blood runs in your veins.*

Oliver's throat felt as if it closed up. He took a step away from Elizabeth. "Dreams can feel oddly real at times, but it's best to remember that they are nothing but figments of the imagination."

Her face fell along with her hand.

The sadness in her eyes had him opening his mouth to say something—anything—when a voice at the threshold of the door filled the room. "My lady," said Jeffers. Of course he would interrupt this moment. "These have just arrived for you." The butler gestured toward the massive display of white roses in his hands. "Where would you like me to place them?"

Oliver watched with a sinking feeling as a small smile peeked onto Elizabeth's mouth. "Do you know who they are from?"

"Lord Hastings, my lady. His lordship delivered them personally with his best wishes for a quick recovery from your illness, and a promise to pay you a visit as soon as you are well."

Oliver's eyes narrowed. It would seem that the man wasn't deterred after all. Wonderful. Just wonderful.

Chapter Fourteen

Elizabeth eyed her navy and white striped walking dress in the mirror as she finished the last gold button on her deep blue spencer. She retrieved her straw bonnet from the dressing table and headed for the door. Lord Hastings was due to arrive at any moment, so she hurried to tie the silk ribbons under her chin.

Because of the *illness* Elizabeth was supposedly recovering from, she had been forced to miss two balls, and a night at Almack's. And she was utterly broken hearted over it. At least, that's what she would tell people when she re-entered Society. But really, she had quite enjoyed herself over the past several days.

Elizabeth had spent more time with her brother than she had spent with him in years. Carver, Rose, and Elizabeth had stayed up intolerably late every night playing games and telling stories. Rose was teaching Elizabeth how to aim a pistol, though Carver—a stick in the mud—would not let her shoot it inside like Rose had. And Elizabeth was teaching Rose how to embroider like a proper lady. Though that was also laughable since Elizabeth was known amongst her family as the worst needleworker of the lot. That included Papa and Carver.

Anyway, it didn't actually matter because she and Rose hadn't been able to concentrate on their stitching long enough to accomplish much of anything. Rose would start to tell Elizabeth about one of her ruses from when she was a thief and they would put down their needlework and glance at it occasionally with an expression of *we should really return to our stitching,* but then they would decide to ignore it for the rest of the night.

Those nursery linens for Mary's baby would never be finished.

But the previous evening, Rose and Carver had felt that *Elizabeth's illness had run its course* and she could reasonably be expected to re-enter society without raising suspicions. So they had all attended Lord and Lady Hamilton's ball. It had gone tolerably well, and Elizabeth had felt rather proud of herself for how much decorum she had displayed. Not a single untoward incident had occurred through the whole evening. Not a single one.

Well. Not a single one—aside from getting her hair tangled up in the branches of a giant fern. She was still convinced the thing had somehow come to life and reached out to grab her as she'd passed by. It was really too bad that Oliver had found her that way. Did he have some sort of alarm bell that rang in his ears whenever she was in an embarrassing situation? He was the one man in the world she wanted to see her as sophisticated and attractive and alluring, and yet, he was the one man who was always catching her with her slipper torn or hair tangled in a fern. It was just as well. She needed a reminder that she had not come to town to impress Oliver. Why did she seem to keep forgetting that fact?

Other than that one small moment—which was hardly even worth mentioning—the evening had gone off without a hitch. Elizabeth's hand had been claimed for every dance and it seemed that no one was the least bit suspicious of the champagne incident. She knew her rescue was mostly attributed to Oliver and the stories he had concocted of her sudden decline the night of Miss Loxley's soirée. But she didn't want to let her mind stray to Oliver again, or the fact that she had missed out on an evening of fantastic entertainment. Apparently, Miss Loxley had hired a traveling carnival to take the stage and perform all sorts of tricks with fire that left everyone in raptures. She was beyond sorry to have missed it.

At the ball, however, Elizabeth had danced nearly every set of the evening, including two with Lord Hastings, and apart from the fern incident, she had successfully avoided Oliver. She was well on her way to pushing him out of her heart for good.

During Elizabeth's days of quarantine, Rose had given her a few pointers about how to appear confident in times of stress, lessons on how to effectively flirt without taking it over the top, and even examples of how to extricate herself from unwanted conversations. Because of those lessons, Elizabeth had been able to smile demurely at plenty of potential suitors, not once trip over her dance steps, carry on polite conversations with gentlemen and matrons, and over all...remain miserable throughout the entire evening.

Not once had she found herself smiling because she felt like it. Not once had she laughed out of instinct rather than force. Not once had she danced with Oliver. But never mind all of that. Everything was going on as planned. Somehow she had managed to hold the attention of Lord Hastings, and he was currently her most serious suitor. Elizabeth would let herself be happy later—when she was married and starting a family and had forgotten all about her unrequited love for Oliver.

Elizabeth finished tying off the ribbons of her bonnet and made her way downstairs to await Lord Hastings's arrival. The previous night, after he had escorted her from the dance floor and back to Rose's side, he had asked for permission to call on Elizabeth and take her for a drive in the park the following day. Rose had momentarily flashed Elizabeth a look that said *do you want to do this? There's still time to tell Oliver how you feel.* To which Elizabeth had flashed a look back that said *Oliver who?* Rose gave her consent in a haughty, motherly way which made Elizabeth want to openly laugh, and then the night had carried on just as she imagined every other ball would: dead boring.

Dancing felt restricting and stale. The refreshments were merely tolerable, the conversation stilted, the smiles fake. And...well, never-mind. What good was it to dwell on the bad? The handsome Lord

Hastings would be there any moment to take her on a drive and that's all that mattered. Things were looking up.

Elizabeth reached the top of the first floor landing just as Jeffers opened the front door and Lord Hastings stepped inside.

The carriage was pulling down the front lane of Dalton Park. Elizabeth knew because she had spotted it from the window where she had been keeping watch the past hour. She shot out of the window seat, her book landing on the floor with a hard thunk before she rushed from her bedchamber to the stairs.

Her breath was racing and anyone who saw her would think her mad. But Elizabeth didn't mind. Oliver was finally here and it was summer, her favorite time of year. Not necessarily because of the weather—although the warm sunshine certainly didn't detract from her admirations—but because it meant she would have a whole month with her favorite person in the world.

Elizabeth reached the landing where she had waited for Oliver to step through the door every summer for the last eight years. Would Carver be with him this year? Her heart still ached for her brother and the grief he wrestled with.

There was a loud knock on the door and Elizabeth's heart echoed its beat. Her hand gripped the oak banister as Henley opened the door. And then there he was. Oliver Turner stepped inside with a bright smile on his face that made Elizabeth's stomach tie into wonderful knots.

He didn't know it, but she loved him.

Last summer had felt like magic. Oliver hadn't declared himself, but something in the way he had treated her was different from every other summer. It was as if he had finally seen her for who she truly was. And now he was back, and hope flickered in her chest.

She waited, holding her breath for the moment she loved more than anything. The moment that had been repeated at the start of every summer since the first day Oliver joined Carver at Dalton Park.

And then it happened. Oliver handed his hat and gloves to Henley, and then with such determination—such certainty and assurance—he turned his sea blue eyes up to Elizabeth like he never doubted for one moment that that was where he would find her waiting for him. Like he had been anticipating this moment just as much as she had.

He smiled fully and raised his hand to her.

Elizabeth smiled back—every part of her aching to be loved by this man, knowing that no one else would ever fill her with as much joy and sparks and excitement as Oliver Turner.

Elizabeth waited there at the top of the stairs. For some reason, her feet would not move from that place. She didn't want to admit what she was waiting there for as she watched Rose enter the foyer and greet Lord Hastings. She gripped the railing—watching, waiting, *hoping*.

Nothing.

He didn't see her. He didn't sense her the way Oliver always seemed to.

Elizabeth cleared the lump from her throat and made her way down the stairs. It was unfair of her to hope for something that Lord Hastings had no way of knowing was important to her.

"Lady Elizabeth," said Lord Hastings with a small bow and a warm smile as she approached. "Good morning. You look well."

Well. He never said she looked beautiful or enchanting. He always thought she looked well. Oh, heavens. Now she was being completely absurd. What did she expect? For Lord Hastings to perform one of Lord Byron's poems to her in the middle of the foyer in front of Jeffers and Rose? She was being unfair and it needed to stop.

Elizabeth smiled what she hoped was her most encouraging smile and curtsied. Seeing him again, dressed in his golden waistcoat and black riding jacket, she was honestly able to say that she found him *very* handsome. His eyes were a deep green and put her in mind of a forest at dusk. He didn't smile overly much, but she could tell by the lines around his eyes that he did laugh from time to time. Perhaps she could bring out the laughter in him more often.

"Do you have everything you need?" asked Rose, with a smile that was tender and supportive, but Elizabeth knew Rose well enough now to see that there was more behind it.

"I believe so." Elizabeth turned to the viscount. "Lord Hastings, would you give me a moment to speak privately with my sister-in-law before we set out?"

"Of course."

"I'll only be a moment."

"Take your time." He bowed again and turned to walk outside. He really was a kind soul. She could certainly do much worse than Lord Hastings.

"What is it?" Rose asked the moment the door shut behind the viscount.

"That's the very question I was going to ask you."

Rose blinked—her face otherwise unreadable. "I'm not sure what you mean."

"You gave me your false polite smile. Why?"

Rose's eyebrows twitched together for the briefest of seconds. "I think you're reading too much into my demeanor."

"That's what you'd like for me to think. But like it or not, Rose Ashburn, Countess of Kensworth, I *know* you now. And I know that you are hiding something from me and that it must have something to do with Lord Hastings. Do you not approve of him?"

Rose sighed and her shoulders dropped. "It does not matter what I think, Elizabeth."

"It matters to me."

Rose gave a soft smile and took Elizabeth's hand. "I do have thoughts and opinions concerning your new courtship with Lord Hastings. But they don't have as much to do with the viscount as they do with another man that I know your heart is still attached to. However, I'm not going to tell you all of these opinions because I feel like this is a decision you need to make for yourself. Only you know your heart and what's right for it, Elizabeth. I trust you to know what's best for yourself." It would be the very worst thing to cry in the foyer just before going on a drive with a potential suitor. And yet, tears were beginning to accumulate behind her eyes.

No one had ever put such faith in her before. Well, no one else, except Oliver.

"Thank you, Rose."

Rose chuckled and squeezed Elizabeth's hand. "Enough of all that. I suggest you get out of here before you're made to endure what I am certain is going to be the most insufferable tea with Lady Hoffman and her daughter. I conveniently scheduled their call during the hour that you would be out on your drive." Those two insufferable ladies were the queens of backhanded compliments. She certainly did not envy Rose. If anything, she loved her all the more for returning to Town and sacrificing the safety and solitude of Havenwood Orphanage to face the claws of the London Tabbies.

Elizabeth kissed her sister-in-law on the cheek. "You are the most wonderful sister in the world."

"I'll be sure to inform Mary and Kate of that next time we are all together." She winked before Elizabeth left the house.

Chapter Fifteen

"Still no new tendré this Season?" asked Kensworth, making Oliver completely miss his shot in the game of billiards they were playing. Oliver looked up from where his stick had just shot right over the top of the ball into the amused eyes of his friend.

Oliver stretched his neck a little to the side. "No. None." Which wasn't a lie. His feelings for Elizabeth were not new. "And I would appreciate it if you would refrain from speaking until I've finished my shot next time."

Kensworth pulled a theatrical frown. "Forgive me. How was I to know that question would make you flinch?"

"It wasn't the question. It was the sound of your voice."

"And here I was thinking you liked my baritone all this time." He shook his head. "Ten years of utter lies."

Oliver forced out a short chuckle but, actually, the statement had hit a little too close to home. He hadn't exactly been lying to his friend for the past ten years—but he certainly hadn't been telling him the truth. Not about his father, and not about Elizabeth. It felt as if every single day his feelings for the woman only grew stronger. He didn't know how much longer he could resist her.

Oliver had been staying away the past week while Elizabeth was at home recovering from her supposed illness. He had been taking great care not to find himself alone with her again by burying himself in social events, paying calls to anyone and everyone he knew in Town, and even joining Kensworth for a round of sparring at Gentleman Jackson's Boxing Saloon. But none of that worked. His mind continued to obsess about how she had reacted to him the last time they had been together and how concerned she had seemed to be about him viewing her as an *untamed creature*. No matter how he tried to distract himself, his heart continued to find its way back to Elizabeth, and he wasn't sure what he was going to do about it.

Actually, he did know what he would do. *Nothing*. Absolutely nothing. He was going to keep his distance until Elizabeth was married off and then he would have no choice but to swallow his feelings for the rest of his life.

At that moment, Hatley stepped into the room.

"Who's telling lies?" asked Hatley. He had heard the tail end of their conversation.

Oh, wonderful. That's exactly what Oliver needed: Mr. Inquisitive on the case.

"Olly. He's not smitten with my voice anymore," said Kensworth.

Hatley cracked the barest of smiles and picked up his cue stick. "You two are infantile, I hope you know that."

"We do," they both said in unison.

Hatley leaned over and took his shot, sinking two balls into two different pockets. It was absurd how good the man was at everything he did.

"How's Lady Hatley faring?" asked Oliver.

Robert's face turned thoughtful. "She's...as well as can be expected, I suppose."

"What does that mean?" asked Kensworth, acquiring that edge to his voice he always gained when he feared for one of his family members.

Robert must have heard it, too, because he chuckled. "Easy, Kensworth. Mary's all right. She's simply distant in mind. I can see that she's terrified of what may happen to the baby, but she's refusing to acknowledge it." He leaned over and sunk another ball into a pocket. "She's taken on all sorts of jobs from her bed. Redecorating the drawing room. Ordering a whole new wardrobe for yours truly. Having the staff bring up nearly every serving dish from the pantry to have it inspected for chips and cracks. And, of course, spending lots of time reading to Jane. But never will she even mention the pregnancy or the new baby." He paused a moment and Oliver could see the way his knuckles were turning white as he gripped the cue stick. "I mentioned the idea of having her redecorate the nursery to make room for the baby and Mary didn't even acknowledge it. She simply pretended she hadn't heard me and continued talking about something else."

"What will you do then?" asked Oliver.

Robert looked at him, a sad smile tugging at his mouth. "Nothing. I don't think there's anything I can do but wait this out with her."

"But you would tell me if there was anything I could do?" asked Kensworth, his question mirroring Oliver's thoughts as well.

Robert nodded. "Of course." But he looked tired. No...more than tired, he looked weary.

Normally Hatley was vibrant and alert and always ready to impart wisdom. But just then he looked almost as if he were giving up on something. It troubled Oliver to see the man look so worn down.

Hatley shot the last ball into the pocket, ending the game. Kensworth shook his head, eyeing the billiards table in sad disbelief. "Blast. Hang you, Robert. That's four times in a row. Can you never show a little mercy on us?"

Robert smirked. "That was mercy. I let you both get a shot in, didn't I?"

"You are goodness itself," said Oliver.

Kensworth set down his stick and looked toward the door. "All right, gentlemen. I'm off to find my wife."

"You're always off to find your wife," said Oliver with a smirk as he returned his stick to its holder against the wall.

Robert pretended to whisper at Oliver. "Devilishly clingy, that one."

Kensworth just laughed and threw his hands up in defeat. "Call me whatever you like. If being married to the most beautiful woman in the world and wishing to spend every spare moment with her means I'm pathetic, so be it."

Oliver made a sound of disgust. "Just get out of here already and quit spouting poetry at us."

Kensworth turned and left the room with a chuckle. Hatley poured two drinks from the beverage cart and gestured toward the sitting area. It wasn't until they were both seated and Oliver had taken his first sip that he realized his mistake.

"I'm surprised you're not out paying a call to some lovely new debutante," said Hatley. Blast. Oliver knew better than to allow himself to be caught in a room alone with Robert when there was something weighing on him. Even worse that it was a secret.

"Mmhmm," said Oliver, taking a sip of his brandy to gain himself a moment to think. Oliver always took small sips, forcing himself to take more time in consuming an alcoholic beverage than was necessary. Knowing what he knew about Frank Turner, Oliver took extravagant precautions when it came to all intoxicating substances. "Just wasn't feeling quite the thing today." There. That was noncommittal. There was absolutely nothing in that to allude to his pent-up feelings.

"Really?" Hatley took a sip of his brandy, one leg crossed easily over the other. "And why was that?"

"No reason in particular. It's simply been a long couple of days, and I—" but then he stopped and looked up at the earl who was studying him with those dark, all-knowing eyes. Oliver chuckled and waved his hand. "Oh, no you don't! No, no, no."

Hatley looked amused as he reached in his jacket to pull out his silver snuff box. "What?"

"I know what you're doing," said Oliver, watching Hatley skillfully flick open the snuff box and take a pinch. "I've witnessed enough of these conversations between you and Kenny to know that you're about to drag me into an emotional tunnel and have me spilling my whole budget before I ever know what's hit me."

Hatley just chuckled. "I don't think I do that."

"Oh, believe me, you do." Oliver rested his glass on the armrest.

"And it almost always starts by you hypnotizing me with that deuced snuff box of yours." He paused, not wanting to watch Hatley take a bit of snuff but unable to look away. "But really, Hatley, you've got to show me how to flick it open like that. Very elegant."

Hatley laughed. "Some other time. For now, why don't you tell what's put that grave look on your face?"

"I don't have a grave look."

"You're not smiling." What was with everyone suddenly becoming so interested in how often he smiled?

"And that makes it grave?"

"When we are speaking of Oliver Turner, the eternally smiling man, yes."

Oliver grimaced. "What a weak picture you've painted of me."

Hatley's brows pulled together with a contemplative look. "You think smiling makes you a weak man?"

Oliver laughed and then pointed to Hatley. "You're doing it again. Keep your bloody psychology to yourself, Hatley."

The man shrugged with a smug grin and a silence fell over the room. Neither of them made a move to stand. At first, the silence was comfortable. But after a time, when Oliver's mind returned to Elizabeth and his father, the silence felt unbearable. And the way Hatley continued to just stare at him, as if he could see Oliver's thoughts written in the air around him, and knowing it was only a matter of time before Oliver cracked, only added to his discomfort.

"Lizzie and I had a row," he finally blurted out, immediately put out with himself for allowing Hatley's hypnosis to succeed.

"A row about what? And if I remember correctly, aren't disagreements fairly common between you two?" Hatley wasn't wrong. Elizabeth and Oliver were never afraid to come to cuffs with one another. It's why their friendship felt so strong.

But when he thought back on the encounter between he and Elizabeth in the back room of Kensworth House, he felt agitated. "This one was different. It was…"

"It was what?"

Oliver's eyes met Hatley's. "I don't know exactly. That's what bothers me. It was something she said to me. Lizzie seemed to think that I only viewed her as an *untamed creature*. Someone who could never make a good wife." He shook his head. "I can't think why she would imagine such a thing. Or care, even."

One of Hatley's brows was lifting, along with the corner of his mouth. "Can't you?" He paused, as if waiting for Oliver to fill with some obvious revelation. "She's in love with you, man."

Oliver sucked in a deep breath right as he had taken a drink and it sent him directly into a coughing fit. After a few moments, he recovered himself from coughing and wiped his mouth with the back of his hand, shaking his head. "Lizzie does not love me." Or...did she? *No.* He absolutely could not allow himself to wonder that. Or even believe it. Because if he believed that—oh, blast, no. That made everything so much more complicated. It made staying away from her more difficult. It made not telling her the truth unbearable.

"Would that be so terrible if she did? You two get on quite well together, do you not?" How on earth was the man's voice so calm? Oliver's world was spinning and Hatley's subdued tone simply did not fit.

"It would be terrible," Oliver said firmly.

"Why?"

"Don't ask me that."

"Why?" Robert asked, undeterred.

Oliver's nerves felt like bees swarming inside him. He needed to get up. To pace. He shot out of his seat and walked to the window across the room. But that wasn't nearly enough walking so he paced back. He didn't want to tell Hatley anything. He wouldn't tell him anything. Remember, he was a closed book. A locked chest. A—

"Because I would manage to hurt her somehow." Oh, yes. Definitely a locked chest.

Robert leaned forward in his seat. "How are you so certain?"

He wasn't certain, and that was the problem. It wasn't as if he had ever been aggressive or spiraled out of control with alcohol before. But still, Frank Turner's words seemed to creep up his spine like a dangerous spider, ready to bite and inject poison at any moment.

Oliver couldn't bring himself to tell Robert about his father or the abuse he and his late mother had endured over the years. So instead, he told a version of the truth. "Surely you know my ability to fall in and out of love at the drop of a hat. What if I pursue Lizzie only to fall out of love with her in a few weeks? Our friendship would be ruined. Her family would hate me." Oliver didn't even realize that was a real fear until he spoke the words and they resonated deep within him. How was Hatley so blasted good at extracting information?

There was a silence. A long one that left his vulnerable words hanging in the air around him, and leaving him even more exposed. "Or perhaps," said the earl, "you've simply never known true love before." Oliver slid his eyes from his boots up to meet Hatley's dark eyes. Hatley leaned back again. "The thing about emotional scars is that they often distort our view of ourselves. Sometimes we think we are seeing our skin, ugly and marred, but really we're just looking at a scar and don't realize it."

"You think I'm scarred?"

"I know you are. We all are, in some way. But our hurts manifest in different areas."

Oliver let out a short laugh, growing more and more uncomfortable. "And mine manifests in the form of falling in and out of love with women, rapidly?" Stupid. If anything, Oliver's flighty feelings were simply a fulfillment of Frank Turner's constant prediction of how worthless Oliver would be to the world. *Better if you had never been born*, were the actual words his father had used.

Robert shook his head lightly, his confidence and gaze never falling away. "The opposite, actually. I think whatever demons you fight leave you feeling the need to be loved by everyone you meet."

Oliver sunk back in his chair, realizing that he was coming out the other side of the Hatley emotion tunnel. How had he let this happen? He hated discussing his feelings. He hated the way that his friend's words felt like a sudden knife to his chest. And he hated the way that hearing the words *need to be loved* conjured up memories of his father slapping him across the face. He shut his eyes against the memories and the heat he felt building behind his eyes. Oliver stood up.

"You're wrong this time, Hatley. I'm just a flirt. There's nothing more to it. No deep underlying pathology. No emotional scars blinding me. I'm just a man who falls in love too much and has too fickle of a heart to form anything lasting. And because of that, I will pretend I never heard what you said about Elizabeth." And for more reasons that he wasn't willing to divulge.

He turned on his heels, ready to storm out of the billiards room and leave the earl and his wrongheadedness behind. He wasn't some weak, jaded man looking for love and acceptance. He could live with being a flirt. He could live with the whisper telling him he would never offer anything of value to the world. But what he could not live with was letting his father's hand reach him anymore. He refused to believe he was broken or misguided or affected in any way by that man whom he had left behind at Pembroke years ago.

Oliver was in control of his life. He could make sure that he never let himself enter a situation he wouldn't be able to control. Marriage left too many things to question—and it was not an option. Frank Turner wouldn't control him anymore.

"Oliver," Hatley's voice caught him before he left the room. "I'm here when you're ready to talk." He wouldn't be coming back to talk to Hatley, though. He'd had quite enough of the earl's thoughts.

"You think too much of your abilities, Hatley. Stick to the billiards table next time."

And then he left.

"Everything all right?" asked Rose, coming down the stairs and spotting Oliver before he left out the front door.

He wanted to groan. Would everyone stop trying to suss out his emotional scars? He flashed his best smile—the smile of a man who was *eternally smiling.* "Wonderful! And you? Are you adjusting well to the life of a countess?"

She laughed as she reached the bottom floor. "Let's just say, it's a rather good thing that I'm a fabulous actress. Carver, however, is not, and is eagerly counting down the days until the Season is over and we can once again escape the eyes of the *ton* and return to Hopewood." Oliver could well understand. The orphanage Rose had founded, and where she and Carver had decided to make their home, was lovely. It was tucked back into the country where rules and propriety and changing your wardrobe four times a day couldn't reach.

Oliver was aware of a sudden jealousy prickling him. Is that what he wanted? He had always assumed Town life was for him. But there was a quiet longing inside him for something he knew he couldn't have. Honestly, the more time he spent in London, the more he tired of it—all of it. The balls, the flirtations, the debutantes, the keeping up of appearances. He even tired of the man he was when he was in Town. Was Robert's assessment of him correct? Was this man he had become not his true self? Did he even know who he was apart from his father and London and the Ashburns?

His heart pulled to Elizabeth again and knew that the only times he had ever felt truly comfortable had been when he was walking with her through the grounds of Dalton Park.

"Well, I must be off. I'll see myself out," he said with a brief bow to Rose and turned toward the door, eager to escape all of these depressing feelings.

"You don't wish to wait until Elizabeth returns from her drive and see how things went?" asked Rose, her amber eyes holding an odd glint.

Oliver paused with his hand on the door knob. "Her drive?"

Rose gave a soft sweet smile that could only mean she had ulterior motives. "Yes. She left about a quarter hour ago with Lord Hastings for a drive through the park."

He turned around and walked back toward Rose. "The park, you say? And…would that happen to be Hyde Park?"

Rose studied his face a moment. "Yes," she said slowly. "But you wouldn't be asking because you plan to go to the Park and check up on her, would you?"

Oliver frowned deeply. "No. That doesn't sound like me in the least." He was backing toward the door.

"Oliver, I'm happy to wait with you in the drawing room for her return where *then* you may ask her about her afternoon. But Elizabeth deserves to go on a drive with a gentleman without your interference." Apparently, her scheme was not unfolding in the way she had hoped.

He opened the door. "Of course she does. I'd never dream of interfering."

Rose followed him out the door. "You're not going to the Park, are you?" Her voice sounded as if she already knew her answer.

"Definitely not." He definitely was.

"I don't believe you," Rose called out, though he was already down the steps and mounting his horse.

"Good. You shouldn't!"

He heard her puff out air and saw defeat in her slumped shoulders. "I would shoot you in the leg to stop you if Carver hadn't taken my blasted pistol away."

"Remind me to give him an extra gift at Christmas," said Oliver with a smile and a tip of his hat.

He wasn't exactly sure what he planned to do once he arrived at Hyde Park. He really should be keeping his distance. But knowing Elizabeth was enjoying an afternoon with another man blinded the rational, thinking portion of his mind.

Chapter Sixteen

Lord Hastings really was a handsome man. Sitting beside him in his curricle as they moved at a sedate pace through the park gave Elizabeth the opportunity to admire his short, honey brown hair and chiseled jawline. And although he didn't seem to talk overly much, he made everything he said count.

For instance, a moment ago—before the large span of silence they were now enjoying—he had said that he preferred Town life to the country because there was so much more entertainment offered. Elizabeth had been able to gather from that statement that Lord Hastings was not an outdoor enthusiast and that he had likely never stepped foot outdoors in the country or else he would have known that country life held much more appeal than London, with its fetid air, no matter the entertainment available.

"Do you enjoy riding?" she asked, hoping to both find a mutual hobby and fill the seemingly never-ending silence.

"I do." Oh. There. Something they could agree on. "But only when I absolutely must. Otherwise I prefer to drive my curricle or ride in a carriage. Not as much road dust or horse hair spoiling my breeches makes a little less work for my valet."

Oh.

Well, never mind if he was a bit...*dull*. And it actually showed a kindness in him to be aware of the workload he put on his servants. She simply needed to focus on the good in Lord Hastings and not allow Oliver's obnoxious assessment of the viscount to cloud her judgment.

"What about you? Do you ride often?" he asked.

"Oh, yes! As often as time and circumstance allow. Obviously, here in Town I am not given much opportunity to ride but, back home at Dalton Park, I ride nearly every day."

His brows raised a little. "Every day? Well, I suppose it is excellent exercise."

"Yes...it is." And then they fell into another silence. Only the sound of the wind moving through the trees and horse hooves beating the ground broke the heavy silence.

Elizabeth moved her lips from side to side to give her something to do.

Perhaps it had only been the champagne, but the night she had met Lord Hastings, she had found him much more personable. Easier to talk to. Then again, that champagne also had her talking to the carved lion head in Miss Loxley's foyer so that wasn't necessarily saying much.

At least five minutes passed without anyone muttering a single word, and the quiet was beginning to drive Elizabeth mad. If this man —a man who supposedly never showed any females any attention— had singled her out, it must have been because he wanted to further his acquaintance with her in some way. So why wasn't he talking? "May I be frank, my lord?"

He smiled softly. "Please do."

She fidgeted with her lace gloves. "I was rather surprised that you wished to call on me after the night we first met."

"Oh?"

"Yes. I"—she could feel her face growing hot—"I remember saying some rather unpleasant things to you and acting in a way that was not at all becoming. Honestly, I wouldn't have blamed you if you had decided to give me the cut direct."

He chuckled a little. The sound was nice. Welcoming, even. "Well, if I may be frank in return—"

"Oh—yes! Please do," said Elizabeth, turning a little in her seat and feeling excited at the chance to have a real conversation with him. Possibly even begin a bit of flirtation. Maybe he would tell her that he had secretly adored her silly antics that night. Or that her beauty had captured him from the moment he laid eyes on her. This could be the beginning of her falling in love with Lord Hastings.

"I'm a little surprised that I didn't give you the cut direct as well."

Hmm. This wasn't exactly the romantic declaration she had been hoping for. She faced forward again. "I see."

She could feel his eyes on her. "Was that terribly rude?"

Elizabeth tipped her head to the side. "Well, I suppose I did give you permission to be frank, didn't I?"

"Blast." The frustration in his voice caught her by surprise. "I must warn you. I'm no good at this." He gestured to the space between them. "You might have heard the rumors that I've never courted a woman before. And it's for good reason—"

"Stop!" she said, putting a hand on his arm and forcing him to stop the horses. Elizabeth looked toward the commotion that had drawn her attention. A little dog had run in front of their carriage, and Elizabeth squinted to see two children in the distance yelling and running after it. Her head swung in the direction of the little mutt and then back to Lord Hastings.

"What is it?" he asked, alarm in his tone.

Did he not see? Could he not hear the children?

"Those children have lost their dog," she said quickly, pointing in the direction of the brown ball of fur that had momentarily stopped to scratch his ear. "We must catch him."

Lord Hastings looked both puzzled and as if he were about to break out in full laughter. "Catch that dog?"

"Yes."

"That filthy looking animal over there, who I imagine at one point was white and is now brown?"

"Yes," she said, exasperation growing. "Will you not go catch him for the children?" She searched his dark forest eyes but saw no hint of the answer she was hoping for.

"No," he said on a chuckle. "I will not. I apologize, Lady Elizabeth, but this is a new Weston coat and I paid far too much for it to have it dashed to bits by that grungy dog." He looked forward again and adjusted the reins to start moving again.

The dog finished scratching and prepared to bolt again, as the children neared—but Elizabeth knew there wouldn't be enough time for them to catch it. If Lord Hastings couldn't be bothered to help, she would simply have to do it herself.

Elizabeth gathered up the skirts of her dress and jumped swiftly down from the carriage.

"Lady Elizabeth!" said the unhelpful man in horror. "What are you doing?"

"Isn't it obvious?" she yelled back as she began running as fast as she could toward the dog, hand on the top of her straw bonnet to keep the wind from ripping it from her hatpins.

Elizabeth had almost made it to the dog when she felt a hand on her arm pull her to a stop. She spun around, ready to do battle with Lord Hastings, when her eyes locked with the set of blue eyes that never failed to make her stomach swoop and immediately long for the sea. *Oliver.* He smiled, and the unexpectedness of his presence made a soft, warm flutter soar through her body. "Wait here, Lizzie. I'll catch him." His hand was still on her arm and part of her forgot all about the dog and wished she could spend the rest of the day right there with his hand gently holding on to her.

"Thank you," she managed to say before he darted off in pursuit of the dog.

Elizabeth continued behind Oliver at a slower, more ladylike jog. All right, so perhaps not ladylike since a lady would have never jumped out of that carriage in the first place. But at least she wasn't running with her skirts up anymore.

Oliver overtook the little dog in less than a moment, but the man and beast performed what Elizabeth thought was the most entertaining dance she'd ever witnessed. The dog moved to the left and Oliver followed, only for the dog to zigzag in the opposite direction. She could no longer contain her laughter when Oliver finally dove onto the dog and wrestled the muddy fur ball. He rolled over and sat up, not letting the dog out of his arms, and stood. Elizabeth's hand flew to her mouth to hide an even bigger laugh threatening to burst out.

Oliver was covered head to toe in dirt. His tan leather breeches were ruined with grass stains. His jacket was covered in cakes of wet mud. It seemed Lord Hastings was correct about the unfortunate mutt's original coloring. Even Oliver's cheek had managed to earn a brown splotch. And yet—he looked more handsome to her than ever. His eyes sparkled and his jacket was strained against the muscles in his arms where he struggled against the efforts of the rambunctious dog. This was the man she loved. Her heart gave a sharp tug that he didn't love her back.

"You're really enjoying this, aren't you?" he asked with playful narrowed eyes.

"What do you mean? You look perfectly normal." She assumed her most serious expression.

"I can feel the mud on my face."

"It adds to your rugged handsomeness," she said with a chuckle.

His smile grew a little serious. "You think I'm handsome?"

Her smile then fell away all together. Thankfully, at that very moment, the two children—an older boy and a young girl—bounded up behind them, panting and red faced from their exercise. "There, there," said Elizabeth bending down to put a hand on the little girl's back. "Take a breath. Your dog is rescued so you may make yourself easy now."

"Thank you for catching our Freddie, mister!" said the boy, who looked to be somewhere around eight years old.

Oliver raised Freddie to look into the little mutt's eyes and laughed. "Freddie, is it? I should have known. Freddies are forever disobeying."

"Truly?" asked the little girl who looked a little older than Elizabeth's three year old niece, Jane.

Oliver assumed that expression he always got when he was trying to entertain Jane. "Oh yes—I once knew a boy named Freddie and he was set down from school for misbehaving more times than I could count."

"That's just like our Freddie, all right," said the boy, giving the dog a reprimanding look. "I'm sorry you had to spoil your clothes to catch him for us."

Oliver smiled and looked down at his ruined breeches. "These old things? Never mind them. I've despised them for years."

"Boy," came the sudden harsh sound of Lord Hastings's voice from behind Elizabeth. She turned and found him and his pristine Weston coat walking up behind them, a frown on his face. "You ought to have had that dog—"

"*Freddie*," Oliver interjected. "The dog's name is Freddie."

Lord Hastings looked to Oliver as if he didn't quite know how to take the interruption. He swung a disapproving look back to the boy. "Dogs should never be in the park without a lead. Do you see what your negligence has caused?"

"Lord Hastings," Elizabeth said in a soft tone, hoping to get the man to stop talking. His shift in demeanor was more than a little shocking.

He looked to Elizabeth, standing a little taller. "Young boys must be shown the error of their ways. And this," he gestured toward Oliver and Freddie, "was certainly an error. Not only have you ruined a gentleman's outfit, but you have delayed our drive. Where is your—"

"That's quite enough, Hastings," said Oliver with an edge to his voice that Elizabeth had never heard before. Of course, she'd heard that he and Carver had been known to escalate their arguments to actual fisticuffs now and then, but she had never seen him look so fierce or protective. "The boy doesn't deserve your wrath. I'm sure it was an honest mistake."

"It was, sir!" said the boy, looking as if he were trying to be brave but might fall into tears at any moment. "We had him on this lead," he raised a limp piece of leather, "but Sally begged me to let her chase him. I let Freddie off of it for only a moment, but then he ran off."

Oliver smiled at the boy. "Like I said, an honest mistake."

"One that should be paid for," said Lord Hastings, refusing to come down from that throne of righteousness he was perched on. Elizabeth did not at all like the man at that moment.

"Since it was not you who suffered any sort of sacrifice today, Hastings, I hardly think you are in a place to make that call." Oliver turned his blue eyes to the boy and the fire that had been present a moment ago had softened. "Now, let us get our dear Freddie back on that lead of yours." He set Freddie down and helped the boy reattach him.

Oliver was so kind and gentle with the boy, and it made Elizabeth want to wrap her arms around him and never let go.

"John," said the little girl. "Miss Hollis is going to be angry at us, isn't she?"

"Who is Miss Hollis?" asked Elizabeth, stepping in front of Lord Hastings to shield the children from any more of his unkindness.

"Our governess," answered John. "She…might have told us to stay put while she went to speak with a friend on the path. And then…"

"You ran off after Freddie without telling her," said Oliver when the boy trailed off, eyes cast down.

Both children nodded. Oliver simply chuckled. "No need to look so glum, children. Don't worry, I'll return you to your Miss Hollis and have a nice chat with her. You see, I'm told I have a smile that can charm anyone out of the blackest of moods." He looked at Elizabeth and winked. He winked! Had he ever winked at her before? No. She didn't think so. Because she would have definitely remembered the way she was feeling—like melting or skipping or giggling.

A hand on her elbow made her jump. "We need to be going or Lady Kensworth will grow anxious." Lord Hastings's voice sounded grave.

Oh. Right. She had to drive back with him. Her heart sank. In her mind, Elizabeth had imagined herself walking with Oliver and the children back to their governess. After, Oliver would have walked her home but taken the long way, allowing them to get lost for a time and explore the less traveled paths of Hyde Park.

Instead, she was climbing into that stuffy curricle with a man who made her long to step on his toes, while she watched Oliver disappear across the park.

The drive back to Kensworth House was a quiet one. But the thoughts inside Elizabeth's mind were plenty loud. Oh, how she ached to give Lord Hastings a stinging set down. The worst feeling, however, was that of hopelessness. He was supposed to be the one to help her move on from Oliver. Instead, he was serving in the opposite capacity. Oliver was even more wonderful in her eyes than he had been yesterday. A large part of her wished he would stop showing up in her life. Maybe every other man wouldn't look so dim if not forced to live in Oliver's magnificent shadow.

The carriage came to stop in front of Kensworth House and a footman approached the side, ready to help Elizabeth down. Lord Hastings held up his hand to the servant. "Give us a moment."

Elizabeth's body went rigid. She didn't wish to spend another moment in that man's company. Handsome or not. She kept her eyes firmly fixed on her hands, tightly clasped in her lap, gritting her teeth in a way that would most definitely hurt later.

"Am I right to assume you are vexed with me over my reaction to the children at the park?" His smug voice irritated her.

"A bit." She prepared herself for his defense.

His weary sigh, however, surprised her. Elizabeth turned her head and saw his broad shoulders sink a little. "You're right to be vexed with me. I'm angry with myself, in fact." She blinked at him, not sure what to do with that statement. He peeked over at her, a crooked smile on his mouth. "I was a pompous coxcomb back there. I can only beg for your forgiveness and ask that you put that memory out of your mind." As it turns out, Lord Hastings wore a crooked smile nicely.

"Well…I suppose we could strike a deal. I might be able to forget your manners in the park if you are willing to forget my manners during Miss Loxley's soirée."

He shook his head. "I should never wish to forget that night."

"But in the park you said you were surprised you did not give me the cut direct."

He turned to face her more fully. "What I was going to say to you before we were interrupted by Freddie, was that I have a tendency to be completely and utterly daft when it comes to women." Elizabeth had to press her lips together to not smile. "Somehow I have gained the reputation of a self-assured gentleman who finds woman beneath him. The truth is that I am shockingly shy and have no idea how to act around the opposite sex. Your manners at the soirée were shocking to me in the best of ways. You forced me out of my comfort and intrigued me. What I am about to admit is humiliating and would be a real damage to my finely crafted reputation, therefore you should know, if repeated, I will deny it to my grave."

She couldn't help her chuckle. "Very well, tell me your secret and I shall promise to keep it. Unless of course, it's just too fantastic to keep to myself."

"I was surprised that I did not ignore you because usually I am not bold enough to approach a beautiful woman." Elizabeth felt a subtle stir inside her at his words. And she was more than pleased he hadn't used the word *well* to describe her. "And now, having you here with me, I have no idea how to act or the proper thing to say. At the park, I shamefully admit that I was hoping to appear masculine and dashing. It was ridiculous, I see that now. Please, I beg you to forget this entire morning and allow me another chance."

She smiled. "I would like that very much." The only thing that would have made his speech any better was if he had taken her hand while making it. Something in her longed to know if his touch would invoke the same fire that she felt from Oliver's.

But no...that was unfair. Elizabeth was determined to no longer compare Lord Hastings to Oliver.

She would give him the fair chance he deserved.

Chapter Seventeen

"I never got a chance to ask you about your morning with Lord Hastings yesterday," said Rose as she and Elizabeth continued down the sidewalk toward Hatley House. Elizabeth hadn't seen Mary since her move to Kensworth House. She had been meaning to visit, but every time she had considered it she'd thought of their last conversation and Elizabeth would talk herself out of it. She remembered that look in Mary's eye—sad and heavy, but unwilling to talk about it with her younger sister who she clearly didn't trust to rely on her to help with her troubles. The rejection still stung.

So, Elizabeth had been avoiding her sister. Robert, however, had sent a note over to Carver that morning requesting Rose and Elizabeth to come visit Mary. *"But under no circumstances must Mary know that I have written on her behalf."* Elizabeth could almost see Robert hovered over a desk, quickly dashing off a note, fearfully looking over his shoulder in case Mary should find him out and spend the rest of the day scolding him for trying to take care of her without her approval.

Mary could be frightening when she wanted to be.

The sun was bright and warm against Elizabeth's skin as she tipped her face up toward the sky, squinting at the light and trying to decide how to respond to Rose. *My time with Lord Hastings was something of an intriguing disaster and I have no idea how my relationship with him will end.* No. That wouldn't work. Since Elizabeth was hoping this courtship with the viscount would see the distance, she didn't want to put him in Rose's black books by telling her about his manners toward the children.

So what to tell Rose? *It was absolutely wonderful and I've fallen madly in love with him!* Definitely not. She was a terrible actress and could never be that convincing.

"Too late," said Rose, pulling Elizabeth to a stop with her on the sidewalk. "You took too long to answer. Now I know you had a terrible time." Elizabeth wondered if she just kept on moving, would it keep Rose from asking any more questions? Worth a try.

"Elizabeth Ashburn, stop right there."

Elizabeth stopped and winced as she waited for Rose to catch back up. Rose crossed in front of Elizabeth and paused. She was a tiny yet fierce woman. Elizabeth watched, resisting a smile as Rose tugged at the bonnet strings under her chin as if she could barely tolerate the thing being on her head. Rose had never been an admirer of fashionable ladies' bonnets. It made Elizabeth laugh to see her sister-in-law so uncomfortable.

"What happened with Lord Hastings?" asked Rose.

"Well…" Elizabeth swallowed and considered.

"The truth, if you will."

Elizabeth sighed. "He was a bit pompous in the beginning and we didn't exactly have the best time."

Rose looked relieved that Elizabeth had suffered a bad morning with the viscount, but then she seemed to remember that she was trying to be supportive of Elizabeth making a match with the man and frowned. "That's too bad."

"Actually, it all ended rather nicely. He and I had a nice talk and I think I would like to give him a second chance."

"Oh. Splendid." Rose's voice hit an octave Elizabeth had never heard from her sister-in-law before.

Elizabeth's mouth tugged with a smile. "Holding back your opinions is killing you, isn't it?"

"Slowly and painfully," Rose sighed with a grin. They linked arms again and continued down the sunlit sidewalk. "Well, if you are serious about him, then I suppose I ought to plan some sort of dinner or outing to allow you two more time together. What do you think it ought to be?"

Something that absolutely under no circumstances included Oliver Turner.

The sound of laughter and voices trickled through the hallway, reaching Elizabeth and Rose before they ever stepped through Mary's door.

"It sounds like we are not the only ones visiting Mary today," said Rose. Elizabeth welcomed that realization. The less time she had to spend alone with her sister, the better. Feelings swarmed through her that she wasn't sure what to do with. She had always complied with her siblings' suggestions and demands. It had never been a problem before. But now, as she was trying to make her own place in the world, it annoyed her to have Mary refuse to see her as equal.

"Are we intruding on a party?" asked Rose as she inched open Mary's door, revealing Carver and Robert standing near Mary, lovely in a modest deep purple dressing gown, resting on a chaise. Miss Vienna Loxley occupied the chair beside her.

The first thing Elizabeth noticed was that Mary was smiling. Albeit, a tense smile. She looked from Mary back to Miss Loxley and felt a tug of jealousy. Jealousy was the last feeling in the world Elizabeth wished to be experiencing. She should be grateful that Mary looked lighter, rather than frustrated she had not been the one to put the smile on her face.

"Come in! Now it most certainly is a party." Mary held out her hand to Elizabeth, squeezed it, and smiled her mother hen smile. "I'm happy to see you, darling. You've met my dearest friend, Vienna, have you not?" Elizabeth swallowed the words *dearest friend.* She had had no idea how badly she wished to be Mary's friend until she had come to London. Now that want stared her in the face and mocked her in the form of a beautiful friend named Vienna.

Of course, Vienna wasn't actually mocking her. In fact, her smile was so warm and kind that Elizabeth could see quite easily why Mary adored her. That somehow made it worse.

"Elizabeth and I were able to chat briefly at my soirée, but it wasn't nearly enough. I want to know all about how you are enjoying your first Season." Elizabeth opened her mouth to respond, but Vienna continued. "I hope it has been nothing like the first Season your sister and I endured together." Vienna and Mary exchanged knowing looks. Looks that said they had gone through battle and back together.

"I haven't heard any tales of your first Season, Mary," said Rose, from where she now stood beside an adoring Carver.

Come to think of it, Elizabeth had never heard her sister speak of her curtsy to Society either. "Was it so terrible?" asked Elizabeth.

Elizabeth looked back and forth between Vienna and Mary, catching the moment that Vienna gave Mary a sad, understanding smile. Mary returned it and then looked to Elizabeth. "It was not the best of Seasons for either of us. But never mind all that. Let's hear how yours is getting on. Any suitors?" Mother hen had appeared again.

Elizabeth could feel her cheeks pinking. She could also feel that all eyes were on her and she did not care for it one bit. The truth was, she would have told Mary about Lord Hastings if they had been alone. But with Vienna perched in her chair looking like an older and more sophisticated version of herself, Elizabeth felt a little crippled. "Not as of yet."

"That's not what I've heard," said Robert, shifting on his feet and clasping his hands behind his back. Robert was known for his unreadable expressions. The man was a master at cards. But the face he was wearing just then said he had a good hand and he wished for everyone to know it.

"And just what have you heard, dearest brother-in-law?" said Elizabeth in the teasing tone she often used with him. Like Rose, he had never been one to pat her head and shoo her back to the nursery.

He smirked slightly. "That Lord Hastings—the Unobtainable himself—seems to have set his sights on you."

Mary gasped and looked at Elizabeth. "Is that so? I'm missing everything being holed up in this room."

Vienna grinned. "I thought I saw a spark between you two at my soirée. He was very dedicated to remaining near you the entire evening." Elizabeth curled her toes inside her slippers, hoping Vienna had not noticed the real reason for Lord Hastings's devotion that evening: making sure she didn't fall over. Mary could certainly never know about that unfortunate slip up.

From the corner of her eye, she could see Carver open his mouth. But then Rose shoved her elbow into his ribs and something between a squeak and a cough was all that left his mouth. They both then smiled innocently.

"Where did you hear that?" Elizabeth asked Robert, trying to turn the conversation away from any topic that could lead to Mary learning of Elizabeth's overindulgence.

"From the informant I've hired to watch you," he said, stone-faced. But then a smile cracked his mouth. "Turner, of course." Something inside her felt shocked by his statement, but she wasn't quite sure what it was yet.

"You and Oliver were discussing my courtship with Lord Hastings?" Interesting.

"So it is a courtship, then?" asked Mary.

Elizabeth sighed. "I suppose, yes. He took me for a drive in the Park yesterday."

"That's wonderful, Elizabeth! Lord Hastings would be a fine catch." Mary turned her eager grey eyes to Rose. "Have you planned any events to help encourage his suit?"

Rose visibly stood a little straighter under Mary's watchful gaze. It nearly made Elizabeth laugh. It would seem she wasn't the only one who felt as if she needed to add an extra inch or two to her person when Mary was looking on. "I had considered throwing a dinner party."

Elizabeth noticed Vienna crinkle her little nose.

Mary noticed, too. "You don't think a dinner party will suit, Vie?"
Vie? Mary even had an endearing name for her friend? Elizabeth was
painfully aware of her jealousy. It didn't suit her. But she couldn't help
it. Mary had never even shortened Elizabeth to Lizzie. Actually, Oliver
and Papa were the only ones to ever call her by that name.

"Dinner parties are just so…ordinary and boring, don't you think?"
Unfortunately, Elizabeth did agree with Vienna. And she knew that
Rose would as well. But she was feeling just petty enough not to agree
out loud.

"What do you suggest?" asked Mary, looking to her friend as if she
held the keys to the world.

Vienna put a finger to her lips in thought. Most women only did
such things when trying to make themselves appear more attractive or
seductive. But somehow, Elizabeth knew that, for Vienna, the look was
one of genuine contemplation. It was very difficult not to like her. But
Elizabeth was giving it her best effort.

Vienna's finger popped into the air, her bright green eyes sparking
with an idea. "A riding party!"

"A riding party?" asked Elizabeth.

Mary's grey eyes lit up. "To Charlotte's house for a picnic!" It
seemed Mary and Vienna could communicate telepathically. "That was
such a hit when we were young."

"Exactly my thought. The weather has been so wonderfully mild as
of late, and her house is only an hour's ride from Town. I think Lord
Hastings would enjoy an expedition, and from everything that I've
heard of Elizabeth"—Vienna looked up at her—"you would more than
enjoy an event that keeps you moving rather than seated at a stuffy
table." Must she pretend that she knew Elizabeth so well? And must
she be so spot on? But she was wrong about one thing.

"I'm not sure. I don't think that Lord Hastings would enjoy it as
much as you think." After all, he had told her himself that he preferred
to avoid riding as much as possible.

Mary spoke up quickly, waving a dismissive hand. "Nonsense,
he'll love it. Everyone loves to ride. Rose, I'll handle writing to our
friend, Lady Stanton, and arrange the whole thing. I will even handle

sending out the invitations so you won't need to do a single thing other than show up." How did Rose feel about Mary bowling her over? Relieved, by the looks of it. Apparently Elizabeth was the only one who felt annoyed.

"Mary, I think it would be better for everyone if we—"

"Darling, you mustn't worry your head about it. I know sitting still and planning is not your forte," Mary said, forcing Elizabeth's hands to clench at her sides. "I'll take care of everything."

"But you should really be resting. Wasn't this sort of thing exactly what the doctor intended for you to avoid by placing you on bedrest?"

Mary's face darkened. The smile she had been wearing a moment ago faded and a cloud hovered in her eyes. "I'm well enough to handle writing letters, Elizabeth." Her clipped tone felt like salt in the wound Mary had inflicted on Elizabeth several days ago.

The whole room felt tense. Everyone seemed to suddenly find their shoes extremely interesting.

"I didn't mean to offend you. I simply want to care for you and the ba—"

"Of course she wasn't offended," Vienna interjected with too bright of a smile. She leaned over and patted Mary's hand. "And this is just what our Mary needs to help pass these dreadfully boring days. Now everyone shoo and allow Mary and I to get to work." Vienna was going to help Mary? Of course she was.

Elizabeth watched Mary lift her hand and reach for her full midsection, but as if deciding against it, froze and laid her hand back down beside her. It broke Elizabeth's heart. Mary was hiding her hurt. It irked her that Vienna seemed to be the newest blockade between Elizabeth and her sister.

But then again…perhaps Vienna was better suited to care for Mary than she was. She certainly seemed to know her better.

"You're sure you don't need my help?" asked Elizabeth, both fearful and hopeful that Mary would see the concern in her eyes.

However, Mary was too busy rearranging her skirts to look up. "Never you mind, darling. Vienna and I will get it all taken care of and send a note over with all of the details."

Elizabeth nodded. Everyone said their goodbyes and began filing out of the room. Elizabeth stopped when she heard Mary say, "Oh, yes. Oliver Turner must definitely be invited."

Elizabeth whipped around. "No!" But she shrunk back a little from Mary and Vienna's wide eyes. "I mean...no, do not invite Oliver."

"Why ever not?" That was a very good question. One with an answer that could not be spoken aloud.

"He...has been under the weather. And you know Oliver. If he's invited he will most definitely attend. But...I think it would only hinder his recovery." It was a bold-faced lie. However, Elizabeth couldn't bring herself to care at the moment. Her only objective was to ensure that Oliver Turner would be forced to keep his distance and give her enough space to fall in love with Lord Hastings.

Chapter Eighteen

"**W**hat's happened?" Oliver asked no sooner than the door to Hatley's study closed behind the butler. Hatley had sent a letter around to Oliver's flat that morning with an urgent message that he was to come to Hatley House straightaway.

At eight o'clock in the morning, Oliver was striding into Hatley's foyer ready to be met with some sort of terrible news. The butler—who liked him much more than Kensworth's butler did—immediately showed him to the earl's study. He had been dreaming up all sorts of terrible scenarios involving Elizabeth or Mary and, because of that, was prepared to be met with the news that Elizabeth had gotten in a carriage accident and her arm had been trapped under the wheel and they had been forced to amputate it. Or that Mary had developed another complication with the pregnancy and was in dire straits.

Only…the earl was lounging behind his desk with his feet propped up on the surface and a book in his hand. "Have you read this?" Hatley asked, dark eyes peeking over the book: *Pride and Prejudice*. "It's good. I was surprised because normally when Kate suggests a novel for me it's some gothic romance that I'm sure she shouldn't be reading. But this…I like it."

Oliver gaped at the man as he forced his racing heart to slow down.

"You've brought me here in a panic because you wished to inform me of a book recommendation from Kate?" Oliver was fond of the youngest Ashburn sibling as much as the rest, but he didn't give a dash about her choice of reading material.

Hatley set the book down. "Why did you come in a panic? No one said you needed to panic."

Oliver let out an incredulous laugh as he pulled a letter from his jacket pocket. He opened it with a flourish and then cleared his throat before reading, "Turner. Get here now. It's urgent. Signed, H."

He looked up at Hatley, whose face held nothing but amusement. "Exactly. Never said you needed to panic."

Oliver let his gaze fall heavily on the earl. "I'm going to run you through." Oliver had raced through the streets of London like the very ground was on fire. The whispers around his name were going to be plentiful.

"Could you possibly wait until after I've found out what happens with Mr. Darcy?"

"Mr. Who?"

Hatley lifted the book with a grin.

Oliver grunted and sank into a chair in front of Hatley's desk. "Why am I here, Hatley?" He pointed a menacing finger at the book. "And it better not have anything to do with your blasted Mr. Darcy."

"A bit surly this morning, are we?" asked Hatley.

"I didn't sleep last night."

"Why?"

He rubbed his hand over his face. "I can't decide what to do about Lizzie. I saw her at the Opera last night and Lord Hastings spent nearly the whole evening at her side. Ridiculous."

"I fail to see the ridiculousness of the situation. Isn't he known as a rather respectable gentleman of good breeding, with a nice fortune?"

Oliver shuddered. "Exactly. He'll bore Elizabeth to death."

Hatley laughed and stood up to come lean against the front of his desk, crossing his arms. "So let me get this straight. You don't want Elizabeth for yourself, but neither do you wish for Elizabeth to be with anyone else?"

"Well, when you say it like that it sounds rather childish, doesn't it?"

"I would answer that question, but I've been told recently that I think too much of my own opinion and I should stick to billiards."

Oliver winced. "Sorry about that. You hit a sore spot during our last talk. I might have been a little sharp when I left you."

"Might have been?" Hatley asked with a grin.

"I've apologized. No need to rub it in."

"Very well. I'll tell you why I've called you here, then."

"Please do."

"I need to ask a favor of you."

"Of course. Anything," said Oliver.

Hatley smiled. "The ladies have all planned a little riding party to Lady Stanton's home just outside of Town for a picnic. Mary, of course, thought it advisable for me to attend as an escort and has volunteered my attendance. I, however, do not feel comfortable leaving her in her state for that amount of time and was hoping I might persuade you to attend in my place."

The ladies had planned a riding party? Why hadn't he been invited to begin with? "The picnic is today?"

"In about an hour, in fact."

Oliver narrowed his eyes at Hatley. Suspicion tiptoed over him. "And just when were you first asked to join this riding party?"

Hatley cracked the barest of grins. "Three days ago."

"And you're only just now deciding you should like for me to go in your stead?" Hatley nodded. "Do the ladies happen to know you are asking me to attend in your place?"

"No."

Oliver narrowed his eyes into the barest of slits. "Scheming, Hatley?"

"Will you do it, or not?"

Oliver looked down and lightly scuffed his boot across the red rug. "Do you happen to know if Lord Hastings will also be among this riding party?"

"I believe so."

Oliver's fingers dug into the arm rest.

"Does that bother you?" asked Hatley, already reading the correct answer in the whitened grip of Oliver's knuckles.

He relaxed his hand and stood up. "Of course not. As I told you the other day, Elizabeth deserves the best. I hope this for her as much as she hopes it for herself." Was that believable enough?

"I thought you said Hastings would bore her?"

"He will. But he will be safe." His gaze dropped to the floor, seeing a memory of Elizabeth laughing instead of the ornate swirling pattern of the rug. "All I want is for Elizabeth to be safe."

"For what it's worth, Turner, I have no doubt she would be safe with you."

Oliver looked up and met Hatley's eyes. "Only because you don't know my whole story."

"Tell it to me."

He couldn't. Even if he wished to, Oliver couldn't get the words out. With words came memories, and those memories still hurt today as much as the day they were created. However, this time, he didn't feel like snapping at Hatley's prodding. He held his gaze and admitted, at least in part, the truth. "I can't. It hurts too much." He swallowed and Hatley remained quiet, giving him the space he needed to collect his thoughts.

"Trust me, Elizabeth is better off with the viscount. He can offer her all of the things that I cannot. I'll go in your stead today, but only because you need to be here with Mary. No matter your scheming, Hatley, I don't plan to interfere with Hasting's suit."

What was Oliver doing here? No. He absolutely was not supposed to be invited. Elizabeth had made it plain to Mary that Oliver was not to be added to the guest list. Although she hadn't said as much to Mary, Elizabeth knew that if that blasted man continued to show up in every corner of her life she would never be released from loving him. And she thought that, for once in her life, her sister had listened and submitted to her desires for Oliver Turner to be left off of the guest list.

But there he was, ruining all of Elizabeth's well thought out plans, walking his horse up next to hers with a smile that sent a warm rush through her chest. Did his blond hair have to look so wonderful peeking out of his hat at the nape of his neck? And why must he have worn her favorite light blue waistcoat under his black jacket? It was obnoxious how well it hugged the contours of his muscular shoulders. Shoulders she had spent a little too much time dreaming of touching. Elizabeth shook her head, ridding her mind of those unwelcome thoughts.

Rose and Carver, Lord Hastings and his younger sister, Lady Olivia, as well as Miss Barley and her younger sister, Miss Marion, were already in attendance and seated on their mounts, waiting to set out. Mary had also invited another single gentleman by the name of Mr. Yates, but he had unfortunately become ill overnight and had sent his regrets that morning. Unfortunately, the atrocious Miss Barley had weaseled an invitation for herself and her sister from Rose, and had not come down with an illness overnight that would have prohibited her attendance. No sooner than Rose and Elizabeth had left Mary's house the day the riding party had been decided, had Miss Barley and her mother crossed their path on the sidewalk and pounced on she and Rose.

Rose was a mastermind when it came to spinning conversations in the directions she wanted them to go, but even the retired con woman walked away from their talk in a haze, wondering how the devil she had been manipulated into extending an invitation to the obnoxious pair. Rose was a bit testy for the remainder of the day, sulking around the house, claiming she had completely lost her touch.

Carver had managed to pull Rose out of her blue devils by sweeping her off to a remote section of Hyde Park, rumored to be a popular dueling ground, and returning her pistol. He had nailed a playing card to the trunk of a tree and had her shoot several rounds until she was smiling again. She had returned home in the best of spirits and Elizabeth couldn't help but long for the type of union Rose and Carver shared.

Which is why she was so spitting angry to find Oliver standing in front of her looking like the most attractive man alive. She would never find her soul mate when he was always showing up and taunting her with what she could never have.

"Mr. Turner," said Elizabeth in a cold tone as Oliver stopped with his horse next to hers, "What a nice surprise."

He lifted a brow in an amused smirk. "Really? I'd hate to see what your face looked like if it was an unpleasant surprise." He winked and lowered his voice leaning closer so his breath tickled her ear. "Don't worry, Lizzie. I won't step on your time with Hastings."

Could he not see that he already was? Just the feel of his breath against her ear was making her head spin. And it was irritating that he did not look the least bit upset by the knowledge that she was wishing for alone time with another man. Not that she was trying to make Oliver jealous by her courtship with Lord Hastings.

But...maybe she had been secretly hoping it would make him at least a tiny bit jealous.

"Olly!" said Carver, walking his horse up next to where they were standing. "Come to play chaperone with us? I'm dreading this day a little less now that I know you get to suffer with me." Luckily the rest of the group was engrossed in conversation and hadn't heard her brother's ineloquent speech. But he wasn't wrong. The day would, unfortunately, be vastly more enjoyable with Oliver present. Everything was more enjoyable with him. And more attractive. And smelled better.

"You know how much I enjoy being tortured by the *ton*," said Oliver with a glittering smile.

"I do. Which is why I was a little surprised when I heard you didn't wish to make up one of our party."

Oliver's eyes slid to Elizabeth's—slow and deliberate, piercing her with one of his looks, conveying meaning in a secret language only the two of them could understand. He raised his brows. Her face filled with heat.

"Believe me, Kenny. I'm just as surprised by my choice to not attend as you are." He smiled wickedly in Elizabeth's direction. "But Hatley did not feel comfortable leaving your sister and persuaded me to take his place." Oliver inched just the slightest bit closer to Elizabeth. She could feel the hairs on her arms stand up from the challenging look in his eyes but refused to acknowledge the sensation. "You don't mind, do you, Lizzie?"

She pressed her lips together in a closed smile before replying, "Don't be silly. Of course I don't mind." Except she did, very much. She wanted to murder Robert for giving up his place. And murder Oliver for acting so smug about finding a way into the party he had clearly been excluded from. Well, murder him or kiss him. One of the two.

Elizabeth turned her eyes to Lord Hastings, poised upon his horse. She was a little surprised when she realized he was watching her from the corner of his eye. Watching her and Oliver? She was suddenly filled with the urge to shove Oliver away from her. He was going to sabotage everything somehow. She just knew it.

Chapter Nineteen

How many times, really, could a woman say, "Oh, Mr. Turner, you're so droll!" and reach out and touch his sleeve?

Five.

Elizabeth knew because that's exactly how many times she had heard Miss Barley utter the insipid phrase. Elizabeth had been forced to ride behind Oliver and the woman who was named after a grain and possessed the eyelashes of a spider. She had listened to her flirt with Oliver, and he had returned her flirtations with charming smiles for the entire ride thus far. One obnoxious smile after another.

How was it that Elizabeth was supposed to be having an afternoon of flirtations that made Oliver jealous—No, wait. Where had that thought come from? She was not here to make Oliver jealous. The flirtatious afternoon was only meant to encourage Lord Hastings. But instead, her thoughts were too focused on trying not to grind her teeth into dust while being forced to watch Oliver prove how effectively he could flirt with the opposite sex.

Miss Barley had used every trick in the book. At one point she had even asked Oliver to ride a little closer to her so that she might retrieve a leaf—or rather, a *nonexistent* leaf—from his hat. They had not even ridden through foliage. The worst part of it all was that Oliver complied with every one of Miss Barley's outlandish requests. And there were many. Elizabeth continued to hope that Lady Olivia or Miss Marion would draw Oliver's attention—if only so that Elizabeth might have received a respite from hearing the woman's nasally voice. But, alas, no. The two younger ladies seemed perfectly content to ride in one another's company, giggling and swapping stories in hushed voices.

Elizabeth envied the young ladies. It would have been nice to gain a female friend in London, rather than constantly be on the receiving end of Miss Barley's haughty sneers anytime Oliver reciprocated one of her vapid compliments. Miss Barley's eyes seemed to claim Oliver, and warn Elizabeth off from interfering. Elizabeth didn't plan to. She didn't have any desire to compete with the woman.

So she told herself. But if it were true, why was Elizabeth laughing loudly at something Lord Hastings had just said, despite having not even heard it? She knew the answer as soon as she received the response she had secretly been hoping for. Oliver looked over his shoulder with a raised eyebrow.

"How funny you are, my lord," Elizabeth said, looking at Hastings over a slightly lifted shoulder like she'd seen other women do when they were trying to look attractive. Was she doing it correctly? She sort of felt as if she looked deranged. And whose attention was she truly trying to gain? Lord Hastings's or Oliver's?

Lord Hastings's. Definitely Lord Hastings's attention. She simply needed to focus on the viscount and block out the ugly jealousy she was feeling toward Miss Barley and the attention Oliver was giving her.

Lord Hastings's brows pulled together but he smiled, evidently confused, but nonetheless enjoying the sudden attention. "Well, I suppose that taking a toss during a fox hunt and nearly being trampled to death might be viewed as humorous. In a sort of dark way, I suppose." *Oh.* Is that what he had just said? Oh, dear.

Elizabeth noticed Oliver's ears strain back like they always did when he was trying not to release a full laugh. She needed to recover herself. It was time to take the game up a step. No, not a game. What she meant was, it was time to ensure her relationship with the man riding beside her.

Elizabeth steered her horse a little closer to Lord Hastings's and looked at him with doe eyes. "It's only humorous because it is so unexpected. I dare say it's very unusual for a...strong gentleman such as yourself to ever lose his seat."

Despite herself, Elizabeth peeked up at Oliver. He hadn't turned back around, but his head was now angled in such a way that she knew he was listening.

Lord Hastings looked confused again. "Perhaps. But if you will remember, the story to which I was referring was inflicted on one of my friends. Not me." Oh, drat. Her face flamed. She should have known it wasn't him. Lord Hastings didn't seem to do anything besides float around to various card parties and bury his head in politics in the House of Lords. He would never engage in something so exciting as the fox hunt. He probably wasn't even enjoying himself on this ride. She still felt uncomfortable that Mary had forced an event on them that Elizabeth knew Lord Hastings would not enjoy.

A weak smile was all she could muster. She looked over her shoulder at Rose, feeling her spirits sinking with every increasing minute of the day. Her sister-in-law returned her pleading look with a firm nod that Elizabeth knew meant *turn around and be confident!*

It was time to pretend she was Rose. Elizabeth turned back and squared her shoulders. But her heart faltered a little when she realized Oliver had been looking back at her. A soft smile played on his lips and for a brief moment, Elizabeth completely forgot about all of her determination to take her heart back from him. She would have given anything to be riding next to Oliver just then.

"Mr. Turner," said Miss Barley, diverting Oliver's attention back to her after spotting his smile toward Elizabeth. "Is it not wonderful to see Lady Elizabeth thriving amongst Society?" Elizabeth was aware of Lord Hastings speaking to her but she narrowed her eyes on Miss

Barley, knowing the woman too well now to trust that her comment to Oliver was a compliment. The conniving woman continued, "Because knowing how close you are with her family and how much you care for her like your own sister, you must be eager to see her well-situated. Or...perhaps I am wrong and your sentiments toward her are not familial after all?"

Elizabeth sucked in a breath, waiting for Oliver's response to the forward woman, and wishing Lord Hastings would cease talking so she could hear him more clearly. She didn't have to hold her breath long, Oliver responded almost immediately. "You are not wrong, Miss Barley. Lady Elizabeth is my dearest friend, and I am most eager to see her established in her own home."

Elizabeth had thought it wasn't possible for her to feel any further pain or disappointment when it came to Oliver. Apparently she had been wrong. His response somehow served to make her heart sink even lower. When would she come to terms with the fact that he was never going to regard her as anything other than a friend? Did he have romantic feelings toward Miss Barley? Would he finally decide to settle down with a woman? And if so, was this how their friendship would look for the rest of their lives? It felt all too wrong.

"...and so I think it's safe to assume that you will be receiving an invitation soon," said Lord Hastings, pulling Elizabeth's attention back to the present. What was that about an invitation? Blast. She hadn't been listening to him again. But in her defense, the man did have a rather monotonous voice. Simply adding a bit of modulation would go a long way to augment his storytelling abilities.

"Right," she said, trying to sound as if she had been attending the entire time. "And this invitation...I should be excited to accept it, no doubt?"

Lord Hastings looked at her with an expression that was the closest thing to warm she had seen from him thus far. "Shall we speak frankly with one another again, Lady Elizabeth?" If frank meant with a little more excitement, she really hoped he would. "My mother has never felt a need to extend an invitation to visit Addington Hall to an unmarried lady and her family before." A visit? To Lord Hastings's country seat?

Elizabeth swallowed. "But…she does now?"

He smiled a little. She had to admit he looked handsome when he did that. Her stomach didn't flip over like it did when Oliver smiled, but she could appreciate the sight nonetheless. "I think she does, yes."

"Oh." She needed to smile. This was good, was it not? He was essentially admitting that a proposal was imminent. Good. Wonderful. Brilliant. This was exactly what she wanted.

Elizabeth looked down at the reins, held a bit too tightly in her hands. She mustered a smile and aimed it at Lord Hastings. "I should be delighted to receive an invitation." There was no going back now.

Oliver suddenly slowed his horse's pace to drop in beside Elizabeth. She resisted the urge to look at him. She wasn't going to let him ruin this for her. "I don't think Miss Barley should have to ride alone," she said to Oliver. Getting rid of Oliver was a must. She couldn't focus on Lord Hastings when she was constantly trying to put out the fire that rushed over her when Oliver was near.

"Neither do I. Which is why I've come to fetch Lord Hastings." Oliver looked around Elizabeth to make eye contact with the viscount. "Miss Barley wishes to bend your ear a moment. Something about hoping to join the commitee that helps sponsor young women who have found themselves in unfortunate situations. You know, the committee over which your mother presides."

Something about Oliver's tone made Elizabeth's eyes narrow. What was he up to? She looked to Lord Hastings and he frowned. "I'm afraid Lady Hastings is not associated with any such committee."

Oliver looked flabbergasted. Completely and utterly flabbergasted. "You don't say? I thought for certain she was. Well, you'd better set Miss Barley straight then."

Elizabeth looked to Miss Barley and noted her wildly possessive eyes staring Oliver down. It did not look like the face of a woman who wished to have a private chat with Lord Hastings over any such committee. What was Oliver's aim?

"Very well," said Lord Hastings, looking as if he'd rather have his hair plucked out one by one than ride beside Miss Barley for even a moment. She could at least admire him for that. "Do you mind, Lady Elizabeth?"

Elizabeth was a little startled when the first thought that popped in her head was, *For goodness' sake, go!* It only served to make her angrier with Oliver. She would have been perfectly content with Lord Hastings's monotone stories if it weren't for that obnoxious best friend of hers.

"I will be sad to lose your company, but I quite understand," said Elizabeth.

He smiled, pleased by her reply. Her eyes widened as he reached out and squeezed her hand—the first contact they had shared other than when they were dancing. "I will return to you soon."

Oh, come on, you rebellious heart. Why won't you beat faster for him?

The moment Lord Hastings led his horse up to the front, Oliver guided his to ride close to Elizabeth—the same way they always rode at Dalton Park. Or, not exactly the same way, because his leg had never brushed up against hers before like it was doing at that moment.

"Shouldn't you be the one to set Miss Barley straight since you were the one to lead her astray?" said Elizabeth through tight teeth and turning to glare at Oliver.

"Oh, no. She might think I'm simply trying to needle her out of position. Better leave it to Hastings." *Unbelievable.*

Oliver's horse, Romeo, tossed his head against the reins, trying to gain the attention of Lucy—Elizabeth's mare. Knowing how much Lucy meant to Elizabeth, Papa had been kind enough to have the horse transported to Town with her. It was nice having this bit of home away from home.

Elizabeth couldn't help but smile down at the two horses that were the best of friends. Anytime they were let out to pasture together, they always played and raced and danced around as if they were the animal embodiments of Elizabeth and Oliver.

She laughed and leaned down to pat Romeo. "Not today, boy. Lucy has to focus." It hadn't surprised Elizabeth a bit the day Oliver had told her he had named his new horse after the Shakespearean lover.

"Poor old chap," said Oliver, with a chuckle. "He's missed his friend, and now that she's with him again, he can't even get her to play." Elizabeth looked down at the grass. Was he actually talking about Lucy and Romeo? She was so tired of Oliver just thinking of her as a friend. "Come on, let's have a race and give these horses something to do. I know you're just as bored as I am on this dull ride." He hadn't looked bored, laughing at all of Miss Barley's jests.

But he was right. She was dying to let her horse run. She knew Lord and Lady Stanton's home wasn't much farther. She itched to spur her horse into a gallop and surprise Oliver before he was ready. It wouldn't take long for him to catch her—it never did—and he would laugh, telling her she was a dirty cheat. Last time she had jumped the start of a race, he had taken her dessert at dinner as penance. She smiled just thinking of it.

"See, just the thought of a race is making you happy. Come on, Lizzie. I know you want to."

Elizabeth's smile fell, and his nickname reminded her that she couldn't act in such a way anymore. He was *still* thinking of her as Little Lizzie. What did she have to do to get him to understand? To see that she was different—no longer that little girl, eager to run with him into any adventure. Things had to change. It was time for her to become a wife and a mother. If he didn't wish for her to fill that role in his life, he was going to have to move aside. Lord Hastings was her future now.

Elizabeth pressed her lips together and sat a little straighter, banishing memories of Dalton Park from her mind. "Ladies do not race during a riding party, Mr. Turner. Lord Hastings would not find it becoming."

"Elizabeth." The way he said her name—almost as a caress—made her look up at him. There was something new in his tone. And his look…if she had thought Lord Hastings's look was warm, this one was pure fire. Her heart raced. What did it mean? Was she imagining it? Was he…jealous?

Her traitorous heart liked that idea far too much.

"Mr. Turner!" Miss Barley's voice sidled into their conversation, effectively putting a stop to whatever Oliver was about to say. "You promised you would tell me about meeting the prince regent! We are nearly finished with our ride and I have yet to hear the story. Do come tell me." She fanned her spider leg lashes at him.

Oliver sighed and broke his eyes away from Elizabeth. "Of course. I'll be right there." Elizabeth could feel Oliver looking at her again but she refused to meet his gaze. Why could he not just tell the woman *no*? Clearly, whatever it was he had been about to say was important. But apparently his dedication to the flirty miss—and every other blasted debutante in London—was more important. Oliver only wanted Elizabeth when he was bored. When he needed a friend. When they were safely tucked away at Dalton Park and no one of the *ton* was around to entertain him. When would she stop forgetting that?

Elizabeth's anger boiled. She was sick to death of being there whenever he was ready to talk.

"Elizabeth. Could we speak later?" asked Oliver, as Lord Hastings rejoined her on his staid and sensible mount.

She snapped her eyes to Oliver. "No, I don't think there will be time."

His brows furrowed. "But—"

"Carver," she cut Oliver off and looked over her shoulder at her brother. "How much farther…?" She frowned at her *chaperones* who had fallen back and floated so far away from the group, looking so deeply lost in their own blissful newlywed world it was laughable. They both only had one hand on their horse's reins—their other hands were entwined together. Mary would have been aghast. No. She couldn't think of Mary just then. She still wasn't sure what to do about her sister and that frightened her.

Oliver cantered back up to Miss Barley's side.

Lord Hastings fell in line with Elizabeth.

She still had an entire afternoon stretched out in front of her—of faking a smile and pursuing a man she didn't love.

And suddenly, she wanted to cry.

Everything felt wrong. Flirting felt wrong. London felt wrong. She and Oliver felt wrong. And the bright lavender riding habit she was wearing definitely felt wrong. None of this was her, and she wasn't sure how long she could keep it up. Would it even be worth it in the end?

Chapter Twenty

Oliver focused on taking three deep breaths in and out of his nose.

Inhale. Exhale.

If he concentrated all of his attention on breathing slowly and purposefully—

Inhale. Exhale.

He would not notice how utterly and completely infuriated Elizabeth was making him.

Inhale. Exha—

Elizabeth's fake tickling laugh interrupted his meditation. Lord Hastings had said not one humorous thing the entire afternoon. Not a single one. And yet, Elizabeth had laughed that obnoxious fake laugh what he imagined was over a hundred times. What did she see in that man? Most would call Lord Hastings an upstanding gentleman. Oliver just found him to be a dead bore. Not one surprising or original statement had left the viscount's mouth since they set out that morning.

Oliver had sworn to himself he wouldn't interfere. But of course, just like every other time he found himself in Elizabeth's company, he couldn't stay away from her. She was a magnet and everything in him was absurdly attracted to her. He was also so inexcusably jealous of

Hastings that Oliver was afraid his skin was starting to physically turn green.

Almost as green as all of those cucumbers Lord Hastings was placing on Elizabeth's plate at that moment. Oliver watched closely to see how Elizabeth would react.

They had arrived at Lady Charlotte Stanton's house a half hour ago and were enjoying—*enjoying* being the opposite adjective of how he was truly feeling—a picnic in her gardens. They were all seated around a table bright with pristine white linens and gleaming utensils reflecting the sun's light overhead. It never ceased to amuse Oliver what fashionable Society thought was a picnic. Miss Barley leaned into Oliver's side, once again a little too close for his comfort, and started remarking on the well manicured paths of the garden and how she should like above anything to explore them before it was time to leave. She was about as subtle as an elephant in a church. She likely wanted to get him alone on one of those paths and find out if his reputation of being a fantastic kisser was well-earned. One thing was for sure: Miss Barley would *never* find out.

She droned on and on, but he mentally clapped his hands over his ears so he could focus on Elizabeth's reaction across the table when Lord Hastings handed her the plate he had so chivalrously prepared for her. Oliver narrowed his eyes as the plate was set in front of Elizabeth. She looked down at it and Oliver didn't miss the split second frown that pulled at her mouth. Her eyes flicked up to Oliver's and locked for one knowing moment before she turned to Hastings and recovered her smile. "Thank you, my lord."

Hastings looked smug at the sight of her smile. He nodded toward her plate. "I believe you forgot to ask for cucumbers so I took the liberty of adding a few to your plate." He picked one off of his own plate and took a large indulgent bite and swallowed. "They are a delicious fruit. You agree, do you not?"

Elizabeth blinked a few times quickly. "Oh, yes. I adore them."

A loud scoff fell out of Oliver's mouth. He covered it with a cough, but it still earned him a sharp glare from Elizabeth.

They communicated in their wordless language. *"Shut it. Not a single word."*

He smiled and leaned back, folding his arms. *"Fine. But I will always know the truth."*

~

The sun was full and warm and Elizabeth hadn't come inside for luncheon, which could mean only one thing.

Oliver walked outside in the direction of Elizabeth's favorite oak tree. It wasn't far from Dalton House, but it was tucked far enough away that you couldn't see it from the windows of the manor. Elizabeth had found the tree when she was ten years old and claimed it as her own. She said it spoke to her, and therefore it belonged to her. It was difficult to believe that had been eight years ago.

She was a woman now. And because of that, Oliver had mentally promised to keep his distance from Elizabeth during his summer holiday. Kensworth still wouldn't return home with him, so he felt as if he didn't have anyone to create the much—needed barrier between him and Elizabeth. Every one of the Ashburns saw Oliver as family—and because of it, no threat to Elizabeth whatsoever. Which was why he was allowed to venture outside, as he was at that moment, prepared for a picnic and looking for Elizabeth, with the blessings of both duke and duchess.

They wouldn't have given him that blessing if they could have read his thoughts anytime Elizabeth stepped into a room.

But still, he loved the duke and duchess as his own parents—actually, he didn't love his own father, so he loved them as something different. Something stronger. He would never do anything to lose their trust.

Oliver's boots crunched over the tall green blades of grass, every step sounding remarkably like a laugh. A mocking laugh saying that he never stood a chance at staying away from his beautiful and enjoyable friend for an entire summer. No—in fact, he'd spent nearly the entirety of every day in Elizabeth's company. Mornings, they spent together riding. The afternoons, taking walks together or playing cards with

Kate. And the evenings, reading by candlelight in the library while the duke and duchess played chess nearby.

Elizabeth's tall tree came into view. It was a peculiar tree, split down the middle, but the two halves were joined together by a small plank of wood he had nailed into the tree to create a secret hiding place for Elizabeth during his first summer at Dalton Park. The sun was golden and there wasn't a cloud in sight, so he knew he would find Elizabeth on the opposite side of the tree, resting her back against the trunk.

He smiled when he approached and saw a slip of green fabric and a bare foot poking out from behind the tree, boots and stockings discarded haphazardly across the ground. Oliver rounded the tree and found Elizabeth exactly as he suspected he would—asleep, bonnet cast even farther away than her boots, a book in her limp hand on the ground, a faint pink strip forming on the bridge of her nose.

Oliver gently used his boot to nudge her bare toes. A small slow smile pulled at one corner of her mouth, but her eyes didn't open. "Oliver," she said in little more than whisper.

His heart shook to life. "Yes?"

This time she jumped and opened her eyes as if she only just now realized he was standing in front of her. So then why had she just—

"Oliver!" she sat up straighter and touched her hand to her wild curls that had come loose from the knot behind her head and then crinkled her nose, evidently noticing the crispness of her skin. "Oh, drat. How long have I been out here?"

He chuckled, retrieved her bonnet, and tossed it in her lap. "Hours."

She pulled a frown and put the bonnet on her head, leaving the ribbons hanging untied. "I never know how I manage to fall asleep." She always said that after he found her this way. An afternoon nap was never what she intended. But the warm summer sun never failed to lull her into slumber. Oliver attributed it to the fact that Elizabeth awoke before the sun and spent nearly all of the day in constant motion. Sleep was something that must only ever sneak up on her.

"One might assume it begins with closing your eyes."

She flashed him an annoyed look and pretended to kick him. He dodged it and chuckled. "Have you brought something delicious inside that bag, or are you simply carrying it as your newest accessory?"

He held himself a little taller, satchel hanging off his shoulder, and pretended to strut. "It's all the rage in Town. What do you think?" Oliver looked down his nose at her and she suppressed a smile.

"I think you're an infantile dunderhead carrying an ugly satchel."

He feigned reproach and clutched the bag. "Now I'm definitely not going to share my delicious food with you."

Her blue eyes glittered. "I knew you brought me something."

"I did. But I fully intend to eat it all myself now."

"You are going to make me apologize, aren't you?"

"To the satchel."

Her mouth cracked with a slight grin but she controlled it. "Very well." She looked at the bag. "Do forgive me, satchel. I was most unkind and I regret my poor manners deeply."

He smiled, enjoying their games a little too much. Elizabeth never found herself important as the other women of Society did. She never shied away from a playful exchange. She never smothered her laugh. Elizabeth was...wonderful.

Oliver plopped down on the ground beside her and began digging through the contents of the satchel. He removed a small sandwich wrapped in linen and handed it to Elizabeth. Their hands touched when she took the offering from him and just that small contact sent a jolt through his body. He wasn't supposed to feel that way about her.

He swallowed and turned his full attention to removing the wrapping from his own sandwich.

She gasped after unwrapping her sandwich. "Cucumbers!"

"Oh, here. I gave you mine by mistake."

They exchanged again but, this time, he was careful not to come into contact with her. He couldn't help but smile when she blew out a long dramatic puff of air. "I was fearful for a moment that you had forgotten my dislike of that horrid green fruit."

"How could I when you've reminded me of your hatred toward it every day since you were ten years old?" He leaned in close to her and

took a big taunting bite of his own cucumber-filled sandwich. She wrinkled her adorable nose and leaned away.

"I despise them."

"I know."

"Loathe them, in fact."

"I know."

"Wish that Adam had stomped them to bits in the Garden of Eden and abolished them forever."

He smiled. "I know."

"Good. Only making certain you never forget." She peeked up at him and he felt his stomach turn over from the almost flirtatious look she gave him. Their gazes held for a moment before she cleared her throat and looked down at her own sandwich—which really couldn't even be considered a sandwich since it was only bread and cheese. "I don't know what it is you see in the fruit."

"My mother loved them," he said and then froze. Had he really just said that out loud? He never spoke of his mother. Never. Not to anyone.

Elizabeth's mouth parted and she took in a breath. She knew this unspoken rule as well. Questions, concern, and uncertainty ran through Elizabeth's sky blue eyes. Her gaze dropped to her sandwich and something in him longed for her to cross the line he'd drawn. The line he'd never allowed anyone in the world to even get close to.

"Go ahead," he said, his voice shaking a little at the permission he was offering. "Ask me."

She turned her face to him, her expression soft and tender. "What was she like?"

A breath released from him like the first cleansing breeze of spring. He shut his eyes to conjure up the soft memories he kept tucked inside his chest. "She was lovely in every way." He smiled as he pictured her. "I have the most vivid images of my mother's eyes crinkling in the corners as she held my hands and spun me around in the pasture as a child. She was the sort of mother who would chase and play and laugh and...she protected me with everything she had." Oliver had to clear his throat against the emotions he felt welling up.

"In the darkest of days, she laughed—just to make sure I always *had a reason to smile. She told the most wonderful stories of adventure and romance and somehow managed to make our very dark life brighter." And then she died and all of his light fled with her.*

Oliver felt the familiar knife twist through his chest at the memory of losing his mother. At the feelings of loss and heartache and fear he had experienced as a young boy when he had learned that the only person who loved him in the world was gone. The only relief from the pain was to force himself to return his focus on the present where he was no longer a helpless child.

With his eyes still shut, he tuned into the world around him. The smell of summer. The warmth of the sun. The sound of birds overhead, and the breeze pushing through the leaves of the tree. He stretched his fingers then gripped the sharp blades of grass under his hands. After a moment, the twisting of the knife subsided a little.

But then an unexpected feeling joined the rest. Warm. Soft. Velvet. He opened his eyes to see Elizabeth's hand covering his. "What happened to her?" She asked gently.

This was the difficult part. The part that had changed his life forever. "She died unexpectedly in her sleep." That night flashed in his mind. Frank Turner's voice loud and angry rising behind the closed door after mother had retired for the night. He could still hear her sobbing into her pillow once Frank had finally let her be. Oliver shut his eyes again, wishing he could go back in time and be stronger for her. Open the door. Protect her from his father as she'd done for him all his life.

"The doctor said it was most likely due to a condition of the heart, and I don't doubt it. My father was hateful and aggressive and...dark. I'm convinced his hate killed her and that she died of a broken heart."

Oliver looked from where Elizabeth's hand was covering his to her eyes. They were sparkling with unshed tears. She blinked and one fell down her cheek. Oliver raised his hand and used his thumb to wipe it away. She shut her eyes and leaned ever so slightly into his touch. How was it that she wasn't saying anything, but he had never felt more comforted?

"You're like her, you know?" she said softly, and his whole body

stilled. Her eyes opened and fixed on him. "Your eyes crinkle when you smile and your laugh has always pushed away my shadows."

He couldn't say anything. He was frozen, soaking up this moment and her words—silently begging them to be true.

"And, you love cucumbers," she said.

He smiled, his hand falling away from her face as he looked down to his sandwich. "But you do not."

There was a small thoughtful pause.

"No," she said simply. "But as long as we are friends, I'll always make sure you have them."

Chapter Twenty-One

Enough was enough. He had tried to be patient. He had tried to give Elizabeth her space that morning. But it was torture watching her bat her lashes at Hastings and lavish him with flattery. Not because he was jealous—although he most definitely was —but because she was terrible at it. This version of Elizabeth was painful to watch. She was rigid and uncomfortable and very clearly enjoying her new change about as much as he was.

He was confused. Why would Elizabeth be throwing herself away on that buffoon? No, buffoons were at least interesting. Hastings was a statue. He wished for Elizabeth to marry an upstanding gentleman who could take care of her in a way that Oliver feared he couldn't—but that did not mean that he wished for her to marry someone who would do nothing but make her yawn for the rest of her life.

Oliver continued hugging the wall and peeking through the crack of the door to the little closet in which he was standing. It was a little desperate to be waiting inside a closet for Elizabeth to walk by, but what could he say? He *was* desperate. He needed to get her alone for just one minute. He needed to talk to her. To understand why she was acting the way she was, and why the devil she was pretending to love cucumbers.

The sound of footsteps approaching drew his eyes to the left outside the closet. Elizabeth and Lord Hastings were walking behind Lord and Lady Stanton, with the obnoxious Miss Barley on the other side of Lord Hastings. The two youngest ladies of the bunch had opted to remain outdoors and forgo the house tour. Rose and Kensworth were nowhere to be found. They were the very worst of chaperones.

But at this moment, Oliver was thankful for it.

He waited until the couples had passed by the closet and then licked his lips and quietly whistled a quick loopy sound that he hadn't whistled in years. Would she remember their call? It was the secret signal he and Elizabeth had used when they had played hide-and-seek in the woods many years ago. Elizabeth—being much younger than he and her siblings—had a difficult time finding anyone when it was her turn to be the seeker. It always hurt Oliver to see her little face so sad when she would search and search to no avail. So he had concocted a secret whistle to help Elizabeth cheat and find him. Carver and Mary never caught on. Unfortunately, he had to be seeker more than he liked, but it was worth it to see her smile.

He wanted to see her smile again.

After his whistle faded into the air, soft and almost undetectable, he peeked through the crack. No one seemed to hear the sound, but Elizabeth's body stiffened. She looked toward the ground, angling her ear back toward him. He smiled and waited.

She turned her head forward again and he felt his heart sink. Was she not going to acknowledge it? But then he heard her say, "Will you all excuse me? I…need to…slip away for a moment."

"Shall I escort you?" said Lord Hastings. The blasted weasel. Oliver knew Hastings would like nothing more than to walk alone with Elizabeth.

"No," she said firmly. But then he saw her shoulders relax. "I… need to seek out the water closet." He didn't need to look at Elizabeth to know her face was likely flaming. He grinned to himself. "You all go on ahead and I will rejoin you shortly."

Lord Hastings looked just as uncomfortable receiving that bit of news as Elizabeth had giving it. He nodded and continued on with the rest of the group down the hall. Elizabeth turned toward the direction of the closet where Oliver was hiding. She glanced around hesitantly, taking a few steps until she was just outside of the closet and whispered, "Oliver? Was…was that you?"

He quickly thrust open the door, grabbed her hand, and pulled her into the closet before pulling the door cracked again. He would have shut it completely but he wanted to be able to see her face.

"Oliver! What the devil are you doing?" She pressed her hand to her chest, breathing as if she had just outrun a lion.

"I need to speak with you," he said.

"So you thought jumping out of a closet and giving me the fright of my life was the best way to go about it?"

He smirked. "Retaliation for all of the years you've jumped out at me."

Her gorgeous light blue eyes looked fully into his and she smiled. Suddenly, he was aware of how small the closet was. She was standing close enough that he could easily lean down and kiss her without ever having to take a step.

No. I can't do that.

But could he?

No.

He swallowed. "You remembered our secret call."

Her lips pursed together and she took a deep breath. "Of course I did." Her eyes held his for a moment and he debated brushing his fingers against hers. What would she think of a gesture like that? He was beginning to fear that if his heart raced any faster he was going to drop dead in that closet. She smelled like oranges and her skin looked soft.

Her expression, however, was cold as ice. When had this happened? Why was she so prickly toward him lately? Hatley's words came to mind again.

Elizabeth is in love with you.

That made no sense. If Elizabeth were in love with him, wouldn't her actions be the opposite of a mistreated porcupine ready to draw blood?

"What are we doing in here, Oliver?" asked Elizabeth, breaking eye contact to fidget with one of her gloves.

"I need to speak with you. And every time I try, Lord Hastings or Miss Barley gets in the way." He peeked through the crack, a little fearful Miss Barley might have sniffed out his location. He considered taking her in lieu of a hound on a fox hunt. Her tracking abilities were unparalleled. "The woman won't leave me alone."

He looked back at Elizabeth and her blonde brows were pulled tightly together. "Getting in the way? What an interesting way to talk about a woman whom you are clearly mad for," she said in an angry whisper.

He gaped at her. "Mad? For Miss Barley? Now, that's madness."

She narrowed those bright blue eyes at him, finally shedding some of the obnoxious proper lady facade she'd been wearing all day. "Admit it, Oliver," she shoved her finger into his chest, "you're in love with her and her beautiful eyelashes."

He let out a short, disbelieving laugh. "Beautiful! Good gracious, that can't be what you believe?" Well, he supposed he could see how she might get the impression, since he had in fact been trying to avoid the painful sight of Elizabeth and Hastings by pouring his attention onto Miss Barley. That, however, had backfired terribly. Now, the woman seemed permanently stuck to him. He half expected to look over his shoulder and find her clinging to the back of his jacket. It seemed he would be giving her the "friend speech" in the near future.

"You told me yourself you thought they were *fantastic*." She changed her voice on that last word and blinked her eyes as if he always spoke in a nasally, obnoxious voice when he discussed other women.

"I meant it in a frightening way. As in—they are so fantastic they haunt my dreams. I fear for my life when she blinks at me. How in the world could you ever believe I would be in love with that woman?"

She looked down and shuffled her feet, lightly kicking his boot in the process. "Oh, I don't know. Perhaps because you have flirted with her constantly."

"You're one to talk," he mumbled.

"What?"

"Nothing." He smiled down at her, resisting the urge to tip her chin back up to him. "Were you perhaps…a little jealous when you thought I loved Miss Barley?"

Elizabeth's eyes snapped to him. "Absolutely not. That's ridiculous. I was only confused by all of the attention you give her and wanted to know for sure."

"Mhmm." She was jealous.

"Wipe that stupid grin off your face!" said Elizabeth. Her heated cheeks and obstinate refusal were having the same effect on him as the champagne had on her. He was drunk off of hope and the inebriation was numbing his better judgment.

"You were jealous."

"I want to slap you. Or step on your toes. Or both."

He leaned down a little closer to her, narrowing an eye and whispering as if it were a great secret. "Exactly which part made you the most jealous?"

"This is absurd. I'm leaving." She turned toward the door but he caught her arm before she could take another step.

"I'm only teasing, Lizzie." He had yet to let go of her arm. He should. But his hand wouldn't move.

He followed her gaze down to his hand resting on the side of her arm—chill bumps running like a wave over her skin—before she looked back up at him. "You've broken two of our rules now," she said quietly, a slight tremble to her voice.

He wanted to break a few more. What had gotten into him? This wasn't good. He could feel his resolve wavering and he needed to let Elizabeth go. But the sight of her and Lord Hastings was tearing him up inside.

"What are rules if not made to be broken?"

She didn't smile. Her gaze challenged him. "Why are we in here, Oliver?"

"Because…" his hand trailed down her arm until his hand clasped hers, lacing their fingers together in a way that was intimate and daring and honest. "You ate cucumbers."

He didn't realize she had been holding her breath until it all released in a puff of disappointment. She yanked her hand from his and crossed her arms in front of her. She was back to prickly Elizabeth. "I knew you would not let that go. It was only a few cucumbers, Oliver. Hardly a reason to get your petticoats in a tangle."

"There was more than just cucumbers and we both know it."

Her eyes narrowed. "I'm not sure to what you are referring."

"Ah—we are going to play the ignorant game, are we? Then allow me to enlighten you." He gestured toward her outfit. "For starters, I know that you cannot enjoy wearing that color."

She raised her chin defiantly. "There is nothing wrong with this color."

"No, there's not. And you look stunning in it, might I add. But I happen to know that bright colors make you feel ostentatious in the worst sort of way. Am I wrong?"

She looked at him as if she wanted nothing more than to argue, or strangle him, or kiss him but couldn't. He wouldn't mind one of those things.

"I thought so," he continued. "And earlier today when Hastings stated that taking a carriage would have been much more enjoyable, you agreed as if your life depended on it, when I know that you would have hated taking a carriage above all things. Not only does your stomach feel weak in closed carriages, but you despise being deprived of the sun and wind in your hair."

She pursed her lips together and looked down to her folded arms, her dark lashes fanning against her cheeks. Oliver lowered his voice and inched even closer. He was taking liberties but he couldn't bring himself to care just then.

Taking her chin gently in his hand, he tilted it up to look her full in the eyes. "What I want to know, Lizzie, is why you have not been honest with Lord Hastings today?"

She dropped her gaze to his chest. Eyes locked on the fabric of his waistcoat. "Because I couldn't."

"Why? You've always been honest with me."

"That's different," she said, a subtle tremble touching her voice.

"How?" Why was he pushing this? What would be the end result?

Her eyes raised and her stare fixed with his—poignant and accusatory. "Because you are not my suitor." Those words strangled him. "I have nothing to prove to you, Oliver. No need to impress you." Her voice sounded desperate and almost aching. It matched the way he felt. What was happening between them? "I'll tell Lord Hastings the truth eventually, but for now…I simply need to have at least a few common interests with him."

"But they are not common interests. You are sacrificing your likes and dislikes to fade in the presence of that boring imbecile."

She pulled her chin from his hand and edged away from him. "Oh, stop, Oliver. That's unfair. You have no right to speak to me like this. You have no claim on me."

No right? No claim? Oliver had to ball his fists at his sides to keep the words from coming out. He had more claim on Elizabeth than anyone. Oliver knew and understood her better than anyone else in the world. He could grab her around the waist and pull her to him, kissing the breath out of her lungs right then and there if he wished, because he knew Elizabeth, and he knew she would want it too.

That thought stopped him and his hands relaxed.

Hatley was right. Elizabeth loved him. It was clear and shining in the challenge of her eyes. They seemed to be pleading with him to see —to see her heart and want her. How long had she felt this way? How had he never recognized it so plainly before? Or, perhaps he had never seen it because he didn't wish to.

But if she loved him, why hadn't she simply told him? Perhaps she knew deep down, just as much as he did, that he was not good enough for her.

"You're right. I'm sorry." He took a small step back. As much as the closet would allow. The space between them felt vast and cold. Elizabeth must have felt it, too. She rubbed her arms and was quiet for a moment before she turned, preparing to leave by putting her hand on the closet knob. But she paused and he heard her take in a deep breath.

She turned around sharply. "Do you know, Oliver, I find it rather hypocritical of you to lecture me on sacrificing my wants and desires for another." He stood perfectly still. What could she possibly mean by that? "You asked me earlier if I was jealous of Miss Barley, and the answer is no. I was annoyed."

His head kicked back at the sharpness in her tone, and the way she was stepping closer to him, closing their distance and leaving him trapped between her and the closet wall behind him. "Oh?" Had he stopped breathing? "What have I done to annoy you, Lizzie?"

"You've been flirting with the woman endlessly. No wonder she will not leave you alone. Not to mention becoming her personal manservant. You were quick to comply with every ridiculous request the woman made, from retrieving the nonexistent leaf from your hair, to swapping places with Lady Olivia at the picnic so you could protect her from the bees—which were also imaginary. You've been giving her every indication that you find her desirable. In fact, you give every woman in London that same indication." Somehow she managed to step even closer to him. "That is not who you are, Oliver Turner. You're better than that." Was he though? "And as you are certainly not a manservant, you must stop acting as one."

"Elizabeth, you don't understand. I'm only providing the ladies of Society a service. It is not that they wish to spend their lives with me. They simply use my attentions to attract those more eligible. Men more like Lord Hastings."

"You truly believe that?"

"Yes."

Her brows pulled together. "Then you are a fool, Oliver. A fool who cannot see the beauty in yourself."

"You think I'm beautiful?" he asked with a smirk.

"Do not try to tease your way out of this. I won't let you this time." She always had a way of cutting right to the heart of things with him. How did she manage to do that? It would be useless to try to side step the conversation with her.

"Very well, Lizzie." He swallowed. "What shall I do then?"

"Drop your act. Be yourself from now on, and for goodness' sake, stop doing every lady's bidding in all of London."

He pursed his lips together and thought on it a moment. Unfortunately, her words rang true. He was exhausted from acting the part of Bond Street Beau. All he wanted was a quiet, happy life with Elizabeth. But if he couldn't have that, he was going to ensure that she had it with someone. "All right, I will do as you say. But only on the condition that you do the same." He only wanted Hastings to marry Elizabeth if the man could properly adore the woman for who she was. Elizabeth should never have to hide her adventurous spirit.

They stood there for a long silent moment, staring at each other—daring one another to admit their hearts. If only he could. If only he could trust himself to love her well and protect her. But his father's words rang too loudly in his ears.

Finally, she broke the quiet and something in her smile grew mischievous, changing the air and making his stomach flip. "Agreed. Shall we have a practice?" Oliver knew that look too well. She was up to something but he wasn't sure what yet.

"A practice could be good. What do you have in mind?"

"I'm going to teach you something." Was her tone seductive or was he simply imagining that?

"Oh?" Suddenly he couldn't breathe. He swallowed, trying to also drag some air into his lungs. "And what's that?"

Her eyes sparkled and a smile bloomed on her mouth. "The word...*no*."

He frowned. To say he was let down by the turn in the conversation would be an understatement. "You're going to help me say the word *no*?"

"Yes. It's time you stopped doing everything for every woman in the world. Stand up for yourself. Claim some happiness of your own instead of always seeking it for everyone else." She squared her shoulders and looked up at him. "Here. Let's practice. Oliver, I need for you to ride all the way back to London to retrieve my blue shawl and then bring it back here for me."

He laughed. "That's a ridiculous request."

"Yes, well, we must start with the easy ones since you seem to be inept at using the word." She shifted on her feet and looked fully in his eyes. "Now, come on, take it seriously."

He couldn't help but smile at her determination. And he would spend all day learning this word if it meant he got to stay in that closet with the real Elizabeth, smelling her sweet orange scent and staring at those blue eyes. It was selfish, and he needed to let her get back to her courtship with Hastings. But for a moment, he wanted to be selfish. Completely and utterly selfish. "Very well. No, Elizabeth. I'll not go to London for your shawl."

She nodded. "Good. Now, Oliver, will you be a dear and go ask the kitchen staff to whip me up a fairy cake before we leave?"

He chuckled. "No."

"Wash my horse."

"Not a chance."

"Give me a thousand pounds."

"No."

"Kiss me." Her eyes locked with his and his heart stopped.

It was a game; he knew that, but his mind couldn't help but hear the request as genuine. But...ah—it was genuine. She was holding very still but her eyes betrayed her. They always did. Her look was shifting the air. Shifting the rules. Daring him to kiss her. Inching toward the imaginary line and drawing him closer with her.

He couldn't. Blast he wanted to—but he couldn't. This whole closet conversation had gotten away from him.

Oliver wouldn't let himself look down at her lips. He tightened his fists at his sides and tried to convince himself that he was making the right decision.

"No, Elizabeth. I won't kiss you."

She blinked rapidly and looked away, the spell and the moment broken. She looked around the little closet and then back up at him with the fakest of smiles. "Perfect. I think you've gotten the hang of it. I'd better go find the others." Elizabeth slipped out of the closet and he let her go.

He wasn't entirely certain what had just happened or how he felt about it. Elizabeth looked...disappointed. Hurt even. But what about Hastings? Hadn't she been encouraging his suit?

Oliver rubbed his hands over his face and groaned. Everything was too confusing—too out of reach. The obstacles in his mind felt insurmountable. And the chasm between him and Lizzie—growing. His place in everyone's life had changed. Kensworth didn't need him anymore. Elizabeth was replacing him. His father was dying. Memories of his mother, fading. And his reasons to visit Dalton Park were dwindling.

Who was he without these people who had given him purpose and identity?

What did he want in life?

Elizabeth.

But he wouldn't let himself have her.

Chapter Twenty-Two

Elizabeth wasn't entirely sure what she was doing, walking as she was toward Mary's house. They didn't live far, but Rose had insisted she take a maid with her. Not because Rose gave a dash about propriety, but because she was afraid if Mary found out Rose had let Elizabeth walk by herself, she would be on the receiving end of quite the dressing down. She was possibly the only person Rose feared in this world. Elizabeth understood the sentiment.

If she was being perfectly honest, Elizabeth didn't care to see her sister. She still felt angry at her. Pushed aside. Overlooked. If her sister didn't wish to include her in her life, well, then fine, Elizabeth didn't want Mary to be a part of her life, either.

Only one, tiny problem…she did wish for Mary to be in her life. And as much as she wanted to make her own decisions and be treated as a grown woman, she also had an invitation in her hand and no idea how to respond to it. Elizabeth was going to put all of her feelings aside and ask Mary to make the choice for her.

Elizabeth had entered the breakfast room that morning to a frowning Rose holding the invitation from the Dowager Lady Hastings in her hand. The dowager had put together a little house party—which, thankfully, Elizabeth had already been prepared to learn about from

Lord Hastings—and requested their presence. Rose didn't seem to like the idea too much but refused to make a comment, saying Elizabeth needed to make this choice for herself. Rose seemed to understand the implications of their family being invited to a private house party at the Hastings's estate in the middle of the Season.

And yet another problem; Oliver had left Elizabeth feelings too mixed up to make the choice for herself. It was either accept the invitation, therefore encouraging Lord Hastings and his suit, or come to terms with the fact that she would never love him the way she loved Oliver and decline the invitation, sending him a clear message that their courtship was over.

Mary was overbearing at times, but she was good at making life decisions. She'd tell Mary the facts—leaving out her unrequited love for Oliver, of course—receive her answer, and then go right back to feeling angry at her sister.

Elizabeth sensed an eerie feeling as she stepped inside the house. The butler's face looked pinched. The house was quiet and dark—but that was probably due to the fact that the day was rather gray outside.

A maid hovered in a corner, her back toward Elizabeth, slowly dusting a picture frame. The butler followed Elizabeth's gaze and the maid must have sensed it. She flashed nervous eyes over her shoulder to him, and he snapped his head back to Elizabeth. "Should my lady need anything, please do not hesitate to ring the bell."

"Thank you."

Something was odd. The staff looked as if they were standing on needles. Or holding their breath.

Possibly because she was stalling, Elizabeth peeked into the nursery to spend a few minutes with her niece. But the governess must have taken Jane on a walk because she was not inside. There was nothing left for Elizabeth to do but inch her way to Mary's room. With every step, some strange awareness prickled at her. Something was definitely wrong. She couldn't explain it. But those feeling were beginning to override her sisterly anger and pulling her down the hallway faster.

When she knocked and opened Mary's door she found her sister lying on the bed, curled up on her side, her face in a pained expression.

Elizabeth rushed in and knelt down beside the bed. "Mary, is everything all right?"

Mary opened her eyes quickly, startled to suddenly find Elizabeth at her side. Her wincing expression fled and she gave a tiny smile. "I'm perfectly fine. What are you doing here?" Apparently Elizabeth and Mary held different definitions of *perfectly fine*.

"Do I really need an excuse to visit my favorite sister?"

Mary gave a ghost of a chuckle and spoke quietly. "Shall I tell Kate you said that?" Her breathing was labored.

"If you'd like. But she will simply tell you that I've said the same to her."

"And Rose as well?"

"Of course."

Mary smiled and it was plain to Elizabeth that her sister was trying to hide something. Mary was putting on her mother hen face. A tiny bit of Elizabeth's anger poked its head up once again.

"What's in your hand?" Mary asked, this time sounding pained.

"Oh. Actually, I have come with a bit of news and…for advice." Elizabeth took in a deep breath, trying to gather her courage and swallow her pride. She stopped short when Mary shut her eyes tight and let out a muffled moan. Elizabeth gripped Mary's arm. "What is it?"

Her sister shook her head, dark brown locks of hair shaking with the force of her movement. "Nothing. Everything is fine. Continue with what you were saying."

"Why won't you tell me what's going on?"

Mary snapped her face to Elizabeth and her eyes were blazing. "Because it doesn't concern you. I can take care of myself." Of course. Typical Mary.

Sting and anger and humiliation snatched at Elizabeth. She stood up and forcefully wiped the wrinkles from her skirts. "Yes, you've made that perfectly clear over the years, Mary." She walked to the door ready to bolt from the room and not look back. Mary could handle herself. Elizabeth turned back, her hand on the knob of the door. "Never you mind. I will stop trying to interfere in your life. I understand our roles perfectly now and if you don't see me as a friend or confidant, I will stop trying to—"

Mary's face contorted. Her body pulled up in a tight painful ball. Her hands gripped the coverlet with such force that Elizabeth wondered if her fingers would make holes.

And then suddenly, she realized.

Elizabeth's hand fell away from the door and she rushed back to the side of the bed. "Mary," Elizabeth took her sister's hand and squeezed it. "It's the baby, isn't it? It's time." This must be why the maid had seemed so unnerved. She, too, knew it was time.

Mary shook her head fervently, not opening her eyes. Beads of sweat were beginning to form on her head. "No. It's not. I'm simply not feeling well, is all." Not feeling well? This was more than not feeling well. Elizabeth stood up.

"Where are you going?" asked Mary in a frantic tone.

"To fetch Robert. He needs to know that things are starting."

"No! Things are not starting," said Mary, sitting up slightly onto her elbows and piercing Elizabeth with her grey eyes. They looked feral. "Besides, he's in parliament right now. I'm just uncomfortable, but it will pass. It's not time yet. It's too early." It was early. Elizabeth knew that. But she'd also heard of women delivering children quite early before. Although the hard truth was most of those babies did not make it through delivery. Sometimes the mothers did not make it through delivery, either.

She needed to call for the doctor.

"Mary, please. I really think—"

"No, Elizabeth." Mary's voice was hard and unwavering. "I said it's not my time and it's not. Sit down." Her voice was somehow both commanding and fragile at the same time. Out of habit, Elizabeth obeyed and sat down in a chair beside Mary's bed. She shut her mouth just like she always had when one of her older siblings overruled her. She eyed her sister as Mary lowered herself from her elbows back down onto her back. Elizabeth heard her push out a shaky breath.

She'd never seen her sister like this before—so clearly frightened but unwilling to admit it. "What advice did you need?" asked Mary.

"Oh." Elizabeth looked down to the invitation she was still clutching. It was bending from the pressure of her grip. It felt so wrong to bring it up now. But what else was she going to do? She couldn't very well just sit there and stare at her sister writhing in pain. "Well, things have been progressing with Lord Hastings and his—" Elizabeth broke off when she saw her sister's whole body clench up in pain again. Mary reached out and gripped Elizabeth's hand with the strength of Goliath. This time, a shriek escaped Mary's mouth.

Elizabeth shot to her feet, her eyes roaming over Mary's clenched body. "This is absurd, Mary! You must let me call the doctor."

"No!" Mary called out through her pain. "No! It's not time yet," she said in a sob this time, still gripping the covers.

Elizabeth's shoulders sunk and everything in her felt helpless. Robert needed to be notified. The doctor needed to be called. The bed linens needed to be prepared. Like it or not, this child was coming.

Elizabeth pressed her lips together as her own agony welled up inside her. After a time, Mary's body relaxed and she looked exhausted. Elizabeth shifted on her feet. "At least allow me to fetch you some tea. Perhaps some chamomile will soothe you."

"Do you promise me you will not call the doctor or Robert?" Blast. How did she know?

Elizabeth let out a tense breath, not sure what else to do. "I promise."

Mary nodded her consent and Elizabeth flew out of her room and down the stairs. She was moving as fast as her feet would allow, but to what purpose? She felt helpless. Scared. What if something happened to Mary or the baby? What if the cost of Mary's poor judgment was her life?

At the bottom of the stairs, Elizabeth sat down and put her face in her hands. Tears of frustration and uncertainty dropped down her cheeks.

It was in that moment that black boots entered her vision. "Elizabeth?"

She looked up and met Oliver's eyes. She blinked a moment wondering if she was imagining what she hoped to see. "Oliver? What are you doing here?"

She stood up and his eyes roamed over her face. He stepped forward and put his hands firmly on her shoulders, as if to protect her. "What's happened?"

"It's Mary," she said, and then quickly recounted everything that had just happened.

Oliver paced a step away and ran his hand through his hair. "Blast. And Robert isn't here. I was told I could wait in his office until he returned, but there's no telling when that will be." He stopped and looked at Elizabeth. "You must call for the doctor."

"I know!" Elizabeth said in a pleading tone, tears welling in her eyes again against her will. "But Mary has forbidden me to. She refuses to see reason. She's denying that the child is coming."

Oliver came to her again, taking her hands in his. The warmth of his skin wrapped around hers and she felt a calm rush over her. How did he always have this effect on her? How did he have such a way of suddenly making everything seem right and whole? "Elizabeth," his voice spoke to her heart. "Your sister needs you to be courageous for her right now. She's not well, and if you do not act on her behalf, you could lose her or the child—or both."

Oliver was right. Mary needed her.

Elizabeth looked toward the top of the stairs and then back to Oliver. She held a little tighter to Oliver's hands, afraid that if she let go, he would take all of the calm and strength she was feeling with him. "I'll ring for the doctor. Will you fetch Robert from parliament?"

"Of course I will." Now was when she should let go. But her fingers would not budge. Instead, she looked down and ran her thumb along the back of his large knuckles. Oliver squeezed her hand. "Everything is going to be all right."

"Will it?"

He shifted on his feet and leaned forward, hesitation and determination both marking his brow. And then he softly kissed her forehead, his lips lingering against her skin for the span of one full breath. "I hope so." He turned around and walked out the door.

"You what?" asked Mary, sounding as angry as a hornet.

"I rang for the doctor." Elizabeth rolled up her sleeves, ignored the fuming look Mary was giving her, and instructed one of the many bustling maids in the room to set the basin of water beside Mary's bed. They all looked eager to finally be of service to Mary.

"You promised you wouldn't!" Mary sounded panicked and near tears. "You promised, Elizabeth. I'm telling you, it's not my time yet. The baby is not coming. It's only...it's only..." Tears were beginning to pour down Mary's cheeks.

Elizabeth sat down on Mary's bed and took both of her sister's hands in her own. She looked into Mary's eyes and, for possibly the first time in her whole life, Elizabeth realized that Mary was frightened. "Listen to me," she said, trying to keep her own tears from falling. "I know you're scared. I know that you've still been hurting over the loss of your last child, and you feel like you can't bear to lose another." Mary shut her eyes, beginning to shake with a sob. "I cannot promise you that everything is going to be all right. But I can promise you that whatever happens, you will not bear it alone. You have me and Robert and our entire family that loves you and wants to help take care of you, Mary. You don't have to hide your fear from us. Let us help." She reached up and pushed Mary's sweat- and tear-drenched hair from her face. "Let me help you."

Mary sucked in a breath between her sobs and nodded. "I'm so scared, Elizabeth. And I don't know what to do with these feelings."

"I know. I'm scared, too. But you're strong, Mary."

Mary's eyes searched hers. "What if I'm not strong enough?" She didn't know whether Mary was referring to her physical strength or emotional strength. But either way, Elizabeth's answer was the same.

"You are. And I'll be here with you the entire time to remind you."

Mary's lips pressed together as a fountain of tears continued to stream down her cheeks. Vulnerability felt tangible. "Thank you, Elizabeth. I shouldn't have—"

Elizabeth stopped her with a shake of her head. "Never mind all that." She didn't need for Mary to say the words she could see written in her eyes. "Just focus on breathing." No sooner did those words fall out than Mary began to grit her teeth with another contraction. Elizabeth drenched a rag in the lavender water from the basin and began to dab Mary's forehead.

She heard a loud door slam downstairs and, with a flood of relief, knew that it would be either Robert or the doctor. She stood to go see which it was when Mary reached out and firmly grabbed Elizabeth's hand. "Don't go anywhere, Elizabeth," said Mary. "I need you."

Chapter Twenty-Three

Oliver stopped on the threshold of the nursery and watched Elizabeth sway her new nephew, Matthew Robert Cunningham, back and forth. Seeing her there—holding that child —grabbed him. He could feel his pulse in his neck and the desire he had suppressed for so long demanding his attention, demanding acknowledgment.

He had never wanted to be a father—or a husband, since the two went hand in hand. But there was Elizabeth, bathed in the pink setting sun shining through the window, filling his senses with a new realization that he wanted a family more than anything in the world. He wanted her and her children. He wanted to love her well. He wanted to deserve her. However, fear was a vise that had crippled him for so long. It was unshakable. It was his friend. It whispered that it would keep him safe from himself.

"How does it feel holding a child you delivered?" Oliver asked keeping his voice lowered to match the quiet room.

Elizabeth's tired eyes raised to him. For a moment she paused her swaying and a smile that sent a tingle down his spine bloomed over her face. Maybe it was the sun setting in the window behind her, maybe it was that he had kissed her forehead earlier and just that small touch had confirmed something for him. Or maybe it was that she was looking at him like she truly wanted him there. But whatever the reason, it had him moving across the room to stand as close to Elizabeth as propriety allowed.

All right—propriety wouldn't allow this. But he stood there all the same.

Elizabeth shook her head, smiling down at the bundle in her arms. "It was all such a whirlwind, Oliver. I was so frightened when we realized the doctor was not going to make it in time." Even Hatley had nearly missed the birth. Oliver had retrieved the earl from the House of Lords and Hatley had only disappeared up the stairs for a quarter hour before he had come down again with glistening eyes and a smile of triumph. All of the weight he had been carrying for months was gone. His child was in the world and his wife was well. Elizabeth had delivered the child and tended to Mary until the doctor had arrived. Every bit of the day was a miracle. The child was early—to an extent that most babies did not survive—but the doctor was pleased with his health and he was hopeful that with proper feedings, the newest Cunningham would survive. Thrive, even.

"I cannot believe I delivered him on my own," said Elizabeth.

"I can."

He was looking down at the new little Lord Cunningham, but he could feel Elizabeth's eyes on his face. He could always feel when she was looking at him. "Why do you always say things like that?" she asked quietly.

"Like what?"

"As if you never doubt my courage or strength."

He met her eyes. "Because I don't."

Her brows were pinched together, studying him, looking for the secret he kept locked away. A few more moments with that look and she would unlock it. "Sometimes, I think you're the only person who feels that way about me. Or…sees me that way."

"Lizzie, I've seen you climb out of enough windows to know that you are full of both courage and strength."

"As I've reminded you repeatedly, it was *one* window. And that's different. Others see my actions as reckless. You've never seen me that way."

"I think the real problem is that *you* see yourself that way." He held her gaze, until he couldn't anymore. He looked down to the baby and nodded. "And just look. This is all the proof you need that you are full of courage and strength. You stepped in when Mary needed you and delivered her child."

She smiled and adjusted the blanket away from the tiny baby's cheeks. "It was quite wonderful." She looked back up at Oliver with a playful look in her eyes. "You know, I was only keeping him for an hour so Mary and Robert could get some rest, but perhaps I will steal him away in the night and keep him as a constant reminder of my courage."

Oliver smiled. "A wonderful idea. I doubt your sister and brother-in-law would object in the least."

"Really, I'd be doing them a favor. Imagine all the sleep they will not lose if I steal him."

They both chuckled. "No need to justify your actions to me, Lizzie. I can't imagine why anyone would wish for the responsibility of a child anyway. You would just be relieving them of a burden." It was meant as a jest, but after the words came out, it didn't feel or sound much like one.

Apparently Elizabeth didn't think so either.

She blinked. "You don't wish for children of your own?" Had he never told her that before? No. He'd studiously avoided any such conversations with her about marriage or children. No one knew that he never intended to marry.

"It was only a jest," he said with a wavering smile.

"No, it wasn't. Do not attempt to lie to me, Oliver. I know you too well." She did know him too well. Which was a little frightening at the moment when he felt as if he had so many secrets pinned up inside him. "Why do you not wish to have a family?"

Oliver shrugged, feeling uncomfortable with the conversation. It was too closely related to his other secrets. "I simply do not." He looked toward the door. "I should be going. It's getting late." He bowed and then moved to take his leave, but Elizabeth hurried past him, and blocked his exit. She gave him a challenging look when he stopped in front of her.

"I don't think Mary would appreciate you using her newborn child as a blockade," said Oliver.

Her eyes were on him again. "It's only me, Oliver. Surely you can tell me why? We tell each other everything."

He stared in her eyes. "Do we?" Thoughts of Hatley proclaiming that Elizabeth loved Oliver flashed through his mind. If she loved him, why had she never told him?

She frowned. "What do you mean?"

"Nevermind." He shouldn't have even begun that topic.

She took a step toward him. "No, what did you mean by that?"

Blast. He had gotten himself stuck in a conversation that couldn't happen. As unwanted as the first topic of children was, moving back to it was his only option to keep him from admitting to Elizabeth that he indeed had one large secret he was keeping from her.

"Fine. I don't wish for children because…I don't trust myself with them." Just like he didn't trust himself to love Elizabeth as she deserved. "You know the model I had for a father. If there is any chance I could ever end up becoming the same sort of man he was, I won't take it."

Her face softened. "You are not your father, Oliver." She shifted the baby in her arms and reached out to lay a hand on his forearm. Normally her touch would be a comfort. Normally he would sink into the pressure of her hand against him and soak in her attention.

But right then he felt restless, vulnerable, *scared*.

He wanted to run away but her hand was holding him still, forcing him to hear her. "You are loving and trustworthy. Gentle and loyal. There is not one sliver of anger or violence in you. I have no doubt that —" her words became thick, "—whoever you choose to love in life will be the luckiest of recipients."

He watched her blink back a few tears.

She loves you.

He was helpless to her words. Numb. The protective voice whispered again that they were just empty words. She didn't know the future. He remembered his mother telling him of a time when Frank Turner had not been so angry. Of a time when he would not wake in the morning and immediately reach for the closest bottle of brandy he could find. Oliver's future felt too much out of his control. All he could do was stare at Elizabeth, speechless.

Finally, she pulled her hand away and looked up at him with the smile she always gave him when she was pretending to be happy with something. "Have you ever held a baby?"

Instantly he took a step away. "No. Nor do I wish to today."

She chuckled a disbelieving laugh. "Oh, come on, Oliver. Surely if I can deliver a child you can be brave enough to hold a sleeping one, for a moment?"

He swallowed the lump in his throat and eyed the bundle in her arms. "But he's so small and fragile."

"Making him all the easier to hold. Now, come here and quit being so cowardly." He did not want to hold that baby. But the teasing grin on her lips was drawing him to her again.

"What do I do with my arms?" he asked, feeling stupid and awkward as he attempted to take the child from her.

She repositioned the baby out of the crook of her arm and into her hands, stepping completely into Oliver's space so that her hair was just under his nose. "His head goes in the crook of your arm, like so." She was putting the baby in his arms, her arm brushing against his chest as she securely settled the baby in. "There. And put your hand under him like this to make sure you don't drop him." Her hand was so soft as it brushed over his and repositioned it.

He should probably be focusing on the baby and making sure he didn't drop him, but he couldn't take his eyes off of Elizabeth. She was beautiful with her hair falling out of her knot and her smile soft with the setting sun. Realization of just how deeply he loved her was settling like stones in his chest.

She didn't move away once the child was settled in his arms.

Oliver couldn't help himself. He reached up and brushed the curls from her face to behind her ear, letting his knuckles graze the soft skin of her cheek. Her eyes raised slowly to his. Something in her expression looked nervous. Or hopeful. Or longing.

"See"—her voice was a breathy whisper—"that wasn't so difficult, was it?" Holding the child? Or…touching her?

"No. It wasn't."

The silence between them was heavy, and the air was sparking with questions and unspoken words. His heart was beating loud and strong, begging him to open his mouth and tell her. Tell her he loved her. Take a chance. Tell her he was scared. Tell her that he'd loved her for a long time but was too afraid of hurting her to act on his feelings. He ached to resolve his worries with her.

The sound of boots approaching from the hallway made Elizabeth blink, breaking their trance, and she stepped back. A moment later, a servant walked through the open door and curtsied. "Forgive me for the intrusion, my lady, but Lady Hatley has requested that I take Lord Cunningham to her for his feeding."

"Yes, of course," said Elizabeth, sounding a little jumpy. Her eyes bounced from the maid to the baby and up to Oliver. "I'm afraid you will have to continue your practice another time, Oliver. Little Lord Cunningham cannot afford to miss a feeding."

She stepped quickly to him and retrieved the child from his arms, not lingering quite as long during the transaction this time. Elizabeth passed the baby to the maid, who turned to leave but then seemed to remember something else. "Oh, and Lord and Lady Kensworth are waiting for you in the foyer. They are ready to take their leave."

Elizabeth nodded, and the maid curtsied—which felt somehow more impressive and unnecessary with a child in her arms—and then she was gone, leaving Oliver and Elizabeth alone again.

Words. He needed to say something. Anything to draw out this moment and make his time with her last a little longer. "Is Kate recovered yet? Will the duke and duchess be able to come meet their new grandson?"

Her shoulders slumped. "No. Carver just received a letter this morning saying that Kate is recovered but Mama and Papa have now contracted the fever. They are both quite ill."

"Oh, that's too bad."

"Yes."

"I will remember them in my prayers."

She smiled. "Thank you."

Elizabeth seemed to be feeling the same need to draw out their time together as well. Her eyes looked as if they were physically searching for a topic of conversation. Finally, he and Elizabeth both started speaking at the same time, but her words caught his ear and made him stop talking first. "What was that?" he asked, both wanting and dreading her confirmation of what he thought he'd heard.

Her eyes darted to her skirts that she had begun fidgeting with the folds. "The Dowager Lady Hastings has invited me to come to attend her house party next week." His mind raced with the implication of that statement.

"Is…Lord Hastings going to be in attendance as well?"

Her eyes met his. "I don't believe I would have been invited if he was not expected to attend as well." His stomach twisted. Hastings's suit was more serious than he had realized.

"And…are you planning to accept the invitation?"

There was a pause before she blinked and clasped her hands in front of her. "Should I?" She was asking him to make this decision for her? Why? But somehow, he knew that answer.

She loves me.

It felt as if two different paths physically formed in front of him. His heart longed for her. His arms ached to pull her close to him and hold her. He could tell her not to go. He could tell her of his feelings and beg her to choose him.

Or…

He could make sure she was protected.

"You should go," he said, choosing to let Elizabeth have the life she deserved. A life with a man who would be constant for her, free of baggage and heartache. He would never trust himself with loving her. But Hastings would take care of her, boring though he may be.

Elizabeth nodded. "I will then." He saw her swallow before pasting that fake smile on her face. "I wasn't sure until now, but...you're right. I should go. And who knows"—a tremble ran through her voice— "maybe this will end up being the start to my forever with Lord Hastings."

He felt as if his heart had just been ripped from his chest.

Chapter Twenty-Four

Elizabeth kept her eyes fixed outside the window as the carriage rolled away from Hatley House. Never in her wildest dreams could she have imagined the sort of afternoon she had just had. Her mind bounced from remembering the agony of childbirth her sister had withstood, to her own bravery in delivering the child. She had finally found her voice with her sister. A few hours after her nephew was born, Elizabeth had curled up on the bed beside her sister and new favorite little gentleman, and bared her soul. She told Mary all that she had been feeling and how she desired to have a friendship with her. Mary cried, Elizabeth cried, and then little Matthew cried—but mostly from hunger. Everything was going to change between her and Mary in the most wonderful way. Perhaps Elizabeth would even consider getting to know Vienna Loxley better as well.

And then Elizabeth's mind turned to Oliver and she remembered the way his lips had felt on her forehead, the look in his eyes when he had admitted to not wanting a family, and then how dashing he had looked holding Matthew. She had refused to let herself cry just then. Everything in her had suddenly hurt. Oliver told her to go to the house party—and he knew what that meant for her. She had her final answer concerning Oliver's feelings for her. Again.

"I've decided to accept the dowager's invitation for the house party." Elizabeth couldn't bring herself to look at Rose or Carver. She was afraid that if her eyes met her sister-in-law's, she would no longer be able to keep her tears inside.

"What house party?" asked Carver.

Rose hadn't told him about it yet?

"Elizabeth…or rather, *we all,* have all been invited to Lord Hastings's country estate for a house party next week."

"Oh," said Carver, sounding slightly let down. Because he hated the idea of attending a house party? Or— "I see. And…does this mean what I think it means?"

Elizabeth had to look at him now. She tried to look as confident as possible. "I believe it does. Lord Hastings—Wesley"—she tried out his Christian name, which she had learned during their last walk in the park, but it just felt wrong on her tongue—"has hinted toward a possible proposal in the future. I believe he intends to finalize the engagement at Addington Hall. I wouldn't be surprised if he had already written to Papa to acquire permission." Until a few minutes ago when Oliver had told her to accept the invitation, she had intended to refuse his hand. Picturing forever with Lord Hastings had become too difficult. But now…

Now things were different. Oliver still did not love her, and it was more than time to move on with her life.

"Elizabeth," asked Carver with a furrowed brow. He looked briefly to Rose and then back to her. "Are you sure this is what you want? Lord Hastings…do you love him?"

She sighed. "Not everyone gets to be in love before they marry, like you and Rose."

"That's not what I asked," said Carver.

She looked in her brother's steely grey eyes. In the past, she would have lied. She would have said whatever she needed to so that he wouldn't challenge her decision or think she was weak. But somehow, that day had changed her. Her desire to prove herself had fallen away and all that was left was who she was and how she really felt.

"No. I don't love him. How could I when it's Oliver that I truly love? I always have and I'm afraid that I always will." Carver looked as if he were going to say something, but Elizabeth hurried on and cut him off. "But tonight he made it clear to me that he will never love me in return. So I will go to Addington Hall and if Lord Hastings proposes to me, I will accept, because I want to be with someone who desires me."

Carver had yet to blink. His brows were pulled deeply together. She was ready for him to disagree, to push her in a direction that he thought would be best for her. Possibly even demand that the carriage be turned around so he could storm into Hatley House and insist that Oliver marry Elizabeth. But he didn't. He sighed and nodded softly. "Very well. We will send our acceptance, then."

Elizabeth let out a relieved breath.

"And Elizabeth," continued Carver but in a different tone than she'd ever heard from him before. It was the same one he used when he spoke to Mary. "Thank you for all you did for our sister today. I hate to think what would have happened had you not been there to intervene. Had I been in your shoes, I don't know that I would have been strong enough to do all that you did today."

Elizabeth smiled, some of her pain melting away. He saw her. Her brother saw her. "I'm more than certain you would have handled it just fine."

Elizabeth and Carver smiled at each other for a moment, a new friendship blooming between them. And then Rose's voice cut through, irritated and clipped. "This is all well and good. But may I just express what I know everyone is thinking and admit that I hope Oliver trips and falls down the stairs?"

A laugh burst from both Elizabeth and Carver. "No!" Elizabeth said through a chuckle. "That is not what I was thinking. Nor will I ever wish for such a thing. I will always hope the best for Oliver."

"I don't know," said Carver. "He is my best friend, and I love him like a brother—but I wouldn't mind seeing him with a few bruises just now. I was really hoping you two would make a match of it."

"You were?" Elizabeth asked, remembering the reason he had given Rose for his hope a few weeks ago. "So that I always have someone to protect me?"

He chuckled. "You mustn't say it with such disdain. I am your older brother, Elizabeth. Like it or not, I shall always hope for someone trustworthy to protect you with all of his being. But that's not the only reason I have hoped for your match." He paused and a sad smile curved on the corner of his mouth. "You two seem made for each other."

Elizabeth felt very unwanted tears prickling her eyes again. "Apparently not." A tear dripped down her cheek and landed on her skirt. She ran a finger over the new dark spot on the navy fabric.

A handkerchief appeared in her lap with the very worst embroidered monogramming she'd ever seen. She smiled tentatively up to her sister-in-law as she wiped her tears. Carver reached across the carriage to squeeze her hand, his face growing serious in a way she couldn't trust as earnest. "Are you positive I cannot simply go beat Oliver to a pulp until he decides to marry you? Because I assure you, it can be accomplished."

"Nice try. You're not getting out of the house party, Carver," said Rose, leaning forward to enter the conversation he was pretending was private.

"Blast," he said, sitting back firmly against his seat. "No offense, Elizabeth, but I'd rather have a tooth extracted than spend the week with Hastings and his family." Well, that made two of them. That thought did not bode well for her future happiness.

Elizabeth watched as Rose scooted closer to Carver and wrapped her arms around one of his. "Perhaps it won't be so bad."

He lifted a brow and looked down at her. "No?"

A flirtatious smile played on Rose's lips. "I'll be coming with you."

That smile only grew and Carver leaned down as if he were going to kiss Rose. Elizabeth groaned loudly, forcing them both to look at her with lifted brows. "I swear to you, if I have to endure an entire carriage ride to Addington Hall listening to you two acting like this"—she gestured wildly in the air toward them—"I will ride my own horse outside the carriage and scandalize everyone who passes by."

Carver just raised his brow again. "That actually sounds rather tempting."

Rose shoved him in the ribs and he winced with a smile. "Fine. I shall refrain from kissing my wife in your presence."

"Thank you for your sacrifice," said Elizabeth.

"But know that one day you will want to kiss your husband when I am nearby, and you had better believe there is no chance I shall allow it after you have forced my own restraint."

It was meant to make her laugh. But instead, dread settled in her stomach.

If she married Lord Hastings, she doubted she would ever be filled with that desire.

Chapter Twenty-Five

Oliver's eyes scanned over the letter that had arrived to his flat a moment ago and it fell out of his hand, fluttering innocently to the floor, as if it didn't contain the heavy information that his father was now dead. Dead.

Frank Turner was dead. His hateful father was gone from the world and had taken with him any chance of reconciliation or forgiveness. A sick feeling formed in his stomach. Should he have gone to see him after the first letter had arrived?

He honestly didn't know how to feel at that moment. Oliver couldn't say he loved his father—it was difficult to love a man who had instilled such fear and pain in him for so long. But still…he felt…sad.

Not knowing what to do with those emotions or the multitude of other feelings swirling around his head and heart that week, Oliver pulled on his jacket and left his flat. Who he needed just then was Elizabeth—the one person in the world who truly knew what Frank Turner had been to him. But, no. He couldn't go to her. She was moving on to Hastings and he had to let her go. She would belong to the viscount soon, and that meant they could no longer continue on as they had previously.

Oliver's feet stopped outside of Kensworth House. He knocked on the door and silently prayed that Elizabeth was not at home. The door opened and, expecting to see the disapproving face of Jeffers, Oliver was taken aback to find a new face on the other side of it.

"Who are you?" Oliver asked.

The younger man stood a little taller. "Norton, sir. May I help you with something?"

Oliver shifted on his feet. "Where's Jeffers?" Although he had never liked the man, it felt wrong for him not to be there that day. It felt as if the world was turning upside down, and he couldn't do anything to stop it.

"Jeffers is taking a holiday to visit his family, sir. I am filling his position until he returns."

Oliver did something he never imagined himself doing at the words "until he returns," concerning Jeffers: he sighed with relief. Not everything was changing.

Norton showed Oliver into Kensworth's study, where he found his friend examining a bookshelf on the far end of the room. "Finally trying to sharpen your mind?" Oliver asked when he stepped in the room. "I hate to disappoint you, but I'm afraid it's too late for your improvement."

Kensworth turned around with a smirk. "In a lovely mood today, I see. Have I done something to put myself in your black books? Shall I send flowers or sweets to revive your affection?"

Oliver sank into a nearby chair. "Brandy. My father died."

He watched his friend's smile fall just as he had suspected it would. "Blast," said Kensworth, running a hand through his hair and moving to the beverage cart. "I had no idea."

Oliver smiled a little. "No, I didn't suspect you would, since I only just found out myself."

Kensworth finished filling the glass of brandy and came to take the chair near Oliver. "But we are like brothers. Shouldn't I have felt that something was wrong when I woke up this morning?"

Oliver chuckled, knowing that Kensworth was not joking. "What sort of something? A nagging deep in your soul, or as if your eggs simply did not taste as wonderful as usual?"

"Undoubtedly a nagging deep in my soul. I still swear the time you returned to school with a broken arm, mine ached for weeks," said Kensworth with a smile.

Oliver never told anyone that he hadn't broken his arm from falling out of the tree like he had claimed. Like all of the other *accidental* cuts, bruises and mishaps, his father had been the author of that break. But he wasn't alive to cause such pain anymore.

"Only because you were jealous of the attention my injury was gaining me."

"I still think I would have looked better in a sling than you," said Kensworth.

Oliver should have laughed, but he didn't feel like it. He looked down and swirled his glass of brandy, lost in memories, heartbreaking and unwanted.

"What can I say to help?" Kensworth asked.

You could get Elizabeth. She would know what to say.

"Nothing." Oliver rubbed at tightness in his chest.

"Do you regret not going to see him?" asked Kensworth.

Oliver shrugged, staring at the amber liquid. "Perhaps...or, no. I don't think so. It—it wouldn't have changed anything between us."

"I see." Kensworth fell quiet again, both men content to remain silent with their drinks for a time. "I think I know what you need," said Kensworth, finally breaking the silence.

Oliver looked up, knowing that feeling helpless was probably killing his friend. "And what would that be?"

"To go visit your home."

"Pembroke?" No. That's definitely not what he needed. He had planned to write to his father's solicitor and demand that the cursed house be sold immediately. Oliver *never* wished to step through the front door of his childhood home again. "Definitely not." The wake and funeral were set to take place in the next few days and Oliver had already decided he would not go.

"Hear me out," said Kensworth, leaning forward in his seat. "You never got the chance to say a final farewell to your father, so it probably feels as if he's not really gone. But if you go, and see for yourself, you will get the closure you need. Trust me. I wish I had faced my grief sooner than I did, rather than simply trying to push it away." But this was much different than Kensworth not being willing to face his fiancée's death. He was talking about a man who had caused Oliver nothing but a lifetime's worth of emotional and physical scars. The man who had made Oliver feel so little and unsure that he couldn't even allow himself to pursue the woman he loved.

No. This was different than needing closure. This was different than never being able to admit to himself that his father was dead. If he were being honest, he mostly felt relieved that his father could no longer plague him. And that made him feel so utterly guilty and unchristian.

"I'm not going back to Pembroke."

"But—"

"No."

Kensworth shut his mouth and nodded. He sank back against his chair. "All right. I won't force you. I just thought it might also be a good excuse for you to help me keep tabs on Hastings."

But that caught Oliver's attention. He narrowed his eyes. "How?"

Kensworth tipped one of his big shoulders, looking stupidly innocent even though Oliver knew very well that whatever he was about to say was premeditated. "Did you not know that Hastings's estate is very near Pembroke?" No, he did not.

"How near?" Oliver asked, feeling a little angry that Kensworth's plan was already working in his favor.

"Very. If I did not misread the directions sent from Lady Hastings, it is in the same village as Pembroke. The estate is called Addington Hall." Addington Hall belonged to the Viscount Hastings? It wasn't all that surprising that he hadn't realized Hastings had been his neighbor all these years. He'd made sure he was never at home more than a week at a time during his Eton days and, even when he was home, his father hadn't exactly been sociable, never requiring them to make or receive house calls.

If Oliver went to Pembroke, that would mean he would be close to Elizabeth. He shouldn't even be considering it. Had he not promised to let her go once and for all?

Oliver downed the rest of his drink and eyed Kensworth. "When do we leave?"

Chapter Twenty-Six

The carriage pulled up in front of Addington Hall and Elizabeth couldn't help but let out a slight nervous chuckle. *This* was the viscount's home.

"Good heavens," said Rose, in awe beside her. "It's nearly as large as Dalton Park, isn't it?"

Elizabeth swallowed and looked at her sister-in-law. "Rose, did you feel a little sick with nerves when you first came to Dalton Park?"

"No. But that's only because I had no knowledge that I was going to marry the heir of it at the time. I would have tossed up my accounts for sure had I known what responsibility was ahead of me."

Elizabeth let out a dejected puff. "Wonderful. You know you could have lied and said something along the lines of, *no need to worry. You're perfectly capable of running a house this size if the time comes.*"

A twinkle entered Rose's eyes. "I would have, but I was under the impression that you cherish honesty."

Elizabeth laughed before she turned to peer out the window at the enormous home once again.

"It's not too late to turn around," said Carver, his face joining hers to look out the window. "I can invent some excuse and have us back in London in a dash."

She turned slowly to look at her brother, who had asked every single day of the past week whether she was truly certain she wished to go to Addington Hall. "Will you quit trying to get out of this house party? What do you think is going to happen? They will dress you up in a funny outfit and make you perform charades?"

The look of terror that flashed through her brother's eyes nearly made Elizabeth burst into laughter. "I certainly am now. Do you think there's a chance of that happening?"

"Most definitely now that I know you despise the idea so much."

He narrowed his eyes. "And to think I left the comfort of Hopewood just to come launch you into Society. Now I can only hope that Mother and Father catch influenza during Kate's come out as well, leaving you responsible for what I know will be a very tedious debut."

"How very mature, brother dearest. I'll be sure to tell our parents you're wishing them ill."

Carver looked like he had a sally on the tip of his tongue but the door to the carriage opened and a footman waited to assist them down. It was then that Elizabeth noticed Lord Hastings and his family lined up in front of the home, waiting to watch her trip out of the carriage. Because she was certain from the way her legs suddenly felt wobbly and unsure of themselves she was going to end this scene by crashing onto the gravel below.

She had never felt nervous around Lord Hastings before. And, even now, she wasn't sure if the nerves she was feeling were because she was going to see Lord Hastings and meeting his family, or because she was afraid she was making a terrible mistake.

No. Not a mistake. She would be lucky to have Lord Hastings —*Wesley*—offer his hand in marriage.

"Lady Elizabeth," said Lord Hastings after Elizabeth had exited the carriage and miraculously managed to not fall on her face. His smile was different from any Elizabeth had ever seen before on his face. It was unrestrained and...genuinely excited. It gave her a flicker of hope. "I trust you had a pleasant journey?"

Well. If he thought that trying to avoid catching glimpses of one's brother making inappropriate eyes at his new bride for several hours was pleasant then, yes, it had been extremely pleasant.

"It was a lovely journey." Perhaps one day she would feel comfortable enough with him to tell him what was really in her thoughts instead of just polite answers.

"I'm glad to hear it." He continued to exchange pleasantries with Carver and Rose and then his eyes were back on her, and she was painfully aware of his family watching from only a few paces away. He noticed Elizabeth's glance their way and grinned. "Allow me to introduce all of you to my family." He leaned in slightly toward Elizabeth so that only she could hear him. "Mama is beyond excited to finally meet you."

Mama was most definitely excited to meet her. The woman's face bloomed when Elizabeth was introduced. Lady Hastings's already rosy cheeks turned two shades deeper with excitement as she began lavishing compliment after compliment on Elizabeth. Elizabeth's hair was *ravishing*. Her smile was *dazzling*. And, oh my, how elegant Elizabeth was!

Elizabeth had been expecting the stoic Lord Hastings's mother to be very like him in temperament. She could not have been more wrong. The dowager Lady Hastings, was the exact definition of motherly. She was neither tall nor lean, and she wore a frilly lace cap on her head. The woman was positively lovely. Lady Hastings was warm and inviting and just the sort of mother that Elizabeth was sure possessed a concoction for curing any illness known to man. Doting mothers were always proud of their ability to heal a headache.

The point was, Lady Hastings was nice. And that made Elizabeth feel a little guilty. She was not standing there admiring the lady's son— the man who would more than likely propose to her soon—but she was thinking about Oliver. Wondering what he was doing at that moment? Did he go to White's for breakfast that morning? Or did he skip and take a ride in the park? If he skipped White's, that meant he had skipped his morning coffee, which then meant he would be ailing from a headache by that time in the day.

Elizabeth finally shook her thoughts of Oliver and focused on meeting the rest of the family and greeting Lord Hastings's younger sister, Lady Olivia, once again. They were all kind. Welcoming. But none of them sparked any particular feelings of joy or excitement in Elizabeth. Which also made her feel guilty. Shouldn't she be filled with the desire to get to know the members of a family that might become hers?

Thankfully, Lady Hastings insisted that they all be given time to settle in and recover from their exhausting journey. Those words almost made Elizabeth laugh on the spot. She never understood why anyone would find sitting in a closed carriage for most of the day exhausting. If anything, it was an exhausting trial just forcing herself to sit there and do nothing.

After Elizabeth was shown her room, she absolutely could not bring herself to lie on her bed and spend the rest of the day motionless. With the help of a sweet maid who had been assigned to attend to her over the course of her stay, Elizabeth changed out of her traveling clothes into a blue walking dress with yellow flowers embroidered across the bodice, and slipped out of her room.

She should be used to enormous homes. But this one felt different. It was foreign and imposing and everything seemed to be made of stone. It felt a little cold. Or perhaps she was just projecting her own feelings onto the house.

Elizabeth wandered around a bit, until she heard laughing echoing from a room down a long corridor. She paused outside the door, and was surprised to find Lord Hastings hunched over a chessboard across from his youngest sister, Lady Georgia, whom Elizabeth knew to be thirteen years old.

"You've gotten better since we last played," he said, sounding impressed.

"Well, that could be because you haven't played chess with me since I was eight years old."

He chuckled, and Elizabeth was relieved to say she enjoyed the sound. And also the way his brown hair was falling across his brow.

"That could be it." He paused a moment. "I'm sorry I haven't been home more often, Georgia."

Elizabeth looked away, feeling that the conversation had suddenly become too personal for her to observe.

However, if she was contemplating marrying the man, shouldn't she be allowed to get an inside look on what he was like before Papa signed the marriage contract? Elizabeth sank beside the door so she could still listen but wouldn't be seen. Eavesdropping was a slightly unsavory thing to do but, apparently, she was getting a lot of practice, and had perhaps become good at it. She would deal with the guilt later.

"I'm sorry for that, too. We've missed having you around," said Lady Georgia, moving a chess piece across the board.

"Well, if things go as planned, I believe I will be home much more often in the future."

"Does this mean you do intend to propose to Lady Elizabeth, then?"

Elizabeth held her breath and leaned a little closer to the door.

"I'm not sure I should actually be telling you this but...yes. I do plan to propose while she is here. And since she prefers the country to Town, I believe we will reside here for the majority of the year."

Was it bad for a person to go from perfectly well one moment to seeing stars the next? And that whooshing sound in her ears, was it normal? And, oh no...she felt as if she couldn't breathe all of a sudden. She put her hands up on her neck as if that would help her grasp the air she needed.

"Checkmate," said Georgia, signaling the end of their game.

Chair legs scraped against the ground. Blast. They were coming.

Elizabeth looked around quickly knowing it would be terrible to be caught lurking outside a room where Lord Hastings had just admitted to his plans of a proposal. Elizabeth practically dove into a room adjacent to her. She pressed her back to a wall of the empty music room and waited, holding her breath, until she heard the clicking of Lord Hastings's boots and the swishing of Lady Georgia's skirts fade down the hallway.

A breath rushed from her mouth and her legs felt weak.

He was going to propose for certain. Lord Hastings was going to ask her to marry him. She would be given the opportunity to become his wife.

It didn't matter which way Elizabeth formulated the statement, it didn't settle well in her mind.

Chapter Twenty-Seven

It didn't matter how old Oliver was. Standing outside of Pembroke always filled him with dread. He was reminded of that old deserted cottage on Dalton Park's grounds that he and Kensworth had found once and determined to be haunted. Oliver had told Elizabeth about it and she had promptly demanded that he take her there. Elizabeth, being the brave girl that she was, had insisted that they go inside. It had been dark, with spiderwebs covering every corner, and boards falling off the sides of the cottage. Although he would never have admitted to Elizabeth, he had been terrified to go into that place. Dreaded it. But Elizabeth had given him a mischievous smile and said that if it was haunted, she simply must go inside because she'd always wanted to meet a ghost.

He'd held her hand that day as they had stepped through the door— so Elizabeth wouldn't be scared—but looking back, he knew it had been as much for his sake as hers.

Pembroke was twice as frightening to Oliver as that old haunted house. He wished Elizabeth was with him to hold his hand. Only she could chase away the ghosts that haunted it.

Once inside the house, he didn't feel much better. Instead he felt as if a vice was clamped around his neck, choking him. His father was dead, but part of him feared that the man would step out from behind one of those dusty curtains or emerge from one of the closed doors.

Oliver walked slowly through the foyer, hearing the boards beneath his feet creak in a way that used to make him cringe. It had never been good to alert his father to his presence. Better to be silent and hide away most of the day. But Frank Turner wasn't there anymore to hear those boards creak.

He didn't make it more than a few steps into the house before his feet just stopped without his permission. They wouldn't go any farther into that darkened home and he wasn't in a mood to fight them. Painful memories were all twisting and taunting around him. Perhaps it had been a mistake coming there. Kensworth was an idiot to think this would bring him closure of any kind.

He knew he had to fully enter that house eventually, but the moment didn't have to be now.

Oh, blast, blast, blast.

He had found her.

Elizabeth had been avoiding any alone time with Lord Hastings since she had overheard him and his sister talking in the library the previous day. And she had certainly been avoiding him since Carver had pulled her aside that morning and informed her that the viscount had asked for his permission to propose. Apparently Elizabeth had been correct, and her potential new husband was something of an over-achiever who had already written to Papa and asked for his permission to wed Elizabeth. Papa had responded that he would defer to Carver to make the decision since Carver had a better understanding of Lord Hastings's character.

Carver gave his blessing.

Wonderful.

No, really, it should be wonderful, shouldn't it? This was exactly what she had wanted. Exactly what she needed—a man who she wanted, and who wanted her in return. There was only one flaw in her plan: Elizabeth didn't want Wesley. She had tried to rip her heart back from Oliver's hands but, hang the man, his hands must be filled with glue because her heart wasn't budging. It was most inconvenient.

And now, Elizabeth had been walking for at least an hour, thinking that surely she would be far enough away from Lord Hastings to avoid him, giving herself a little more time to make up her mind. But he had found her.

Elizabeth pasted a smile on her face as Lord Hastings approached on horseback.

"There you are," he said, and with a smile as wise as his horse, came to stop and dismounted. "I was beginning to think you had lost your way." Thankfully, the sound of more hooves came from behind him and Carver appeared. She nearly sighed with relief. They wouldn't be alone after all.

He noticed her eyes settle on her brother and he smiled. "I asked Lord Kensworth to come with me to find you. I thought it would be more proper this way." Much more proper. Also, far less romantic, had she actually been hoping for a bit of romance with him.

"Hello, darling," said Carver pulling his horse up beside them but not dismounting. "Lovely day, isn't it?" That put-on smile made Elizabeth want to pinch her brother. He was up to something, she could feel it. He never smiled like that unless he was especially proud of himself. What had he done?

"The loveliest. I'm afraid that's why I've been out wandering for so long. I hope I haven't ruined any plans Lady Hastings might have made for us."

"None at all." Lord Hastings paused a moment, his brows pulling together slightly. "There was an outdoor luncheon and a bit of lawn games with a few of our neighbors, but nothing other than that." So, she had ruined plans. Poor Lady Hastings. Elizabeth really hadn't meant to be gone so long. But sometimes when she made her way into nature, she lost all sense of time. Especially when the weather was so mild and agreeable as it had been lately. It was a problem. A wonderful problem, Oliver had always said.

"I'm terribly sorry. She must think I'm the very worst sort of guest for getting lost to my own devices all day."

"If she is disappointed, it is only because she was hoping to get to know you better." Why must he be so kind? Ever since that day in Hyde Park when he had admitted to Elizabeth that he was shy, she had never again seen that harsh, pompous side to him. Unfortunately, she had also yet to see any sort of fun or life from the man either. He was simply always…nice.

Elizabeth pulled in a deep breath through her nose and forced herself to keep smiling. "Well, then. I shall go back straight away and make it up to her."

"Shall I walk with you? I'm sure Lord Kensworth wouldn't mind riding a bit behind so we might…talk a little more privately." Lord Hastings shot an inquisitive look to Carver. The two were in cahoots, it seemed.

Thankfully, that gave Elizabeth the opportunity to give her helpful brother a look that said *don't you dare leave me with this man or I will cut your hair off while you are sleeping.*

Carver digested the look Elizabeth gave him and with an amount of ease that would have impressed Rose, he said, "Actually, Hastings. I was hoping you might be able to show me around the estate a bit before we are needed to change for dinner. I don't think Elizabeth minds, do you darling?"

Lord Hastings's brows knitted together.

Elizabeth smiled sweetly. "I think that's a wonderful idea. I'm feeling rather tired after my walk anyway." She saw the slightly saddened look that swept over Wesley's face, so she quickly added for encouragement, "Perhaps we might have time to talk…privately, as you suggest, after I've rested."

His smile returned. It was a nice smile. *Nice.* Why did that word keep popping into her head? And why did it sound so negative?

No matter. There would be plenty of years to learn to love his niceness after they married.

Elizabeth watched the two men ride off and part of her felt a little dejected that Wesley had not even tried to kiss her hand, or squeeze it lightly before he left her. Even a wink would have gone a long way to encouraging some flutters. Nothing. The man must have devoted his life to the study of propriety. There would be no surprises in life with him.

At that moment, she heard a cat meow above her head. Elizabeth paused and squinted up into the tree she had been crossing under. There was an adorable little kitten perched on a high branch sending out cries of help.

"Oh, no. Are you stuck?" asked Elizabeth, unashamedly talking to the white kitten in the tree. "Don't worry, I'll help you." It was a rather small tree. She'd certainly climbed higher ones before.

As Elizabeth was bunching up her skirts and preparing to climb the tree, that annoying voice in her head was telling her to stop and think before she acted. These sorts of adventures had never ended well for her in the past, and she was trying to act more refined and polished these days. Not to mention the fact that she was not at Dalton Park but on Lord Hastings's estate.

But Lord Hastings wasn't around, now was he?

Telling that voice to stuff it, Elizabeth started up the tree in the direction of the kitten. Just as she had suspected, it was the easiest climb of her life. She was on the branch just under the kitten. It would be easy to reach up and retrieve the animal if her stupid bonnet wasn't so large, obstructing her vision.

Elizabeth untied it and tossed it off, relishing the freedom of that small act. Reaching up, she took the kitten gently in her arms and began to climb down. When she had almost reached the lowest branch, the kitten jumped from her arms to the ground and darted off.

Elizabeth gave a mock scoff. "And that's the thanks I get for rescuing you from a tree?" She looked down, noting that the drop was not much, and decided to jump rather than climb the last little bit. But just as always in her life, there was a slight hitch.

Everything would have gone smoothly had a branch not snagged her hair on the way down. But of course, it did. And now Elizabeth was standing beneath the tree, being held captive by a rogue branch that felt as if it were slowly ripping every hair from her head. She looked up and immediately winced at the sharp tug of her hair. Like a claw, the branch had somehow grasped, twisted, and intertwined itself into the style that only a few moments ago had been a nicely polished and pinned style.

"Just wonderful!" she said with a rather juvenile stomp. But she didn't care about looking mature at that moment. She felt angry. Why couldn't things simply go her way for once? Why could she not, just this one time, act exactly how she pleased and not have any looming consequences?

Elizabeth reached up, careful to not tilt her head again, lest she be further punished by that cursed branch. Her fingers stilled when she heard the approaching sound of hooves again.

No! He's back?

Could this day get any worse? Lord Hastings was going to ride up and see her tangled in this vindictive branch and ask how the situation came about. She was going to have to tell him the truth and would bet a pony he wasn't going to like it.

She sighed, preparing herself for her fate as the horse stopped and she heard the sound of Wesley dismount and chuckle.

Wait. That wasn't Wesley's chuckle. That wonderful sound belonged to—

"Do I even want to know, Lizzie? How the devil do you always manage to get your hair tangled up in shrubbery?" asked her best friend in the world as he approached her from behind.

Her eyes widened and her breath caught in her chest. The sound of his voice washed over her making chill bumps fly across her skin. She tried to whip around to see him but the branch said no. She hissed at the pain stinging her scalp.

"No, don't move." Oliver came into the periphery of her vision.

First, his boots. Should the sight of slightly muddy top boots really cause a woman so much anticipation? Next, she could see his cravat as he came to stand just beside her—ridiculously close—and then she could feel his warmth as he stretched out tall with his hands above her head, working to free her hair. He smelled intoxicating. "This is rather impressive. What were you doing to make this tree so angry with you?"

But her mind was still reeling. How was Oliver here? And acting so nonchalant? Like he fully expected to see her today and they had planned it all along? This must have had something to do with Carver's triumphant smile. She should have known better than to assume her brother would have not interfered in her life. But, at the moment, she couldn't say she minded.

"I...was rescuing a kitten," she said in a bit of daze, holding completely still as Oliver tended to her hair. What was it he smelled like? It was fantastic.

He tilted his head down, hands still in her hair, and smirked. "A kitten? This isn't like one of your footpad stories, is it? A heroic action to cover up the fact that you were simply climbing trees for fun again?" He smiled fully and her eyes fell to the dimple on his right cheek. He hadn't shaved yet that day. It was unfair how attractive the man looked with a beard.

"It ran off as soon as I reached the bottom."

"A likely story."

"It did!"

"And what color was this kitten?" he asked, narrowing his sea blue eyes.

"White with a little black speck on its right ear. Now will you please focus on my hair so I do not have to make a home out here under this tree?"

She heard the small chuckle again—one that no one else would have been able to hear, but she was able to detect it because his chest was right beside her face. The fabric of his jacket brushed against her cheek. She swallowed.

"I think we are going to have to cut it," he said.

Elizabeth gasped. "No!" Images of her entering Addington Hall and sitting down to dinner with half of her hair cropped an inch from her scalp flashed through her mind.

Again, that chuckle, but this time louder. "Only kidding. It's done." He lowered his arms and Elizabeth felt the release of the branch.

She sighed and rubbed the now sore spot on her head. "Thank you."

"You might want to take a peek in a mirror before you thank me. I'm afraid I've quite thoroughly ruined your coiffure."

"At least we didn't have to cut it. And luckily I have a bonnet somewhere around here that I can use to hide the devastation until I've time to fix it once again." She glanced around, looking for the accessory that, for once in her life, might have served a good purpose had she left it on.

The cream bonnet was resting by Oliver's boots. He picked it up and smiled at her. Elizabeth held out her hand but Oliver swatted it away. He slid the bonnet on her head and bent slightly to see what he was doing as he tied the ribbons under her chin. Unfortunately, he was wearing his riding gloves and she couldn't feel the warmth of his hands. It was odd how much she had come to crave his touch.

If this whole situation had happened with Wesley rather than Oliver, Elizabeth guessed the viscount would have assessed her situation and then dashed off home to obtain a chaperone before he began to untangle her hair. And she could never in a million years picture him tying the ribbons of her bonnet under her chin. Perhaps Wesley was the better gentleman. Was it so terrible that she did not wish for a perfect gentleman all of the time?

Was it so awful that she wished for romance—stolen kisses and longing glances? She wanted to feel her heart race and her cheeks flush. Both of which were happening with Oliver standing so closely in front of her. She'd seen his jaw lined with stubble many, many times over the years, but never until that moment had she had such an urge to run her fingers slowly across it.

Oliver was ruining everything again. She was supposed to be putting him behind her. Why could he not simply have left her alone and given her heart a chance to love Wesley? Instead, he was popping up out of nowhere, with a handsome jaw of sandy scruff, his hair a bit too long, curling around his ears and neck, and he smelled—

"What are you doing here, Oliver?" she asked, in a curt tone, cutting off her own unhelpful thoughts.

He finished the bow under her chin and dropped his hands—but did not step away and give her the space she needed, however.

"Rescuing you, as always."

She narrowed her eyes. "I mean, on Lord Hastings's property. Are you stalking me?"

He gave her a crooked smile. "Yes, darling. You see, I'm hopelessly in love with you and I've followed you all this way because I've come to find that London no longer holds any value without you in it."

But see, the thing about Oliver's sarcasm is that he was so good at it, that sometimes it sounded rather like he was telling the truth. Like just then, Elizabeth knew it was a sarcastic jest, but her poor, stupid heart did not seem to understand the concept.

She held his gaze for a few breathless moments. Not daring to say anything lest something horribly wrong and vulnerable fell out of her mouth.

"Well," he finally said, breaking first. "Those reasons *and* because…my father died."

Elizabeth sucked in an audible breath. "When?"

"Last week."

"Last week? So long ago. Why didn't you tell me?" It hurt that he hadn't informed her. No one had.

He didn't say anything at first. But his eyes looked saddened. "Lizzie, I…I'm trying to find my way through life without you." His look grew meaningful. "Because I know that very soon, I will lose my best friend and have no choice."

There were no words that felt adequate enough to speak at that moment. It all felt so painful.

Elizabeth stepped closer and wrapped her arms around Oliver's middle. He didn't push her away or delay even a moment. Instead, Oliver wrapped his arms around her and pulled her in close, resting his chin on her head as if he needed that embrace to hold him up. Elizabeth knew what Frank Turner had been to Oliver. And she also knew that Oliver despised talking about it. She didn't push him on it. She simply wished to hold him.

Chapter Twenty-Eight

"I t's hot," said Kate with a pouty face. "How much farther must we walk?"

Oliver shifted the picnic basket on his arm and looked sideways at Elizabeth. It was her idea to have a picnic, and so she was the one calling the shots.

Elizabeth laughed. "We could have left you at home, you know. Your grumbling is not helping your chances of being invited next time."

Although, Oliver was happy that they hadn't left her behind. It was good to have a buffer between him and the ridiculously beautiful Elizabeth. If only she had an obnoxious personality to lessen his attraction. But no, she had to be absolutely wonderful.

"What makes you think I wish to come next time? I'm not even sure I wished to be included in this picnic. I was perfectly content reading my book before you dragged me away," said Kate.

Elizabeth cast a quick nervous glance to Oliver and then back to Kate. "You needed some sunshine." Interesting. So Elizabeth had forced Kate to come along? Could it be that she felt the same strong spark he had been feeling lately? Oliver knew his reason for keeping away from her, but what was hers?

No, he was being ridiculous. Elizabeth only saw him as another brother.

Elizabeth paused beside a patch of wild flowers and began to pick them. Kate looked at her sister and rolled her eyes with a smirk before pointing to a nice large tree a little in the distance. She took the basket from Oliver as if she knew instinctively he would stay with Elizabeth. "I'm going over there to set up the picnic. If you take too long, Elizabeth, I shall eat both yours and Oliver's portions." She turned and walked away with a grin.

"Don't you dare," said Elizabeth to her sister's retreating figure.

Oliver watched, willing himself not to stare as Elizabeth crouched down and gathered the blooms in her hands. She was humming a soft tune. Everything about the woman was lovely and pure and enchanting. She looked up at him with a quiet smile and handed him her blooms. "Hold these, will you?"

"Of course." He took them from her and their fingers brushed fire against one another. Did she feel it, too? "Do you realize this will be our last summer like this?" He hadn't actually meant to say those words out loud.

Elizabeth stood and brushed her hands against her skirts, her eyes sparkling with the light of the sun. "Like what, exactly?"

He looked down at the flowers and shrugged. "You're coming to Town this Season. Everything will change. It is very likely you will be married by next summer."

"You have more faith in my success than I do," she said on a small laugh.

He didn't feel like smiling. "I'm certain of it."

Their gazes fixed on each other. The air felt heavy and thick with feeling. Was he the only one fighting this attraction?

Oliver had been both anticipating and dreading this last summer with Elizabeth. He fully intended to spend as much of it as was possible with her. It was selfish, but he wanted to steal as many memories with the woman as he could before he would have to let her go to another man. He would take those memories and hold them close to his heart for as long as he lived. It was all he could have of her, and he would take all that he could carry.

Elizabeth must have felt something—most likely the fear of losing their strong friendship—because her eyes glistened with moisture. She blinked quickly and looked away. When her face turned back, her sadness had vanished and her eyes spoke of mischief. "The summer is not over yet. Let's have a race," she said.

Oliver smiled. "Where to?"

"To the tree where Kate is waiting."

"Very well. Winner gets to eat the loser's dessert tonight."

Elizabeth laughed. "What is it with you and desserts?"

"I know, it's becoming a problem isn't it?"

She bumped his shoulder. "Only if you continue to take mine."

"Well, then, you must learn to run faster."

Elizabeth looked up from her lashes, a wicked grin on her pink lips. And then her eyes dropped to his boots. "You must tie the laces of your boot before the race."

"What?" He frowned and looked down before realizing it was a trick. In fact, it was the oldest trick in the book and he had fallen for it. His boots did not even have laces.

Oliver looked back up to see Elizabeth sprinting off, skirts gathered in her hands, laughing like a villain. He took off behind her, catching her quickly and grabbing her hand to try to slow her down. She glanced over her shoulder, still running, and her blonde locks rushing against her face, a full smile spread across her mouth. They were both laughing as he tugged on her hand a little harder to slow her down.

"Let go!" she said, trying to rip her hand free. "I will not lose my dessert to you again!" But he just grabbed hold again, tugging her back until his arms could wrap around her waist. He picked her up, spun her around to set her down behind him. Their laughter filled the air, each competing to be the loudest. Oliver tried to make a break for the tree but this time Elizabeth caught his arm and tugged him back forcefully. They both stumbled over each other and fell to the ground, laughing like children.

"You cheat!" he said, laughing and lying on his back to catch his

breath. He looked over to Elizabeth who was lying beside him—also trying to catch her breath between laughs. He smiled and held the bouquet he had been holding toward her. She took the flowers and smelled them, looking as joyful and content as he felt.

"You're just as big a cheat as I am," she said.

"You're not wrong." They had both cheated at games since they were young. Even now, spending time with her in this familiar way felt a little like cheating.

Their laughter eventually died out, but she seemed just as content to lie there on the grass staring up at the blue sky as he was. The sun was hot as it blanketed their faces, but he didn't mind. Oliver raised his arm to lay it on the ground above his head. He could feel Elizabeth's hair against his fingers and see her chest rising and falling from the corner of his eye. He could easily imagine spending every day for the rest of his life like this. Elizabeth was the only woman he had ever been able to imagine in his future—the only woman he wanted in his future. To spend the days adventuring, raising children, running across the grounds of their own estate sounded like a dream. Maybe having her within the walls of his childhood home would even erase some of the painful memories.

No. He would never subject her to that life. He was not going to marry Elizabeth Ashburn.

He watched her fingers trace the soft petals, mesmerized by her tender movements. "Speaking of Town..." her voice trailed off.

"Were we?"

"A moment ago, yes." Her lashes raised to peek at him, looking almost shy. "Which unfortunate debutante was able to steal Oliver Turner's attention this past Season?" She dropped her gaze to the flowers again.

He closed his eyes, wishing he could tell her the truth. He wished he could tell her that he had been chasing women the past few Seasons in attempts to shake her from his mind and no other reason. But no one —not one woman—measured up to Elizabeth. It was as if she were painted in bright colors and everyone else in muted tones.

Those words could never be spoken to her. It would cross a line he could never return from. "Miss Surrey was intriguing."

Elizabeth smiled, but her grip tightened on the stems of the flowers. What was he supposed to think of that? "Oh? And do you foresee this intrigue lasting?"

He rolled his head to look at her. Her sights were fixed on those flowers, which gave him the perfect opportunity to admire the way the sun made her golden blonde hair look like light, sweet, dripping honey. He wanted to run his finger across the freckles on her nose and cheeks. Did she know how beautiful she was? And what was it she had asked him? Oh, yes. Did he see his intrigue in the woman he had only made up a moment ago lasting? "No, I do not. I'm not sure I was made for anything lasting." At least, that was the excuse he was using from then on out.

She finally removed her gaze from the flowers and rolled her head to look at him. Her eyes perfectly matched the sky above. It was agony having her mouth so close to his that he could feel her breath against his lips, and yet he could not close the space between them. "Perhaps, one day, you will find someone who makes the idea more bearable."

He already had.

Oliver sighed, discreetly feeling the curls lying against his fingers. He wished for time to stop. For the two of them to lie under the summer sun together for the rest of their lives.

Kate's voice cut through the air, proving that wishes did not come true. "I was not jesting! I am moments away from eating all of your food!"

Elizabeth smiled, dimples appearing in her sun kissed cheeks, before she sat up. He made to follow her, but the next thing he knew, Elizabeth's hand was on his chest and pushing him back down. He only had a moment to relish that action before she sprang from the ground and ran as fast as she could toward the tree, only looking back to yell, "Your dessert is mine, Turner!"

How had that woman so fully captured his heart? He feared he would never recover.

~

Oliver continued to hold Elizabeth in his arms for several minutes. She made no attempts to step back out of his embrace, and he had no intention of letting her go anytime soon. With her near, he felt as if his pain could no longer reach him.

"Are you staying at Lord Hastings's house, then?" she asked, her voice muffled by his cravat.

"Actually, as it turns out, Lord Hastings and I are something of neighbors. Pembroke is not far from here. I've come to settle my father's estate business."

He felt her shoulders stiffen. She pulled back to look at him. "Neighbors?" Why that word seemed to offend her so much, he didn't know.

He nodded, hesitant to confirm it because of the wary look in her eyes.

"But—that means…" Her voice trailed off and her expression looked spooked. Elizabeth turned her face away and squinted into the distance, as if seeing something that wasn't there. Finally, she shook her head from whatever painful daydream she looked to be having. "Nevermind."

"No, tell me."

Her lips pressed together and then she leaned in again to settle her head against his chest once more. "It's nothing. How has it been, staying at Pembroke?"

He sighed. "I've only spent one night there and I'm not sure how many more I can take. My father is gone but…his memory still feels far too alive in those walls."

"I can imagine. Why did you need to come?"

For you.

"I needed to look over Frank's ledgers with his solicitor before I can sell it." Almost without thinking, Oliver raised his hand and stroked down the side of Elizabeth's hair. Oddly, she didn't even seem to notice. Or maybe she just didn't mind.

"You're going to sell?"

"I certainly cannot live there," he said.

"No. I think it's a wise choice."

This time it was he who pulled away to look at her. "You do? You don't think it's a bit...cowardly of me to want to run as far away from the place as possible?"

She smiled softly and reached up to touch the side of his face—something she had most definitely never done before. She ran her thumb back and forth against his jaw, tracing the movement with her eyes. "I would never think you a coward for taking care of yourself, Oliver."

His gaze dropped to her lips. This was not a spontaneous thought to kiss her. It was something that had been lurking and taunting him for years. But seeing her here on Hastings's property and knowing that, very soon—he would not have a right to hold her as he was or talk to her intimately like they always had or entertain the idea of kissing her—well, all of those thoughts were begging him to put all of his fears aside and embrace his desire.

And he might have, if she hadn't tensed up and dropped her gaze toward the ground. "I must go," she said with a cold tone. What had he done? He could have sworn she wanted him to kiss her only a moment ago.

Or...perhaps she really did have feelings for Hastings. That thought tore at him.

Either way, he wouldn't be able to sleep at night knowing he had upset her. "Lizzie, have I upset you?"

"No," she said, pulling out of his arms and most certainly looking upset. She started to walk away, but then turned back sharply. "I'm here for Lord Hastings." She threw the words at him like a dagger.

"I know."

Determination hung in her eyes, and her hands were fisted at her sides, gloves straining against the tightness. "He's asked Carver for permission to marry me."

Oliver blinked. "I see."

"And...you should know, I've made up my mind about it, and I'm going to accept his offer when he proposes."

Oliver's legs felt weak. Those words shouldn't have come as such a shock for him. It's what he'd been planning for and convincing himself was the right thing for her for years. Hastings could love her better than he could. Offer her more. But all he could seem to think of was how Hastings didn't know that Elizabeth despised cucumbers, and read romance novels ironically, and sometimes fell asleep outside under a tree on warm days and would need to be awakened before the sun burned her skin.

"If that's what you want."

"It is." Then why didn't she look happy? "And this"—she gestured in the air between them—"what we are…must change. I have to make room in my life for Wesley." *Wesley.* Oliver had never hated a name more.

"I understand."

She rubbed her lips together, blinking as she nodded mutely. They had always known this day would come. Their friendship must change. He found a small comfort in the fact that it was evidently just as difficult for her as it was for him.

"Good day, Oliver." She curtsied, turned, and began walking away. He watched as she froze again after taking two steps. She whirled around, a new determined and inquisitive look on her face. She opened her mouth but hesitated a moment before she finally asked, "W-why do you smell so good today?"

He nearly laughed from this sudden change in topic as well as the serious knit of her brows. He couldn't resist a smile as he used his tongue to push the mint leaf forward to bite between his front teeth. "Mint. From the garden outside Pembroke."

She eyed his mouth for one long moment, and if he wasn't mistaken—he saw a great deal of longing. Did she ever give Hastings that look?

"Thought so," she said, sounding utterly put out by that mint leaf. Elizabeth turned around again and stomped off in the direction of Addington Hall, leaving Oliver more confused than ever.

Chapter Twenty-Nine

Oliver shoved his hands through his hair and leaned his elbows against the desk as the solicitor closed the door behind him on his way out. He had been sitting at that desk poring over his father's ledgers with the solicitor since he had left Elizabeth earlier that day. It was a little more than shocking to learn that he actually had quite a bit of money to his name now. His father had been paying his staff a ridiculously low wage—an unfortunate fact that didn't surprise Oliver—and there were several tenant homes on the estate's property that were bringing in a high return.

For some reason, Oliver had always thought his father was just barely scraping by. He'd never imagined that there would actually be a large inheritance once Frank Turner died. The meeting with the solicitor might have even been considered uplifting had the man not mentioned the letter Frank had written to him right before his death.

Apparently, his wonderful father had written to the solicitor days before he died, inquiring to see if an entail could be placed on the house, but he had died before anything could officially be put in place. Frank had made it clear that he suspected his greedy son would attempt to sell the house before his body had time to go cold in the grave and wanted to ensure that it couldn't happen. Frank Turner was nothing if not a prideful man, and he wanted to make sure that the Turner name stayed associated with Pembroke for generations. It was odd to Oliver that this seemed to be a last minute thought for his father. Or perhaps it was the first time he had been sober enough in years to consider it. Either way, he wasn't surprised to learn that Frank Turner's hatefulness had transcended the grave.

A knock sounded on the door of the study. It was five knocks in a familiar beat.

"Come in, Kenny."

His friend opened the door and stepped inside. "I knocked on the front door, but decided to let myself in when there was no answer from your staff."

"That's because I don't have a staff," Oliver said. "Most of them quit their posts the day Frank died. They couldn't get away from this cursed house soon enough." Oliver had hired a maid of all duties and a lad from the village to tend to his horse while he was staying at Pembroke. It hadn't been a problem when he was only planning to stay another day or two. But now...

Kensworth cast a glance around the dark, dusty room. Oliver followed his friend's gaze to the paper on the walls that was peeling at the top and to the chairs that looked as if no one had ever sat in them despite being decades out of date. A cloud of dust would certainly be released if anyone were to sit on the aged fabric. There was a fire in the grate, not because the temperature was cold, but because he needed something to make him feel comfortable in that house—and the bleak décor just wasn't filling that need.

Kensworth leaned against the mantle. "Homey," he said with a smirk.

"What are you doing here, Kenny?" Oliver asked, sorting through the papers on his desk and feeling annoyed at every aspect of his life.

Apparently his friend sensed it because for once he did not try to engage in banter. "I came to tell you that Hastings asked for my blessing to marry Elizabeth."

"I know."

Kensworth raised a brow. "You do? And how would you know that?"

Oliver leaned back in his chair, putting the papers aside for a minute. "I saw Lizzie earlier."

"When?"

"She was on a walk. Her hair was caught in a tree."

"And I'm guessing you helped her untangle it?"

"Yes."

"And you two...talked?"

"Yes."

"Alone?"

Oliver looked up at Kensworth, leery of the string of questions. "Yes," he admitted slowly.

Kensworth crossed his arms and leaned his shoulder against the mantle with a look of boring disinterest. However, it was the nothing-in-the-world-could-ever-affect-me sort of look people put on when they are trying very hard to cover up the fact that they are very interested in the answer to whatever they are about to ask. "And...did anything fruitful come from this talk?"

Oliver narrowed his eyes. "All right, cut line. What is this? What are these questions?"

"Nothing." Kensworth looked offended that Oliver would even suspect something. Which meant he had ample reason to suspect something. Oliver let his look grow more accusatory, which finally broke his friend down. Kensworth released his arms with a huff. "Fine. I suppose I might have been hoping that you learning of Hastings's intentions would have finally forced you to declare yourself to Elizabeth."

Oliver ran a hand over his face. "How many times do I need to tell you that I do not love Elizabeth?"

"It doesn't matter the number, I always know when you're lying. It's plain to see that you love her as much as you love your right hand. She's a part of you. You need her."

"I do not need her," Oliver growled out. "And besides, I'm left-handed."

"I don't see why you're being so stubborn about this."

"It's not stubbornness. I simply do not love Elizabeth."

Now Kensworth looked angry. He crossed the room and bent down to rest his large hands on the desk, calloused knuckles on display, leveling Oliver a glare.

"Trying to intimidate me, darling? It won't work. I know you adore me," said Oliver, deflecting the tension as best he could. He was taking a page out of Kensworth's own book.

His friend didn't smile. "Why are you lying to me? There's more to this but I haven't figured it out yet."

Oliver rolled his eyes and hoped to God Kensworth didn't really see what was going on. "You're trying to see too much into things. Believe it or not, a man and woman may be friends without falling in love."

This time Kensworth let out one short laugh—loud and full. "That's the biggest load of nonsense I've ever heard. Of course a man and woman cannot be close friends without developing feelings. And in yours and Elizabeth's case, falling in love."

Oliver's mind grabbed on to one very important word. "Did you say, '*and* Elizabeth's case?'"

Kensworth smiled a devilish smile. "You only get to be informed of such details *after* you've admitted your love for my sister."

Oliver stood and started walking toward the door, he was done going in circles about his feelings for Elizabeth. He was planning to show his friend out. But as he passed Kensworth, the man's arm shot out and caught his chest, not letting him take another step. "Why are you hiding your feelings?"

"Why are you playing matchmaker?" The man's persistence was beyond irritating.

"Because you are acting a fool. And because I care deeply for you and Elizabeth and want the best for both of you."

Oliver shot his gaze to Kensworth. "If it's the best for both of us that you want, then you will let this go and marry Elizabeth off to Hastings as soon as possible."

"Why?" His hand was still on Oliver's chest.

"Let me go, Kensworth."

"Oh, my whole title. This is serious, isn't it?"

"I'm warning you to let me go."

"Not until you tell me why you won't admit your feelings for Elizabeth."

Something in Oliver snapped. He threw Carver's arm off him and he spun to face him. "Because I will hurt her! My father was an alcoholic as well as abusive and he hated me more than anything in this world. His blood runs through my veins. And if there is any chance that I will ever be the same father to my children, or hurtful to Elizabeth in any way, I will not take it. Now, I'm begging you to drop your persistence and allow me to let go of her." Oliver's voice echoed off of the walls, making the silence that followed feel that much heavier.

"Blast," muttered Kensworth. "Why did you never tell me that? You always made it sound as if you and your father simply had differences of opinions."

Oliver scoffed turning a half circle and thrusting his hand into his hair. "His opinion being that I should never have entered this world and mine being that a man shouldn't hit his wife and child." He paused and dropped his hand, giving a light shrug when he knew that Kensworth was still waiting for an answer to his question. "I never told you because…I was ashamed. Like it was my fault somehow. The duke has always been such a good father to you. Sometimes it was unbearable to see the comparison between our upbringings. Your father loved you and mine despised me. So, I simply hid it. It was far easier to pretend it didn't happen rather than speak of it."

Kensworth pushed out a heavy breath through his nose. "I'm so sorry, Oliver. And here I was, pushing you to return to a place I cannot imagine is very pleasant for you to visit."

Oliver breathed. His chest felt a little lighter to finally admit the things he had been hiding. "It's all right. Now I know your whole ploy was simply getting me here so you could play matchmaker." But he instantly regretted bringing the conversation back to Elizabeth. Before Kensworth could open his mouth again Oliver hurried on, "Besides, although I'm loath to admit it, you were right. It's good I came and faced the demons of this place again. Especially since I've decided to live here from now on."

"What? Why the devil would you do that?"

To prove Frank Turner wrong. He thought Oliver was a good-for-nothing spendthrift? He was going to make his father roll over in his grave. "The estate is much more profitable than I originally realized. I think it would be a shame to sell it." He looked around the room as if he were envisioning a beautiful home with fresh paint and new paper and curtains rather than seeing all the corners he used to hide in as a child. "I think I could fix it up and make it livable."

Oh, no. Kensworth was scowling. That wasn't good. "Livable for you and Elizabeth?"

Oliver turned away. "No, Kenny. I already told you, Elizabeth is going to marry Hastings and I am not going to stop her."

"But you do love her?"

Oliver shut his eyes and clenched his teeth together, letting the heaviness of those words weigh on him. "Yes. I do love her. That's why I'm letting her go."

He felt Kensworth's hand clasp his shoulder and grip it. "For what it's worth, there is not a single man in the entire world who I would trust with my sister more than you. Don't lose her because of your fears." But did he even have her to begin with? Had she not told him earlier that it was Hastings whom she wanted?

Kensworth walked toward the door and paused before he left. "Oh, and Olly…a few months ago during the ball that Mother held in honor of Father's birthday, I overheard him telling a friend how blessed his life was because he had been given a loving wife, three fantastic daughters, and *three* wonderful sons: myself, Robert through marriage, and you. He said he would always claim you because he loved you as if you were his own son. So don't think for one moment that Frank Turner is the only father you have had in this world."

An uncomfortable sting hit Oliver's eyes. It was completely unacceptable as a man to cry in front of one's friends. Therefore, Oliver choked back his feelings and grimaced. "You do realize that if the duke is claiming me as a son, that would make Elizabeth my sister? Definitely couldn't shackle myself to her, then."

Kensworth just shook his head and chuckled before leaving the room.

Chapter Thirty

"You're sure you're all right, dearest?" said Lady Hastings for the second time since Elizabeth had claimed a headache and the need to go lie down after dinner rather than participate in a round of charades as the dowager had suggested.

"Oh—quite well, I assure you. I think I simply spent a bit too much time in the sun today. I shall be well tomorrow." Elizabeth smiled sweetly at the dowager while trying to discreetly edge out of the dining room.

Everyone had finished eating and the ladies were all going to make their way into the drawing room and prepare for a game of charades, while the men retired to the library for port until everything was set up.

But Elizabeth had other plans.

Lord Hastings stepped close to Elizabeth, keeping his voice low. "Is something amiss, Lady Elizabeth? I cannot shake the feeling that there is something you're not telling me." This was the closest he had ever stood to her before. And although she didn't exactly feel flutters, she could acknowledge that she didn't feel revolted either. Perhaps that was a good sign.

"As I said before, it's only a slight headache."

He slightly narrowed his eyes. "I mean is something wrong *other* than the headache. You've seemed a bit…out of sorts during this whole stay. You're sure I haven't done something to upset you?" Well, he was upsetting her a bit at that moment.

She cast a brief glance around the room noticing that everyone seemed to be pretending to give them a moment of privacy but doing a poor job of it. Would it have killed him to simply walk her out into the hallway to have this personal conversation? Surely they could be trusted to be alone together for that length of time? But never mind that…she hadn't changed her mind about marrying him—especially after her little visit with Oliver earlier that day.

For a small moment, she had completely lost her head. Oliver had held her and looked at her differently and possibly even flirted with her. But that was the problem. Lately, he had seemed to think he could act in such a way with her, and then return to acting as nothing other than friends when others were around. She was exhausted from waiting around for him to wake up and realize she loved him.

But Elizabeth knew her moodiness and avoidance had not been fair to Lord Hastings. She did the only thing she could think of to encourage their relationship. "I can assure you, you have done nothing wrong…Wesley." His name felt odd on her lips. But it apparently sounded good to his ears because a warm smile spread across his face.

He bowed with his hands clasped behind his back—ever the proper gentleman—and gave her the space she needed to walk away. "Rest well, Elizabeth." Oh, dear. He had used her given name in return. Elizabeth felt as if she had just jumped off of a cliff and was plummeting toward her fate. Except she wasn't sure she had meant to. There was supposed to be a rope to grab hold of. Or a ladder. Or a ledge. But no, she was falling—arms and legs flailing in the air and nothing to do but drop.

Or…perhaps there was one last resort she hadn't considered before. A net all the way at the ground that would catch her at the last moment.

She smiled to herself and, before she left the dining room, Elizabeth made sure to catch Rose's eye—giving her a look that conveyed her need for Rose to follow her out.

Her sister-in-law smiled and looked to the dowager. "Please excuse me a moment. I'd like to make sure Elizabeth gets settled in her room, and then I shall join you all in the parlor for charades."

Charades.

Elizabeth turned a dripping sweet smile to her brother and spoke loud enough for the dowager to overhear. "Oh, Carver! You were just telling me how much you've missed playing charades! Perhaps the dowager has some fun costumes you might add to the performances as well?"

The dowager clapped, her face brightening like the sun. "What a splendid idea! Georgia, you and Tom go fetch the old trunk of hats and masks from the nursery!"

Unfortunately, Carver wasn't the only one throwing daggers at her over that idea. All three of Lord Hastings's younger siblings—especially his seventeen-year-old brother—looked as if they were wishing a carriage would run Elizabeth over at any moment.

Wesley, however, looked rather amused by the idea as if he sensed it was a prank directed at Carver. Perhaps he had a sense of humor buried under all that rigidity after all?

See. Marrying him wasn't going to be so terrible.

"How much do you trust me, Rose?" asked Elizabeth, shutting the door to her bedchamber after she pulled Rose inside. Elizabeth pressed her back to the door as if someone might bust in on them at any moment.

Rose eyed Elizabeth suspiciously. "Why are you asking me this?"

"Just answer the question."

"I don't give answers to questions before I know all of the facts," said Rose, crossing her arms stubbornly.

Elizabeth groaned. Now was not the time for her sister-in-law to be digging in her heels. "Very well. Do you trust me to not make a stupid decision?"

"No," Rose said flatly. "And I don't like the way this questioning is going, either."

Elizabeth gaped at Rose. "No? You don't trust me to not make a stupid decision?"

Rose blinked, unfazed. "You make rash decisions, Elizabeth. I love you, of course, but since you're asking, I feel the need to be blunt."

"When are you not blunt?"

Rose smiled. "When I'm pretending to like someone whom I don't truly care about." That was at least a little flattering. "Tell me what all this is about."

Elizabeth crossed her arms mimicking her sister-in-law's pose. "No. You've already admitted that you won't trust me, so I'm afraid I cannot include you on the details of my plan."

Rose groaned. "A plan? What sort of plan? I thought your plan was to get Lord Hastings to marry you? Which, by the way, *was* a rash decision but I've stood by you anyway."

"It was not rash. I've given it loads of thought. And it is still my plan. But I also have a separate plan. One not at all related to the first."

Rose raised an eyebrow.

"All I need from you is to know where Oliver's home is located."

Rose's face looked impervious to emotion. She stared at Elizabeth as if she was working out all of the possible scenarios that could include Elizabeth needing directions to Pembroke. "I feel another rash decision in the making," Rose finally said.

"Quite possibly." Nerves hummed through Elizabeth's stomach. "But if I don't do this, I'm afraid the question of *what if* will haunt me for the rest of my life."

Rose's whole demeanor softened. She still looked torn, but also as if she suddenly understood. And since Rose had been begging Elizabeth to tell Oliver of her feelings since the beginning, she figured her sister-in-law would be willing to help. She was right. "It just so happens that your brother went to visit Pembroke earlier and he told me how to get there in the event there was an emergency while he was gone."

Elizabeth smiled, her nerves taking flight in her stomach again. "Truly? And you'll tell me where it is?"

Rose nodded and smiled. "But I don't wish to know anything else about what you're planning. I'd like to be completely ignorant to the whole scheme in case you bungle it and blame gets tossed in my lap."

"Deal."

A few minutes later, Rose was leaving Elizabeth's room after having relayed thorough directions to Pembroke. Elizabeth watched as Rose disappeared down the long hallway and then she waited, listening for any other approaching footsteps before she left her room and headed in the direction of the family's wing of bedchambers.

Chapter Thirty-One

Oliver had just settled into a chair and extended his boots toward the warmth when he heard a rider approaching the house. He glanced at the clock on the mantel and saw that it was after eleven: much too late for a casual visit. His heart picked up speed thinking that it might be Kensworth coming to inform him that someone had died.

Or worse: that Elizabeth was engaged.

He shot from his chair and peered out the window. Oh, not Kensworth. There was a young man dismounting from a horse and tying it up to the post outside the house. Oliver wasn't sure whether that sight was supposed to make him more or less anxious.

Oliver opened the front door of the home and called out a quick, hesitant greeting, waiting for the young man to climb the steps. When he reached the top, the gangly young buck peeked up from under his hat. Oliver blinked rapidly at the blue eyes, as incandescent as illuminated sapphires, staring back at him. "Elizabeth?" he asked in a loud whisper.

She grinned. "Dashing fellow, aren't I?"

Without saying another word, Oliver took hold of Elizabeth's elbow and guided her quickly into the study. He shut the door behind them, his hand on the knob and his back to the door, fearful that his maid might discover Elizabeth and think—well, what would she think, exactly? Elizabeth was dressed like a young gentleman. A young gentleman who had no idea how to tie a cravat.

Her hair was tucked up inside the hat on her head and the jacket she wore looked a little too big for her shoulders. The breeches—hang him, Lizzie was wearing breeches—were form fitting to every single one of her womanly curves. No one would ever take a look at that figure and believe she was a boy. He had known her to pull some ridiculous stunts in her time but this was by far the most absurd. Still, why couldn't he keep from grinning?

"I'm not even sure where to start," he said, still taking in this new ensemble and shaking his head.

Her eyes were bright with a twinkle of mischief. The twinkle that had stolen his heart several years ago. He had a bad feeling it was going to get him in trouble somehow that night as well. "I will now and for always be jealous of you men and your breeches." She took a few long, exaggerated steps and then thrust her hands in the pockets. "I had no idea what I was missing! So functional."

He couldn't help but chuckle. "Lizzie, please tell me you stole these clothes and there is not some poor chap somewhere wearing your dress."

A triumphant smile marked her mouth. "I stole them from Wesley's brother's bedchamber when he was downstairs." Her statement, however, only served to remind Oliver that Elizabeth was on an intimate name basis with Hastings and that, if word got around about this little adventure of hers, it would effectively end the relationship she was hoping to gain with the viscount. Why was she even there? Had she not earlier that day proclaimed that their friendship was officially over as they knew it?

Which is why his smile dropped and his words came out clipped. "What are you doing here, Lizzie?"

Her eyes darted away and she bit the corner of her bottom lip. "I like these pockets. I feel as though I could fit so many things in them. What do you carry in your pockets?"

The fire crackled and she stopped to inspect it while moving her hands around anxiously in her newfound pockets. Something was amiss. Why was she there? Why was she nervous?

"Did something happen with Hastings?" he asked, jumping to conclusions and already mentally running the man through if he had hurt Elizabeth in any way. His mind told him to stay put by the door—far away from this unpredictable, anxious Elizabeth—but his feet had other ideas. That was nothing new. His feet were forever disobeying him.

"No," she shook her head, not meeting his eyes until he stopped right beside her. Her eyes flicked up to his—something lurking he couldn't put his finger on.

He guided her shoulders to face him and then began assessing her silly cravat. "You simply felt like dressing up and proving to me that you are good at many things—but tying a neck linen is not one of them?" He smiled, hoping to set her a little at ease. Something about her looked like a spooked animal, caught in between the moment of escape or attack.

She blinked a little faster than normal. "I thought I did a rather admirable job of tying this knot." She patted the wilted, pathetic neckcloth.

"It's a catastrophe." He should be prodding her for answers. No. He should be telling her to leave. "Here," he untied it and began forming a new knot, never thinking the action was too intimate until he heard Elizabeth's breath tremble. His eyes moved up to meet hers and found her staring at him in a way that ignited a fierce desire in his chest. One he'd been smothering and holding dormant for so long. He was losing the fight.

"Why are you here, Lizzie?" he asked again, his fingers stilled against the cream fabric at her neck. She seemed frozen. "I'll ask you again. Did something happen with Lord Hastings?"

"No, but something will soon."

His brows drew together. "What *exactly* do you mean by that?"

Clearly they did not share the same understanding of the word *something.*

A shaky breath fell from her parted lips. "He's going to propose tomorrow. There's no doubt in my mind. And"—there was so much tension built up around Elizabeth. It was getting to Oliver too, making him feel as jumpy as she looked—"after he proposes. He will...kiss me. I've never been kissed before."

"And?" he managed to mutter despite the fact that all of the air had been snatched from the room.

"And so...I came here hoping that just maybe...you would teach me." Shock ripped through him.

Oliver's hands dropped from the linen and he took one wide, *very wide*, step away from Elizabeth. Brows pinching together, he turned a half step away from her, facing the fire and scraping his hands over his face. He groaned into his palms half disbelieving and half angry at what he was hearing.

"Oliver—"

"Let me get this straight," he dropped his hands and turned narrowed eyes at the woman who still looked much too beautiful dressed in a hat and gentleman's jacket. "You stole a pair of breeches, recklessly rode on horseback through the night to my home, risked your reputation and your relationship with Hastings—to ask me to prepare you for a kiss with your future husband?"

She blinked her wide blue eyes at him. "My *first* kiss," she said as if it made all of this in any way more acceptable.

He wanted to groan again from the injustice of it all. Not only was he going to have to live without the woman he loved for the rest of his life, but he was going to know exactly what it would feel like to hold her and kiss her before he had to hand her off to another man.

No, correction: he *wasn't* going to know those things because *he wasn't* going to kiss her.

"Lizzie, you do realize that if I do what you ask, it would no longer be your first kiss when"—he could barely bring himself to say it— "Hastings kisses you." If word ever got back to the viscount, Oliver would certainly be called out to meet the man at dawn.

Actually, no he wouldn't…because he *wasn't* going to kiss her!

Elizabeth cleared her throat and tucked a finger into her cravat in attempt to loosen it. The sight drew an unamused laugh from Oliver because he knew the suffocating feeling she was experiencing all too well.

"I realize that," she said. "But…I'm comfortable with that outcome."

"You are?" his words came out strangled. "Why?"

She swallowed, clearly as unnerved by this whole situation as he was. And then her eyes met his, lit by the firelight and conveying an unspoken message in that wordless language of theirs. "Because, in a strange way, I feel that my first kiss belongs to you anyway." It was official, he couldn't breathe and might never again. He couldn't move. And he was almost certain his heart had stopped. The tension between them felt strong and terrifying.

Had she just…declared herself to him? Did Elizabeth love him as much as he loved her?

Fear gripped him. Strangled his thoughts. Oh, how much he wanted Elizabeth. He wanted her smiles and her laughter and spirited joy for the rest of his days. But so much of him was terrified that one day he would snap. One day he would break and he would wake up with the same temper his father had. That he would be every bit as worthless as Frank Turner.

"Elizabeth…I don't think I can do this for you."

He watched her eyes close, pressing shut against his rejection. She deserved to know that he wasn't rejecting her, but himself. But he knew that if he told her the truth, she would deny it. She would believe in his goodness of character as she always did and convince him of something that could be harmful to her in the end. He wouldn't do that.

Her eyes shot open again, an angry blue fire glowing within them. "Fine." She thrust her hands in her pockets as if she had been doing it her whole life. She jerked her shoulders up and down in a violent shrug. "If you're not up to the task, then just forget it. I thought you were supposed to be the most fantastic kisser in London but I suppose I was mistaken. I'll find someone else to help me." Her statements, each one more ridiculous than the last, were almost too much for him. And something about the way her cheeks flamed when she was angry never ceased to grip him with attraction.

"First of all, I am a fantastic kisser, so you weren't wrong to come to me. Second, where are you going to find someone else to tutor you in the middle of the country before tomorrow?"

"Anywhere."

"Anywhere? Oh, in the pasture perhaps?"

"Perhaps!"

"Or in a tavern? That's an idea. You could simply pop in and ask a parlor full of men which one would like to kiss you." His animated suggestions were making fumes all but pour out of Elizabeth's ears.

"I'm sure someone would oblige me."

"Oh, I'm certain they would." He was smiling at her ridiculousness. Elizabeth was a bit wild but she wasn't stupid. And finding a complete stranger in a tavern and asking him to kiss her was not something she would do.

Although, the competitive smile she was suddenly giving him made his stomach sink. "Do you know, that's actually given me a wonderful idea." She lifted her chin slightly.

"Oh?"

"Wesley has any number of young strapping footmen. I will simply ask one of them. I daresay someone would be helpful enough to educate me," she said, glaring at him and beginning to walk in his direction toward the door.

Educate her? Oh, he bet they would…

Oliver reached out and grabbed her arm to stop her before she passed. He sighed as they both looked down to where his hand was holding her arm softly. "No, you will not ask anyone else."

"I won't?" Her voice was soft as velvet now.

"No." He met her eyes and swallowed. "I'm going to teach you."

Chapter Thirty-Two

Elizabeth's heart was galloping in her chest. Oliver was going to do it. He was going to kiss her.

Her legs felt weak and she was slightly worried that she might faint before he ever got the chance. This was madness and Elizabeth knew it. But—it was important. She needed this. She needed for Oliver to kiss her now, before it was too late, or else she would wonder for the rest of her life what it would be like.

Yes, inventing a ridiculous story about needing him to teach her because she was too nervous to go into a kiss with Hastings uneducated was complete lunacy. But it was safe. And it gave her a reason to kiss him without having to lay her heart on the line. It also gave him a chance—one last chance—to admit his feelings if he harbored any for her.

Elizabeth's eyes met Oliver's intense dark blue gaze and her legs shook again. His eyes roamed over her face as if contemplating how to proceed. She turned to fully face him, hoping to push past the awkwardness of their decision and get on with it.

"All right. Thank you," she said squaring her shoulders to him and running her eyes briefly over the thin layer of shirt that draped over his muscular shoulders.

He looked down and rolled up his sleeves, exposing his forearms and making her mouth go dry. Was he preparing for a boxing tournament? Why was he doing that? And how did the man manage to make comfortable look so very attractive?

Yes, she'd seen him like this dozens of times over the past ten years. He and Carver always played cricket without their jackets. And then there was the time that her brother and Oliver had shed their jackets and cravats and jumped into the lake together. She'd never been able to shake the memory of how he looked rising up out of the water. But all of those times had been much different from this one, and Elizabeth was painfully aware of it.

"Go ahead, then," she said hastily, her nerves practically pinching her skin. Would he just kiss her already?

The tension that had marked his face since she had first stepped foot in that room fell away and a playful smirk took its place. He took a small step closer and nodded toward her head. "I'm afraid I'm not quite comfortable kissing a gentleman."

"Oh…right," she said, suddenly remembering how she was dressed. She looked down, knowing there wasn't much she could do about that now. Oh! But, her hat. She lifted it off her head, feeling her hair fall in long wild coils around her shoulders. She tossed the hat onto a chair and looked back to Oliver. "Better?" she asked, wishing her voice wouldn't crack.

"Much better," he said in a husky tone.

Elizabeth watched as Oliver's eyes traced her hair. Now *he* looked nervous. Oliver, the biggest flirt in London, looked nervous to kiss her. A small smile grew on her lips at the thought.

His jaw flexed and he turned away, his hands clenched at his sides in a way that made Elizabeth think maybe he was going to decline the kiss after all. He paced away, energy and tension coursing through him, before he turned around and started pacing to her in fast strides. Her breath caught at the sudden determination and wildness of his eyes. They were kindling, and made her feel the need to take a few steps backward. He followed her—simultaneously advancing her back and back and back until she bumped into the wall behind her.

Oliver stopped too, so close she could smell him and see shadows on his jaw and the lines his hands had taken to push through his sandy hair. He lifted his hand and rested it on the wall behind her, making her feel trapped in the most wonderful of ways. No—not trapped, safe.

Elizabeth's heart raced faster and her breath was falling out in shaky waves that, quite frankly, embarrassed her. But she wanted this kiss more than anything. She lifted her eyes to his. His stormy gaze held hers and the way he smelled and looked and how the air felt stiflingly warm around her all overwhelmed her senses.

This was her Oliver. Her best friend. But the way he was looking at her just then was unlike any look she'd experienced from him before, and somehow, she knew that he didn't see her as a friend any more than she saw him as one.

His eyes fell to her lips. "A true gentleman will be mindfully considerate of a lady's first kiss." She swallowed. Apparently the lesson was beginning. Elizabeth pressed her hand to her stomach in attempt to still the fluttering. "He will be slow and deliberate in his movements to make sure to give the lady plenty of time to deny the kiss." Elizabeth watched and tried to remember to breathe as Oliver began to drop his head to her level. True to his word, moving slowly— achingly slow. "If...a kiss is what you want, this is where you will need to give him an indication that the contact would be welcome."

Before she had time to overthink it, she felt her eager hand raise up to rest on his chest. She could feel the strength of his muscles and his heart, beating every bit as quickly as hers. His gaze lowered to look at her hand pressing against him before he looked back up at her. He dropped his hand from the wall to slowly slide it into the back of her hair, flooding heat from the top of her head down to her toes. Elizabeth closed her eyes and allowed herself to memorize everything about the moment in a way that she knew would likely haunt her with pain later.

With her eyes still closed, she felt his breath on her lips, the scent of mint lingering in the air between them. "Lizzie, are you sure you want this?" he said in a whisper.

She didn't open her eyes, just nodded.

"Then I'll kiss you now."

And then his lips pressed into hers, light and warm and soft and everything she imagined they would be. She could feel the slight scruff of his facial hair and barely taste the flavor of mint. In that moment, she couldn't move. She was frozen—a stone statue, engraved with the words, *"Hopelessly devoted to Oliver Turner."* Now and forevermore she would be a permanent fixture in his home. Never would she leave. This was where she belonged.

Except, her stone cracked and life fluttered within her as Oliver's mouth slowly and delicately slid across hers, coaxing her lips to move with his in a graceful dance. Elizabeth had never felt so loved or protected. Sharing this with him was both familiar and comfortable, but also completely unnerving and electric. She had never experienced anything like it in all the world. Embroidery was forgotten; kissing Oliver would be her new hobby.

All too soon, he paused and pulled away, lingering only a breath from her mouth. "There," he said, his voice gravelly and restrained.

But no. She wasn't ready for that to be it. If this was going to be the only time she ever got to feel Oliver's lips against hers, she was going to make it count.

Elizabeth's eyes opened and she slid her hand up his chest, over his shoulders to the back of his neck, taking a moment to appreciate the corded muscles she felt there. She took a small step away from the wall to close the distance between them. Oliver's brows pulled together and he looked more unsure now than ever. She raised her other arm to wrap around the other side of his neck, and lifted up onto her tiptoes to reach his mouth again. She took in his guarded expression before closing her eyes and pressing her mouth to his for another soft kiss.

His lips wouldn't move, but she wasn't deterred. She knew that Oliver wanted this kiss as much as she did. She could sense it. Her mouth silently begged him to respond. To show that whatever was between them—wasn't only in her imagination. But he wouldn't move. His hands hung at his sides and his mouth, unmoving.

She broke away and looked at him. His eyes were still open and he looked—fearful. As if he were restraining himself with everything he had.

"Oliver," she said, moving a hand to rest on his jaw. "Kiss me."

His eyes bounced between hers, a debate running through them, and then his hands grabbed her waist and pulled her to him and he kissed her. *Really* kissed her. Passion and fervency wrapped around her in the form of his arms, tightly encircling her waist as his mouth moved with hers. They both conveyed all of the tension and feeling and heat that had never been spoken between them. Elizabeth tightened her arms around him in return, relishing the feel of being held firmly within his strong arms and wishing he wouldn't ever let her go.

He broke away, breathless, gripping the back of the jacket she was wearing. "Elizabeth," he sighed, a look of utter pain etched in his face.

Elizabeth's heart dropped. He was still holding her, but she could feel him emotionally moving away. His blue eyes looked into hers, trying to say something, but unwilling to actually voice it. "That shouldn't have happened."

Pain pushed through Elizabeth like a knife. "What do you mean?" she asked, blinking back tears.

He let go of her and backed away. Elizabeth wanted to reach out and grab him, pull him back, beg him to love her as she had been so certain only a moment ago he did. There was more between them than simply friendship, she knew that now. But why Oliver was still pushing her away, she didn't understand.

Elizabeth watched him continue to back away from her, looking at her as if she were something he had just broken but could not put back together. "I'm sorry. You need to leave right now."

Elizabeth felt like anger and embarrassment and hopelessness all at once. She looked down to her boots as mortification swept over her. What had been the most wonderful moment of her life was quickly becoming the worst.

Her heart was throbbing in her chest as she pushed away from the wall and past Oliver. She sailed through the foyer, feeling her unruly curls bounce around her face and shoulders, and moved as fast as her legs would allow until she was out the front door. She heard Oliver's footsteps behind her but she didn't stop or look back. Hot tears rushed down her cheeks and everything felt terribly wrong. Embarrassment clung to her like skin and she wanted to claw it off.

"Lizzie, you cannot ride back alone. Wait for me to fetch my horse and—"

"Leave me alone, Oliver. I can manage on my own," she yelled over her shoulder, feeling something snap inside of her.

"I'm sorry I hurt you, Lizzie. That's the last thing in the world I wanted to happen. It's why…" his words trailed off.

Elizabeth placed her right foot in the horse's stirrup and mounted. She looked down at Oliver's face for what she somehow knew would be the last time as an unmarried woman. She wiped her tears and forced her breath to be steady. "This is goodbye, Oliver."

His lips pressed together—still red from their stolen kiss—and his brows creased deeply. He shoved his hand through his hair and looked as if he wanted to speak what was on his mind, but some emotion was holding it prisoner. He shut his eyes. "Goodbye, Lizzie."

Chapter Thirty-Three

The golden sun was resting on the horizon and Elizabeth watched the rest of its ascent with a wool shawl wrapped around her arms. She hadn't been able to sleep after leaving Oliver. Hadn't even bothered trying. Instead, she had changed into a dress, taken up her shawl, and mindlessly made her way to the garden outside of Addington Hall where she'd sat down on a bench and stared numbly into the sky until it went from black to pink to orange.

Everything hurt. How was it possible for her body to physically ache when it was only her heart that had been broken?

The sound of gravel crunching nearby shook Elizabeth from her numb trance. It was officially morning. She turned her head down the path of the garden and saw Wesley approaching. He was dressed in a deep green jacket and tan waistcoat. A soft smile on his mouth. Somehow his smile only made her ache more.

He was a good man, and he was handsome, and he was kind, but she didn't love him. She was terrified that she never would.

"Good morning," he said as he came to stand in front of her. He bowed slightly and she offered the warmest smile she could muster. "May I?" He gestured toward the bench.

"Of course." Elizabeth's voice came out hoarse and she hoped

Wesley would not know it was because she had spent the entire night crying on that bench. What must she look like at that moment?

"Couldn't sleep?" he asked as he sat down beside her. She almost couldn't believe he was willing to have this small clandestine meeting with her.

She swallowed, afraid that her pain would bubble over again. She shook her head mutely.

He nodded and looked out toward the garden. It was a lovely garden. Very well maintained with lots of different species of flowers. And the water fountain in the middle of the garden was nice as well. It would have made some lady very happy...

"Elizabeth," said Wesley in a different tone. One that was more nervous and hesitant than she'd heard from him yet. Perhaps it was because he was sitting alone with her in a garden? She imagined he thought this a very scandalous tête-à-tête. "I believe you are aware of my feelings toward you."

Elizabeth forced herself to breathe. This was it. This was the moment she had been working toward since she stepped foot in London. Only...it didn't feel at all like she had hoped or imagined.

"Yes—I believe I am," she said, not willing to meet his eyes. It felt wrong. It all felt so wrong. Especially given her feelings toward Oliver and the kiss that she could still taste on her lips.

"And I am aware of your feelings toward me," said Wesley, causing Elizabeth's eyes to shoot to him. He smiled weakly. "Or—I should say, your lack of feelings for me."

"Wesley—"

He held up his hand. "You have nothing to defend. I only brought it up to say that I think I understand the situation between you and...Mr. Turner." How did he know? Were her feelings that evident?

She hurried to interject, "There is no future between myself and Mr. Turner." The words stung but they were true.

He nodded. "I know that as well. Which is why I wanted to make my intentions clear from the beginning. Elizabeth, I'm very fond of you. I hold you in great esteem and I would be honored to have you as my wife." She felt tears prickling her eyes for countless reasons. "I am under no illusions that I hold your heart, or that it does not belong to Oliver Turner. However…" that however gave her hope somehow. "I believe that you and I would deal amiably together."

He turned to face her, his knees brushing against hers. She looked down, noting the close contact they had never shared before. He continued, "My hope is that over time, we can develop a trusting friendship that could grow into love. I know that I can be too serious and strict—a fault that I believe you will help remedy within me." She smiled as he smiled. And then he reached up and lightly touched her face. "I'm not sure why you and Mr. Turner's futures do not coincide, but I cannot say that I'm not thankful for it. Because, Elizabeth, I truly do wish for you to be mine. To be with me now and always. And I hope that you will say yes and become my wife."

He wanted her now and always.

Elizabeth watched with shaky breath as Wesley tilted his head down and brushed a soft kiss over her lips. She closed her eyes and focused on him. On the warmth of his hand on her face. On the caring words he uttered. On the future she could have with him—a man who wanted her.

A tear escaped the corner of her eye and Wesley pulled away slowly, still holding her face gently in his hand. He was a good man. That he would be good to her, Elizabeth was certain.

His kiss had not evoked butterflies or breathlessness, but it was sweet and secure. Elizabeth took in a purifying breath and smiled. "Yes, Wesley. I would be honored to become your wife."

Oliver's eyes swept over the letter from Kensworth for the tenth time, but the words did not hurt any less than the first time he had read them.

Elizabeth and Lord Hastings are to be married on the first of April. The contracts have been signed and everything has been finalized. I know it will be difficult, but I beg you attend the ceremony.

It went on to state that the ceremony would be held in Hastings's parish. That meant in one week, Elizabeth would be married. In one week, Elizabeth would start a new life—one without him.

Anger coursed through Oliver's veins. He crushed up the parchment and threw it at the wall. He'd spent three weeks in that cursed house. No matter how much sunlight was let in, it still felt dark. But what did it matter if he enjoyed living there or not? He imagined anywhere he lived without Elizabeth would feel dark and empty, too.

Except now he was going to have to live in a home that neighbored the one housing the woman he loved, but could never have, for the rest of his life. It was pathetic. He could have simply gone back to London and finally taken up residence in the townhouse he had inherited. However, he couldn't bring himself to leave knowing Lizzie was still nearby. He hadn't seen her once since the night they had kissed, but there was a quiet comfort in knowing she was still near him. Is this how he would spend the rest of his life? Slowly torturing himself in a house he despised, and living in close proximity to a woman he loved more than his breath but could not have.

You could have her.

But, no. He knew it was better that she had chosen Hastings.

It was better.

Chapter Thirty-Four

"My darling girl, how beautiful you look!" said Mama as she handed Elizabeth a small bouquet of flowers.

Elizabeth looked down at her pale pink gown and ran her hand across the bodice, trying to soothe her nerves. It was her wedding day. It was a time to be happy and joyous. Not to feel like sobbing. And yet…

"Is Kate feeling any better?" asked Elizabeth.

Mama and Papa and Kate had all finally overcome each of their illnesses just in time to spend a few days before the wedding with Elizabeth and Wesley's family at Addington Hall. Having them there made a place that felt looming and uncomfortable a little more like home. Papa's laughter boomed through the walls, and Kate had tiptoed into her room almost every night to slide under the covers and gossip until the early morning hours.

And although Wesley had unfortunately been forced to spend the last two weeks in London tending to business before they wed and went off on a wedding trip, Elizabeth had begun to picture her future there. It wasn't exciting or unpredictable—but it felt sure and certain and it gave her hope. Her heart would mend. She would have a family. A home. She would be happy.

She *would* be.

And she would be even happier when she learned to keep her mind from straying to Oliver and that last night they shared together. It hurt more than she ever thought possible to think back on that kiss. The kiss she was afraid would haunt her dreams for the rest of her life. But still, she didn't regret it. She didn't think she ever would.

It was a cruel form of torture knowing that Oliver was so close. Carver had told her that Oliver had decided to keep Pembroke, something that made no sense to Elizabeth. Why would he live somewhere he despised? Honestly, she wished he would sell. She feared that he would continue to pop up at unexpected times in her life and wreck any sort of intimacy she might gain with Wesley. And yet, despite the fact that seeing him would twist her with pain, part of her hoped that she would spot him in the back of the chapel later that day. He was her best friend. It was going to hurt to not have him there.

"I'm afraid Kate is still not feeling well this morning," said Mama, clasping Elizabeth's hands in her own. Elizabeth looked up into Mama's light blue eyes, the ones that most closely resembled her own. "I'm afraid she's relapsing. She won't be able to attend the ceremony. I'm so sorry, darling."

"Oh." Elizabeth's eyes dropped to Mama's hands. "Well, that's all right. Shall I go in and see her before we leave for the chapel?"

"No, love." Mama smiled softly and squeezed Elizabeth's hands. "We cannot risk you catching whatever it is Kate has before your wedding trip."

Wedding trip.

Elizabeth sighed. "No, we wouldn't want that."

Mama frowned. "Darling…are you quite sure that—"

Elizabeth cleared her throat to muffle Mama's words. "I think we should be going now, don't you? I don't think it's exactly polite for the bride to be late to her own ceremony."

A tight smile pulled at Mama's mouth. "Of course. Let us make our way toward the carriage."

At that moment, Papa stepped into the room, sunshine from the window glinting off of his silver hair. His smile was wide and full just like she remembered seeing it everyday since she was a girl. She paused, looking hesitantly to Papa. "Well? How do I look?"

His eyes glistened as he stepped forward and wrapped her up in a tight hug. "You look more beautiful than ever, my darling." Elizabeth had to shut her eyes tightly to keep from crying. Refraining from crying seemed to be all she ever did these days.

He pulled away, but held on to her shoulders, his grey eyes searching hers. "Elizabeth, my wonderful darling daughter. I hope you know how very proud I am of you." He paused and took a deep breath, his face changing into something deeper. "You, my little love, have always been my heart and my adventure. Ever since the day you were born, you have inspired me to run instead of walk. To laugh in the face of difficulty. I know you have always seen yourself as young and unrefined but, my dear Lizzie, I hope you know that your courage has sparked more life and hope in our family than anyone else ever could dream." Elizabeth pressed her lips together, no longer winning the struggle against her tears. "Never settle, my love. Never stop daring. Dreaming. Living. And my hope for you today is that this will be just the beginning of the adventures yet to come in your life."

Elizabeth's tears continued to roll down her cheeks as Papa's words settled deep within her heart. Her mind flashed to she and Oliver splashing through streams, laughing, racing their horses across the meadow, reading books together under the oak tree, whispering together in the closet. And the fire in his eyes before he had kissed her.

Papa's large weathered hands cupped her face and he wiped her tears with his thumbs. Mama came to stand beside them, placing a hand on her back.

In that moment, it was clear to her that Papa was not picturing Wesley in the future he was hoping for her.

"You do not want for me to marry Wesley, do you Papa?"

He smiled. "I want nothing more than for you to be happy, my Lizzie."

She knew what he meant. And she knew that she had to be honest with him. "Oliver does not love me." The words fell out of her mouth, but he didn't look the least surprised to hear them.

"Do you know that for certain?"

Elizabeth took in a breath as her mind raced back over every inter-action they'd shared since she came to London. No. She didn't know for certain because she had been too scared to ask him or tell him how she felt.

"No—but when I told him that Wesley was going to propose, he didn't object."

Mama put her hand on Elizabeth's back. "Oliver has always put your needs before his, ever since he began visiting Dalton Park. Are you sure he didn't think this was what *you* wanted most?"

Elizabeth's hands flew up to cover her face. Had she made a mistake? Yes. How had she not simply told Oliver how she felt, putting aside her fear of rejection, and lived? Now, it was her wedding day and it was too late. She had promised herself to a man who she could never love.

"Elizabeth," said Mama, in her kind voice. "It's time to make a decision. What do you want to do?"

"Is it not too late for choices?"

Mama smiled. "It's never too late, darling."

She took a moment to think. What did she want? If she risked everything and went to Oliver, only to find out he did not love her, would it be worth it? Could she risk her vulnerability? Could she risk a future she knew for certain Wesley could give her?

Her answer was clear.

"Take me to the chapel. Wesley is waiting."

Chapter Thirty-Five

O liver slammed the shovel deeper into the dirt. He wasn't digging anything in particular, he just could no longer sit inside that blasted house and watch the minutes tick by knowing that within the hour, Elizabeth would become Lady Hastings. It was agony.

He thrust the point of the shovel into the hole he had been digging for the last hour. Maybe this would become a garden when he was finished. Or just a place to bury his heart. *Blast.* Even he found himself unbearable in this blue deviled state.

"Oliver!"

He froze with his hand on the shovel at the sound of a familiar female voice. He turned around. "Kate?" He squinted in the direction of Elizabeth's younger sister running toward him from a carriage waiting at the road.

He dropped his shovel and moved to meet her with quick strides. "Kate. What's wrong?" said Oliver, his panic evident in his tone.

She stopped in front of him and smacked him hard across the arm. "*You* are what's wrong!"

"Ow!" he rubbed his hand over his shoulder and scowled at the youngest member of the Ashburn Family. Goodness, she had grown since last he saw her. Although her sudden maturity did not make his heart quake in the way that Elizabeth had all those years ago. "What was that for?"

"For being a dolt! Now, fetch your jacket and let's go!" Her blue eyes, almost the same shade as Elizabeth's, flashed angrily at him. Kate was like Mary and Elizabeth mixed up into one dramatic woman. She was a bit frightening, just then.

He shook his head. "What are you talking about?"

She stepped up to him as if she were as big as her brother and attempting to tower over him. "We are not fools, Oliver. You love Elizabeth and you are meant for each other. But because of some unknown reason you are being a fool and you are going to lose her!"

His heart began to race, but all he could think to say was, "Do your parents know you are here? Shouldn't you be at the chapel?"

She rolled her eyes, completely exasperated with him. "They believe I'm ill again and resting in bed. I waited as long as I could for you to make up your mind to come after Elizabeth on your own. But, since that didn't happen, I knew I needed to light a fire under you."

"Kate, you shouldn't have come."

"No, I shouldn't have *had* to come. You love Elizabeth. I know it. Everyone knows it. You should have come after her on your own. Now come on, fetch your jacket and let's get in the carriage."

"And then what will we do?" he asked, feeling like his mind was not catching up fast enough.

"And then you will stop the wedding and tell Elizabeth that you've been very, *very* stupid and you want her to marry you, not Lord Hastings!" Stop the wedding? No, no, no. He couldn't do that. Could he?

He shook his head, beginning to pace. He could feel his resolve dropping. Oliver's eyes drifted back toward Pembroke. His fear was still present, still lurking and taunting him, but his desire to have everything he always wanted, to love Elizabeth now and for always, was beginning to overcome it.

"My blood runs through your veins. One day you'll be just like me, and my father before me, and his father before him. We Turners are all the same and there's no use pretending you're any different."

He shut his eyes as memories of his father mixed with joyful summers at Dalton Park.

"Oliver!" Kate's voice cut through the air.

He opened his eyes.

She put her hand on his arm. "If you don't go now you're going to lose Elizabeth forever. Is giving in to whatever it is you're afraid of worth that price?"

"I don't know what to do, Kate. I love Elizabeth, but I'm terrified I won't be enough for her."

Kate's brows creased. "You already are enough for her, Oliver. Don't you see that? No one knows her like you do. No one has ever made her smile or laugh as you do. And I'm confident Lord Hastings certainly never will."

"But what if—"

"It's time to stop asking what if. Live your life now, don't wait to see what happens later. You'll miss it if you do."

An incredulous short laugh fell out of his mouth and he dashed his hand through his hair. "When did you learn to talk like this?"

She shrugged with a grin. "I read a lot of romance books."

"Too many."

"There's no such thing."

"Kate," he said, letting his face grow serious again, "has Elizabeth told you all of this?"

"She didn't have to. It's written across her face every time she looks at you—it always has been."

Oliver pressed his lips together and ran his hand along the back of his neck. Kate was right—something he never thought he would think.

His hurts and his fears had been keeping him from living the life he wanted. It was time to let go of those things. It was time to trust himself and let go of his father.

"We'd better hurry if we are going to stop that wedding," Oliver said, watching a smile beam over Kate's face.

Oliver and Kate stood shoulder to shoulder overlooking the empty chapel. "I'm sorry, you just missed them. The bride and groom left together about a quarter of an hour ago," said an older man sweeping the floors at the other end of the small chapel.

Oliver thought his legs might give out. In fact, they did. He grabbed hold of a pew and sat down. Kate moved to put her hand on his shoulder as he dropped his face into his hands. "She's gone. I'm too late," he said.

Kate stayed quiet but kept her hand on his shoulder in silent support. After several minutes, she said, "I'm so sorry, Oliver. I really thought we would make it in time."

"How am I going to move on now, Kate? How am I going to spend every day for the rest of my life without her?" The weight of the consequences of his decision fell on him like boulders. He felt sick.

"I don't know, Oliver. Hopefully, in time…" her words trailed off. Apparently she knew how unhelpful they were. "Come on. Let's at least get out of here."

He nodded and stood, all too ready to get away from the chapel. And there was no way he was going to live in that blasted house a day longer. Living as Elizabeth's—Lady Hastings's—neighbor would be nothing but torture.

Oliver had the carriage stop before Addington Hall could come into view. He was making sure Kate returned to her family safely, but his heart could not take facing the happy couple. "I'll walk back to Pembroke from here."

"Are you sure?"

"Quite."

Kate didn't argue. She knew the pain he was facing.

Oliver stepped out of the carriage and raised his hand to Kate as the carriage pulled off.

Oliver's feet took him not to the house, but to the tree where he had untangled Elizabeth's hair. He could still picture her standing there, both helpless and defiant as he lingered, taking as long as possible to unwind her hair from the branch. His pain and guilt wrapped around him like a straight jacket. Elizabeth—his best friend in the world—was married. The love of his life was married to another man. His mind didn't want to believe it, and he wasn't sure what he would do now.

Oliver walked to the trunk of the tree and rested his back against the jagged wood. His heart felt beaten and singed. Elizabeth was gone. His mother was gone. Kensworth was married and no longer needed him like he once had. And his father had left the earth without ever seeking any sort of reconciliation.

Emptiness flooded Oliver.

He was given a chance to love Elizabeth and had lost it. He had let his father's words define him and control him to the point of losing himself. He had lost everything that mattered most to him. His back slid down the tree as he found his way to the ground. Unable to control his pain any longer, Oliver put his face in his hands and wept. He wept for what he'd lost, he wept for what he wanted, he wept for the choices he should have made but didn't.

He felt himself unraveling. The frayed edges of his life would hold no more and he seemed unable to control their confusion. But, in the midst of their breakdown, he recognized something else, too. A memory arose from within, awakening his senses and drawing from him a smile amidst the pain. Possibly even healing.

Chapter Thirty-Six

"Hello, darling. Are you hurt?" Oliver asked, carefully approaching little Lady Elizabeth holding the bloody cut on her arm. Oliver had only seen glimpses of the girl since he had arrived at Dalton Park two days ago. He knew she had been curious about him, perched as she had been on the stairs and looking down with a hesitancy marking her face. He had smiled at her that day, hoping she would know she would be safe around him.

"Yes…" said Lady Elizabeth, casting a glance to the large bleeding cut on her arm.

He stepped closer, careful to move slowly and not spook her. Kenny had run off with Lady Mary and his neighbor, Miss Claire, to hide somewhere in the forest. Oliver had been seeking them when he had come across Lady Elizabeth. "May I see your cut?" he asked, kneeling down beside her.

She nodded and extended her small arm toward him. He knew from Kenny that the girl was only ten. But she was so petite he thought she looked even younger. He gently assessed the cut and knew immediately from the way it was bleeding that it was going to need stitching. But he was not going to be the one to break the news to the girl.

"This looks painful. How did you manage to claim this impressive scrape?"

She smiled guiltily and looked up above her head. "I jumped down from the tree. A limb caught my arm on my way down."

"I see," said Oliver, untying his cravat from around his neck. "Well, my dear, you must be more careful in the future." He began tying his linen around her arm to contain the blood until he could get her back to the duchess.

"Why?" she asked, her big bright blue eyes shining up at him.

Oliver couldn't help but laugh. "What do you mean, why? We must all be careful on adventures so we don't get hurt."

She gave a small pout. "You sound like Miss Emma."

"Miss Emma sounds smart."

"She's boring."

Again, he found himself smiling at the girl. "Boring perhaps, but also safe."

Lady Elizabeth made a thinking noise as he finished off the bandage by tying a little bow. He felt proud of himself for how well he'd cared for the girl. He wished Mama could see him in that moment, and the thought filled Oliver with an ache.

"I don't want to be safe. I want to be wild like a fox."

"Hmm. Even if being a wild fox gets you more bloody scrapes such as this one?"

She smiled and stood, dusting off her skirts with her small hands. "Scrapes always heal. Even the bad ones."

Oliver watched silently, and a little in awe, as the girl rushed off in the direction of the house. The large setting sun in front of her made her small form look as only a silhouette.

He sat there for a time, as the girl's words sunk somewhere deep within him.

His scrapes would heal.

Chapter Thirty-Seven

Oliver entered the foyer of Pembroke and made his way to the study where he planned to bury himself with estate work and planning for the sale of the house. And then he would go back to London and...he didn't know exactly. Nothing felt like the life he wanted anymore. All he knew was that he certainly did not wish to return to the way he had been, flirting and courting every woman he met, aimlessly running through life to avoid anything real or lasting. But, he couldn't stay at Pembroke, either.

He sat down at his desk and began moving papers around.

But then the sound of leather squeaking had his eyes rising to the chair in the corner of the room. He dropped his papers.

Elizabeth.

"I hope you don't mind that I waited in here for you." She spoke, and he wondered if she was real. Was he imagining her there in her beautiful pink dress, bouquet lying in her lap? She stood and moved slowly—hesitantly—across the room to stand in front of his desk. The air slowly filled with the scent of orange and then he knew...he couldn't have imagined that.

He stood, sending his chair scraping back against the floor. "Tell me now," he said, his voice urgent and pleading. "Are you married?"

Her eyes filled with tears and she bit her lips together. And then, she shook her head. "I couldn't do it," she said in little more than a whisper.

Relief flooded Oliver's body and a full wonderful breath released from his chest. "Elizabeth," he said, starting to move around the desk to her but she held up a hand.

"Let me talk first, please."

He froze and stared at her. Her golden hair was pinned in loose beautiful curls at the back of her head and small sprigs of white flowers were secured throughout. He watched as she took in a deep breath. "I adore you, Oliver. I always have. My heart has belonged to you from the first day you stepped into Dalton Park and smiled at me. I've been so stupid to hold it inside for so long, but I was terrified to tell you and have you reject me. I didn't think I could bear it. But now—now I know that what I truly cannot bear is to go another day without telling you how I feel. So here I am to tell you that I love you. Only you."

She paused and a laugh escaped with her tears. "I cannot bear the idea of living a life that doesn't include you in every single day of it." She took a step toward him, and he took one toward her. "I know that sometimes I don't think before I act, but you should know that I've been thinking of you every day for the past ten years. Sell this horrid home. Marry me, Oliver." She took another step to him. "Selling this house will not make you weak. It would be very brave to choose to let go of the pain your father caused you." She took another step, until she was standing in front of him, and she reached out to lace her fingers through his. "Build a new life with me. Us. Together." She raised one of his hands and kissed his knuckles. "Let me love you."

He stared into her eyes and then laughed—his joy and relief pouring out. "I came to the chapel, Lizzie. I came to stop you."

"You did?" Her eyes began to pool.

He nodded. "A man told me the bride and groom had left together and I considered very briefly going and throwing myself off a bridge."

"Wesley and I did leave together. After I called off the wedding, he offered to bring me to you. He was remarkably understanding and said that he just wanted me to be happy."

Well. That made Oliver feel a tad guilty for wishing the man would be run down by a carriage.

Oliver smiled and took in a deep breath as he stared into his favorite pair of sky blue eyes—eyes he now could—would—get lost in for the rest of his life. He moved one hand to her jaw and another to her lower back, pulling her in close to him. "My darling Lizzie, I have something very important to tell you."

She spoke on a breath. "And what's that?"

"You are beautiful," said Oliver, making Elizabeth laugh. He smiled and his eyes dropped to her lips. "And you terrify me." Those words, coupled with Oliver's thumb now dragging across Elizabeth's lower lip, had her trembling in his arms. "My darling best friend, I love absolutely everything about you. I have for several years now."

"Really? Then why did you not tell me? Did you think I truly loved Lord Hastings?"

"No. Or—possibly. But it was more that I *hoped* you loved him because I was afraid that I would never be able to take care of you as you deserve. Several years ago, I went to my father and told him how much he had hurt me. He laughed at me and said not to judge him so harshly because it was only a matter of time before I was just like him. He said his blood was in my veins. Those words have kept me prisoner since the day he spoke them."

Elizabeth rested her hands against his chest and moved in closer so that he could look deeper into her eyes and see the truth that she already knew about him. "Who you are is not determined by the blood in your veins. You are what you love. And you love goodness, Oliver. You love joy. You love family. And now I know that you love me. I will help mend the scars your father caused everyday for the rest of our lives—if you will let me."

He smiled down at her, his hold around her waist growing tighter and the bond between them strengthening. "Have I told you I love you?"

"Yes," said Elizabeth, letting her gaze fall to his mouth.

"Hmm. Well, then, have I told you that I want to light candles all around the room and dance with you?"

"No," she said softly, feeling her face bloom with heat. Oliver noticed and moved his thumb to run across the flush of her cheeks.

"Have I told you I want to hold you and kiss you from night until morning?"

"No, you haven't." She could no longer keep the tears from pooling in her eyes or the smile from tugging at her lips.

"Have I told you that I want to chase you on adventures for the rest of our days?"

"I don't think you have."

Oliver bent down slowly and whispered across her mouth, "Will you marry me, Lizzie?"

Elizabeth paused for a moment, staring at his mouth and savoring the question her heart had longed to hear. She raised her eyes to meet his and smiled playfully. "I asked you first."

Oliver only gave her enough time to suck in a quick breath before he wrapped her fully in his arms and captured her mouth with his. He kissed her long and fully, holding her close to him, and allowing her to revel in the realization that she was loved by the person who knew her most in the world.

THE END

Acknowledgments

Thank you to my wonderful readers who have taken a chance on me and picked up another one of my books! I'm so grateful that you guys love the Ashburn Family as much as I do.

A special thank you to my wonderful editor, Emily Poole. Emily, this is our third book together and I feel so lucky to have you as an editor! Thanks for letting me keep my modern voice in a Regency world but making it sound so much better.

Another person who makes my books a million times better is Kari Kulak. I'm not only blessed that she helps me with plotting, beta reading, and proofing; but I also get to call her family!

Chris, my ridiculously handsome husband, thank you for all the countless hours you spend in the behind the scenes work of bringing my book to life and taking the kids out of the house so I can write.

Ember and Reese, it will be years before you ever get to read these books, but I hope that one day you do, and they inspire you to follow your own dreams.

A huge thank you to all of my family members who cheer me on and keep me sane! I love you guys!

Thanks to my Sweet Regency Romance Authors for supporting me, answering silly questions, and being amazing writing friends.

Martha, Ashley, and Carina, you ladies keep me going everyday and keep me from crying more times than I can count. I feel so blessed to have met you through this writing career and get to call you friends!

Also by Sarah Adams

It Happened in Charleston Duology:

The Match: A Romantic Comedy (book 1)

The Enemy: A romantic Comedy (book 2)

It Happened in Nashville Duology:

The Off Limits Rule (book 1)

The Temporary Roomie (book 2)

Standalone Romcoms:

The Cheat Sheet

Regency Romances:

To Con A Gentleman

To Catch A Suitor

About the Author

Born and raised in Nashville TN, Sarah Adams loves her family, warm days, and making people smile.

Sarah has dreamed of being a writer since she was a girl, but finally wrote her first novel when her daughters were napping and she no longer had any excuses to put it off.

Sarah is a coffee addict, a British history nerd, a mom of two daughters, married to her best friend, and an indecisive introvert. Her hope is to always write stories that make you laugh, maybe even cry; but always leave you happier than when you started reading.

Printed in Great Britain
by Amazon

36583205R00158